About the Author

INGRID FRY was born and raised in Berkhamstead in the UK, but spent much of her childhood commuting with her family between England and Austria. Emigrating with her parents to Melbourne, Australia many years ago, she has called Australia home ever since.

A business development consultant, writer and minder of a husband and a beagle with superpowers, she lives in a leafy suburb on the outskirts of Melbourne. Lakes Entrance is her second home, and it was from there, much of the Crystal Sphere series was developed.

In her spare time, Ingrid enjoys pistol shooting at the local gun club, dancing her socks off at The Caravan Music Club, and is a passionate karate nerd, well on her way to a black belt in karate. Ingrid models the belief that it is never too late to achieve your dreams, and age is definitely just a number.

You can find out more information about Ingrid via
her website www.ingridfry.com.au
Email: Ingrid@ingridfry.com.au

Other Books
by
Ingrid Fry

Crystal Sphere Series

Descent into Darkness
Journey to Hell
Quest for Light
Search for Truth
Battle for Blood (forthcoming)

Content Warning: The Crystal Sphere Series is intended for mature readers and contains sexual situations, violence, and other representations that may cause some readers distress. Please prepare accordingly.

National Library of Australia Cataloguing-in-Publication entry:
Creator: Fry, Ingrid, author.
Title: Journey to Hell: Crystal Sphere Book 2 / Fry, Ingrid.

ISBN: 978-0-6486816-2-5

Tale Publishing
Melbourne, Australia

Tale

For my #1 Beta Reader, Cheryl Hutchinson

Follow Maggie's music playlist on Spotify!

Type *all* of the following ridiculously long code
into the Spotify search bar:

spotify:user:zs8xyxpxzbt1mjcir59qz1jzw

Click the Follow Button for Crystal Sphere

Chapter 1: The Cathedral

'You cannot drink the cup of the Lord and the cup of demons; you cannot partake of the table of the Lord and the table of demons.' — *1 Corinthians 10:21*

'Maggie, you're naked. Please, put this on.' Jason held out a white choirboy's gown. 'I didn't want to interrupt, but we need to get the hell out of here.'

I nodded and felt Luca, the priest, shudder. I was clinging to Luca like a koala, with one hand pressed against the gash on his shoulder blade, and the other clutching a bloodied crucifix. He was bloodied and naked too, except for a clerical collar and a pair of Homer Simpson jocks.

Luca unwound my arms from around his neck and lowered me to the ground. The marble of the cathedral floor was icy against my feet.

Ashley found a spare habit and gave it to Luca, all the while looking at him suspiciously. Luca ignored him and instead gazed at the cathedral ceiling as though in a trance. His face quivered as he raised his hands to his head. The veins on the side of his neck bulged as he bent forward and groaned.

I seized him as he swayed on his feet. 'Luca! What's wrong?'

He coughed and spluttered, and his face swelled and turned blue.

'He's choking! Don't just stand there, help him!'

Jason and Ashley sprang to life at my request, but Luca

clenched his fists and warned them off. 'Keep away!'

He stood up straight and his eyes rolled back in his head. White zombie eyeballs stared back at me. His body began to shake, arms stretched out rigid, veins standing out in stark relief as his muscles twitched and shuddered. He screamed, and the sound chilled me — it came from the depths of hell. His face distorted into a cavernous screaming mouth, and the sickening sound of his scream reverberated around the walls of the cathedral.

Jason moved forward, his face ashen.

'Leave him!' Drom shouted from the front of the church. 'Wait!'

'We've got to do something!' Ashley said.

I covered my ears and tried to close my mind to the terror and pain radiating from Luca. I wanted to vomit.

Sudden silence. Luca stood paralysed and open mouthed, his eyes fixed on something far away.

Jason moved forward again.

Drom shouted. 'I said wait!'

We stood transfixed. Luca appeared to be impersonating one of the church's marble statues — still, pale and frozen.

A movement, a black fluttering, glistened between his lips. Two insectile legs and quivering antennae emerged from his mouth. A large, black cockroach slithered out and took purchase on his bottom lip. It stared at us and hissed.

'Shit!' Jason and Ashley said, pulling out their guns.

'No!' I screamed. 'Don't shoot!'

Luca jolted to life and spat out the insect. Picking up a nearby Bible, he smashed it on the roach and brought it down repeatedly until it was no more than an orange pulp on the marble floor.

I touched his shoulder. 'Luca, you can stop now.' He started as though awakening from a nightmare.

'*Stronzo!*' he said, brushing his hands together at a job well done.

A familiar click came from behind me as Jason cocked his revolver.

'Don't!' I said. 'Don't shoot him.'

'You know what happens now, Maggie. He turns into a black hole and takes everything with him. We've got ten seconds.' Jason took a bead on Luca. 'Ash, get her out of here. Now!'

I stepped in front of Luca. They'd have to shoot me first to get to him. 'Wait, please! He saved my life. He's not dead. He killed his roach. Don't you get it? He won!'

Ashley tried to grab my arm. 'Move!'

I raised my crucifix. 'Back off!'

I had the top of the blood encrusted crucifix wedged in my fist with the point sticking out between my second and third fingers. 'I've killed with this before. Don't make me hurt you.'

'Don't shoot!' Drom yelled. He was at the front of the church using his power wand to dispatch the last of the roaches. In true traceur style he vaulted over the pews towards us. He flew over the top of those fifty pews like a gazelle. Poetry in motion. God, he was impressive.

'Chill, guys. Luca's clean. Maggie's right, he's no threat. I can sense it.'

Jason noticed Drom's attention was caught by my current state of undress, and he stepped in front of me. 'Why is it you always end up naked? It's so annoying.'

'If I recall correctly, you're the ones who actually pulled my clothing off. So, what? You're annoyed at yourself?'

He sheepishly handed me the white gown again. 'Point taken.'

I slipped it over my head and immediately felt as though I should be going for a medical examination.

Ashley chuckled. 'My name's Doctor Beringer, please come with me.'

I glared at him. 'Shut up, Ashley.'

Luca picked up the spare habit he had dropped and slipped it over his shoulders.

'Are you all right?' I asked him.

'Yes and no.'

'You can't be alone tonight; you need to be with us. After everything that's happened — we'll help you.'

'Okay,' he said, softly.

Between the five of us, we got things sorted. Luckily for us, the police — who were already swarming through the city because of the gang riots — arrived after all the drama in the church was over. A familiar face appeared through the busted down door. Detective Inspector Johnston. He rocked back and forth on his heels. 'How come I'm not surprised to see you lot here?'

Luca took him aside and spoke to him, pacified him, and sent him on his way. Luca must've been persuasive — the Detective Inspector wasn't a man to be fobbed off easily, if at all.

The church maintenance crew arrived shortly after to board up the door to the cathedral. Once the church was secure, we all piled into Ashley's battered truck and headed back to the Hyatt hotel. We made the short trip in silence as each of us tried to process the horror that had befallen us. I reckoned it'd take a couple of lifetimes to process what we'd been through in the last few days. But what worried me more was the premonition descending into my mind.

It rang out loud and clear. This wasn't over.

We hadn't seen anything yet.

* * * *

Once we were back in our hotel suite, Jason whispered, 'I'm going to duck out and get you some new clothes.'

'Nah, leave it to me,' radar ears Ashley said. 'I'll get the clothes dude on to it. Like before.' He pulled out his phone. 'I'll get new duds for the Padre too.'

4

'Please, no red silk dresses or stiletto shoes.'

I had a new respect for stilettos after having jammed the heel of one through a villain's eyeball. I didn't want to be reminded of that incident ever again though.

'I'm stupid, but not that stupid,' he replied.

'I know. Sorry.'

Jason hugged me. It felt so good to be back in his arms. I'd thought I was going to die in that church with a million roaches setting up house in my body.

Jason turned and headed for the kitchenette. 'I'll get us all some drinks.'

Ashley finished his call and whispered in my ear. 'What's with Luca and the Homer Simpson jocks? Aren't priests supposed to wear horsehair underpants or something?'

'I have no idea what they wear, but this one's obviously a fan of Homer Simpson. I do know one thing about him though.'

Ashley was always keen for a bit of intel. 'Yeah, what?'

'Luca's never had a woman. Ever.'

Ashley looked horrified. 'You're kidding me.'

'It's what he said. Never.'

'*Never?*'

'Never.'

Ashley raised his eyebrows to the max. 'And how come this came up as a topic of conversation while you were being tied upside down to a cross and covered with a million cockroaches?'

'It's a long story.'

'Oh, I'll bet it is.'

'Shut up, Ashley.'

Ashley scratched his chin. 'I need to do something about this. It's not right. It's my duty to fix this.'

'What are you going to do?'

'I'm taking Luca out tonight. I'll shout him a high-class hooker. It'll give him something to remember for the rest of his poor celibate life.'

'Don't you dare, he'll be appalled! You're sick. The poor bloke has been through enough today without you adding more emotional problems for him to process. He's been possessed by a mutant roach, had to kill six of his crazed, possessed brothers with a crucifix and expel the roach from his body by using every ounce of his spiritual and physical energy, but all you can think about is sex?'

Ashley flashed me a cheeky grin. 'It'll help take his mind off things.'

I rolled my eyes. 'You're wanton and wicked.'

He laughed. 'It's why you love me. By the way, aside from all the roaches, you looked great in church today — naked as the day you were born. I certainly look forward to seeing what each new day brings these days.' He raised his pinkie finger and wiggled it at me.

I raised the crucifix. 'In your dreams, mate.'

---

[1] *Maggie's Playlist: Dancing with Demons — Palisades*

Chapter 2: Luca

'But he said to him, "Behold, there is a man of God in this city, and he is a man who is held in honour; all that he says comes true. So now let us go there. Perhaps he can tell us the way we should go.' — *1 Samuel 9:6*

Luca had ducked out to the twenty-four-hour clinic to get his shoulder looked at, and Jason was on the phone ordering food via room service. We'd learned that horrific events, terror and action did nothing to stem our appetite. In fact, these days, we were always as hungry as hell. It seemed our norm to feast after danger. I guess one used up a lot of fuel fighting for one's life. So, after another nightmare of a day, everyone just wanted to eat and chill out, except maybe Ashley, who still was obsessed with finding a hooker for Luca.

'Let it go,' I said.

'I can't. It's a travesty. He's a good-looking bloke, and he's never going to know the delights of a woman.'

'He's married to God, for Christ's sake.'

'What a load of—'

'Ashley, it's what he's dedicated his life to.'

'It's a load of crap. It's all about power and control.'

'True, but people believe in religious structures and they'd die for them. Look at religious extremists.'

'Don't get me started.'

'Me neither.'

'Champagne?' he offered.

Reaching across to the drinks trolley, I picked up a glass and held it out to him. 'Need you ask?'

'Just checking. I thought maybe your new holy friend has changed your evil ways.'

'That'll be the day.'

'Thank God.'

'Amen.'

'I love you, Maggie.'

'I love you too.'

'What's with the love fest?' Jason asked.

'We love you,' Ashley said. 'Did you know Luca has never had a woman, ever?'

'He's a priest.'

'It's wrong.'

'He's obsessed with this,' I said.

'No wonder. Its Ash.'

'It's not right. It's a sacrilege,' Ashley said.

Jason laughed. 'According to your religion. By the way, how did you find out that fact, Maggie?'

'It's a long story.'

'I'll bet.'

'Don't you start!'

'This is doing Ashley's head in, isn't it?' Jason said.

'Yep, he wants to hire a hooker.'

Jason tsk-tsked and rolled his eyes. 'I give up.' He hurried off to the kitchenette to get more beer. Drom was lying back on the couch. I pushed over a foot stool and said, 'Here, put your feet up. You must be exhausted.'

'Thanks. It's been a big day.'

'I can't thank you enough for rallying the troops and being there for me. You're amazing. I think I was channeling you in the church today. I was doing some serious parkour on the church pews. I couldn't believe myself.'

Jason returned with two beers and handed one to Ashley.

They clinked bottles, sculled the contents in four seconds flat, with Adam's apples bobbing rapidly.

'You were awesome,' Jason said, wiping his mouth with the back of his hand. I jumped as Ashley let out a huge belch.

'How'd you know?' I asked.

'We saw everything. Drom did some weird mind meld thing and we were in your head. He was linked into you, and he connected us into the loop. Kind of like a head Skype.'

'Oh, that's awful!'

Jason scooped me up in his arms, and carried me into the kitchenette. 'I need a word.'

'What are you doing? Put me down. I can walk you know. My legs aren't painted on.'

He kissed my forehead. 'I enjoy carrying you. It makes me happy.'

'I reckon you enjoy using your new super powers.'

'Yes, that too.' He deposited me in the corner of the kitchenette, right where Ashley had given me a clandestine bondage experience. I touched the bench and the energy took me straight back there. I gasped as my body flooded with erotic sensations.

'You okay?'

'Um, a bit hot and flustered is all.'

Jason fiddled with the zip on his jumper. 'Maggie, I don't know what to say.'

Ashley sauntered in and helped himself to another beer from the fridge. I'm sure he just wanted to listen in to what was going on. He was the ultimate sticky beak.

'I saw and felt everything you were going through in the cathedral,' Jason said.

Ashley looked grave. 'Make that we.'

'It's the worst thing I've ever experienced,' Jason continued. 'You were so brave ... fighting off those priests and hordes of roaches. We couldn't get into the bloody church to get you out.

Ash had to go back and get his truck. I had, we had, to function while seeing and feeling what was happening to you in there.' His face twisted with emotion. 'My God.' He gripped my arms.

'I'm sorry you had to go through it too,' I said. 'It's more than enough for one person. Now we're all traumatised. Drom shouldn't have done it. What on earth was he thinking?'

'I don't know that I'll ever be able to sleep without a can of heavy-duty bug spray beside me,' Ashley said. 'What a head fuck.'

Jason stroked my face. 'How are you? Really?'

'Surprisingly fine. I lost it towards the end, but I'm okay now. I'd rather face a load of roaches than that arsehole Dylan. He seriously got to me, with the syringe an' all. I can deal with bugs better, believe it or not.'

Ashley looked shocked. 'You can't be serious?'

'Deadly.'

'You're kidding?' Jason said.

'No. I'd choose bugs over humanity any day.'

They had absolutely no idea how to respond to that bombshell, except for the usual.

'Another beer, Jace?'

'Yep, great, mate, thanks.'

I wandered into the lounge and sat next to Drom. 'How come you mind melded with the guys? It freaked them out. You're one helluva wizard to be able to do that, by the way. I'm in awe of you, but Jason and Ashley … they can't deal with it.'

'To tell you the truth, it was the first time I've done it. I'm sorry, but I knew time was of the essence. When my mind received your call for help, I linked into the guys without even thinking about it. It was an automatic speed dial. Then I couldn't disengage them from my head. We were stuck in a telepathic videoconference loop. I'm sorry; I didn't mean to do it. We were all so discombobulated by the experience it was hard to function. It was insane.'

'Welcome to my life. I knew I'd connected with you, Drom, but I didn't realise everyone was there with me.'

'You had too much going on. It's something I won't forget in a hurry. You were incredible, so courageous.'

'I must have been channeling your parkour skills; there's no way I could ever have done what I did in that church. I'm a corporate couch potato, a computer nerd. How was it possible?'

'I was locked into you, Maggie; I was you. I wanted to do more, have you leap up those cathedral walls, but your body couldn't cope.'

'Wow. I thought so. I was amazed at myself leaping across those pews. I knew it couldn't be me.'

Drom looked pale and tired, as if he'd had all the energy sucked out of him. I squeezed his shoulders and they felt tight and knotted. 'Hey, Ashley, can you ask Mel at reception to organise a masseur for a couple of hours? Drom's cactus, and I think it would behoove us all to partake in some relaxation. I'll pick up the tab.'

'Great idea. I can save you some cash if you want.'

'How so?'

'I'd be happy to massage you for free.'

'I walked right into that one, didn't I?'

'Yep. Are we on?'

I narrowed my eyes, spun on my heel and headed for the kitchenette.

'I'll take that as a no?' he called out.

Food and drink were flowing freely, the drink probably too freely. It was a post-war after party. What the hell. We had a lot of bugs to get out of our heads.

Luca had returned and was sitting on the window ledge, looking out at the city.

I touched his shoulder. 'It's beautiful, isn't it?' He winced. 'Oh, I'm sorry! How is your shoulder?'

'Very sore, but I'll be fine. The twenty-four-hour clinic did a great job patching me up. It's not serious.'

'What about your head?'

'That's another story. Not good. I can't understand or come to terms with what happened. I killed my brothers. How am I going to explain it? No one will believe me. I can't believe me.'

'Luca, you were incredible today, and you expelled the roach. Your brothers tried, but they couldn't. They were doomed, but they're free now. I know others who died the same way, and they're free.'

I thought of Adam in the hospital morgue, of how I'd connected with his spirit after Jason had shot him and he'd said he was free. I wasn't sure about the rest of the roached humans we'd killed. I hoped they were free too. 'Luca, you have incredible spiritual strength to resist as you did. You saved me against all the odds. You don't realise how powerful you are.'

'But what shall I say? How shall I explain this? What *is* this?'

'You'll know what to say and what to do. You believe in God's will, so what's happened is it. Don't doubt yourself.'

Luca closed his eyes, put his head back, breathed in and then exhaled. He flicked his head, as if trying to dislodge cockroaches. 'Thank you. I'll try.'

'Stay with us tonight?'

'Yes. I need to. I have nowhere else to go. No one who would understand.'

'Somehow, I may have let it slip about your celibacy, and now Ashley thinks it's his mission to ... to, ah ... fix things,' I said quietly. 'Just letting you know.'

Luca smiled. 'Maybe it's not such a bad idea.'

'Jeepers, that wasn't the reaction I was anticipating.'

'After today, anything is possible.'

'Too true. Can I get you a glass of red, Luca?'

'Please. Can you make it a large one?'

I gave Luca his wine and he headed off to watch the TV. I

sat on the window ledge and looked out over the city.

Ashley wandered over. 'Penny for your thoughts.'

'I gave Luca the heads up on your anti-celibacy plan, and, astoundingly, he said maybe it's not such a bad idea.'

Ashley looked surprised. 'Dead set?'

'Yep. I didn't expect that. Seems a shame his first time would have to be so impersonal, with a lady for hire.'

'Nah, it's different for blokes.'

'How so?'

'It just is. We don't get so hung up with feelings; we just want to get our rocks off.'

'Charming. He's a priest. I'm sure feelings and a spiritual aspect mean a lot to him.'

'Nope. Trust me. How old is he? Maybe early thirties? No sex ever? He wants to get his rocks off. Why are you so worried about it anyway?'

'I'm not worried. I was just thinking about things.'

Ashley scrutinised my face. 'Oh, my Lordie, you've got the hots for him.'

I felt myself blush. 'I have not.'

'Maggie, Maggie, Magster. You can't lie. Ha. You've got the hots for the Padre, and you want to be the one. *The only one who could ever reach me, was the son of a preacher man, the only boy who could ever teach me—*' Ashley sang softly.

I pulled away. 'Shut up! You're drunk and ridiculous. Grow up.'

Jason wandered over and gave Ashley another beer. 'What's up?'

'Maggie's got the hots for the preacher dude, and she's not happy with my plan to outsource to a hooker.' Ashley laughed at the horrified expression on my face.

'He's drunk and being an idiot,' I said to Jason.

'Fair dinkum? You're thinking of offering your services as a charitable endeavour?' Jason said, playing along.

I was fair dinkum going to kill Ashley. I glared at him. He winked in response.

I'd play this game too. I flashed them a big smile. 'Luca did defeat the Dark Force, slaughter six of the evil minions and save my life, so it's the least I could do. It would be a charitable endeavour, but only with your blessing of course, Jason.'

He laughed. 'I might believe you're serious, Ms. Maggie.' His phone rang and he moved away. I poked my tongue out at Ashley.

'You might fool Jason, but you can't fool me,' he said.

'You know I've always taken a great interest in spiritual affairs.'

I sat on the couch next to Drom. 'How are you?'

'Much better. I'm starting to unwind. Can't wait for that massage but.'

'Me too. I need to ask you a favour, but if you're not up to it, please say.'

'Sure, what is it?'

'Hang on, I'll get my mobile … oh, damn, I keep forgetting; it's lost. Jason's finished, I'll use his.'

I flicked through the photos on it to find one of Boo. I showed her to Drom. 'This is our dog, and I'm worried about her. Can you tune in and find out if she's all right? My senses are fried at the moment. I can't get anything.'

'No worries.' He took the phone, rested his fingers on the image, and was quiet for a moment. His eyes narrowed and his forehead creased. 'I must be too tired.'

'Why, what is it?'

'All I get is an image of a dog sitting next to a Tawny Frogmouth. They're on the roof of a two-storey house, looking out at the view. That can't be right.'

'It's perfect!'

Drom seemed surprised. 'It is?'

'Yep. You haven't met our dog yet,' I said, giving the phone back to Jason.

Boo was on the roof and all was well in the world. She was obviously making the most of her new powers of levitation. I felt happier knowing she was safe. I couldn't wait to give her a big hug and a roast chicken dinner.

A sharp knock at the door of our suite made us all jump.

Ashley carried out his usual gun routine. 'I've got it. S'okay. It's the clothes dude.'

Jon came in with shopping bags hanging off his arms and a huge smile on his dial. 'Ciao, greetings and salutations!' He looked exceptional as usual.

Jon eyed me up and down. 'Good grief, Maggie, I arrived in the nick of time. And this must be Luca,' he said, shaking Luca's hand. 'I think you'll love what I have for you. Smart casual, man about town, with some accessories to give you a bad boy edge.' Jon passed him a few bags and Luca seemed excited.

'If you don't like anything, or it doesn't fit, leave it in the bags; I'll have someone collect them in the morning. Ciao bella.' He waved at Jason and Drom, kissed Luca on both cheeks, repeated the procedure with Ashley and me, and then he was gone.

'Bedroom's free, Luca. Go try on your new duds,' Ashley said.

Luca nodded and headed off. Ten minutes later, he poked his head out the door.

'Come on, man,' Ashley said. 'Watcha doing in there?'

'I need Maggie for a minute. I need help, some fashion advice.'

Oh my. Fashion advice from me?

Jason laughed. 'Fashion advice from Maggie? Perhaps not such a good idea.'

'Oh. Ha Ha. I'll be right there, Luca. Don't listen to him.'

Ashley's face was like thunder as I walked into the bedroom and closed the door. His head would be spinning. I laughed to myself. I didn't know where he'd got the idea I had the hots for Luca. I didn't. Ashley could be so annoying. He was a troublemaker with his crazy ideas.

Luca was standing in front of the mirror. He turned to me. 'What do you think?'

'Wow! I mean, really, wow!'

A beautiful, short leather jacket set off his physique. Underneath he wore a white 'V' neck T-shirt, black jeans, belt buckle — not too ostentatious—and low heel boots.

'So, what's the problem?'

Luca held out a selection of bracelets. 'I don't know what to do with these. Aren't they for girls?'

I took a leather strap and tied it around his wrist. 'Believe it or not, I think they're to give you the bad boy edge.' I followed up with a couple of beaded bracelets, and noticing two rings in the packet popped one on each of his hands. I pulled out a chain. 'Here's a necklace — a crucifix!' Good on you, Jon. I undid the clasp and fastened it around his neck. 'The crucifix has to go inside your T-shirt, not on the outside, so you only see a hint of chain. Ta-dah! Mega cool with a touch of bad boy.'

Luca looked sad. 'There's no doubt I'm a bad boy.'

'You're a saint, and now a handsome, well-dressed one at that. We're all here for you, no matter what happens.'

He smiled. 'Thanks. I appreciate it.'

I opened the door. 'Come on, let's go out and show the guys.'

Luca was greeted with a round of applause and slaps on the back. Ashley looked at me suspiciously.

'What?' I said

'I was wondering what sort of "advice" you gave him.'

'I helped him fix his bracelets.'

He laughed. 'I'll bet you did!'

'Shut up. You're irredeemable.'

Jason grinned.

Ashley directed his gaze at me as he said, 'Well, guys, Luca and I are ducking out for a while. Don't wait up, kids.' He threw his arm around Luca. 'Come on, Padre, lets you and me get us some action.'

I felt bummed out at the thought of Ashley bedding a hooker. I knew we weren't together anymore — he could do whatever the hell he wanted. But I felt as if he was cheating on me, and right to my face. Our recent off the wall, erotic pinkie swear energy exchange had bonded us and reignited our feelings. Or so I'd thought. His actions made me feel betrayed and heavy hearted.

Jason came over looking concerned. 'Why so sad?'

'Just a bit tired, I guess.'

'Come to the bedroom and we'll get you out of the choir robe. That'll make you feel better.'

'Okay.' I headed off with him hot on my heels.

We were about to close the door when Drom said, 'Ah, guys, I need to tell you—'

Jason closed the door and yelled, 'Hold that thought, Drom. We'll be out in a sec.'

Drom yelled back, 'No, I really need to—'

'Save it. We'll be out later!' Jason shouted.

'You should talk to him. It might be important.'

'It can wait.'

---

2 *Maggie's Playlist: Son of a Preacher Man — Sarah Connor*

Chapter 3: Mind Meld

'Red silk ribbons cutting my skin, red silk ribbons, love or sin? Blood and lust, I see it all. Mirrored thoughts spread their pall. Minds display their secret wares. Nothing hidden in your glass-eyed stares. Your minds to me are an open book, where horror lurks in every nook. What blocks it out? What stops the flow? Champagne and sex, it's this I know.'
— Maggie McLaine, Journey to Hell

Jason stood in the middle of the bedroom and pulled off his top. His lean muscular body was nearly healed, the scars barely visible. Noticing Luca's clerical collar on the floor he picked it up and clipped it around his neck. He grinned.

I giggled. 'Oh, it's Father Jason!'

He strode over and pushed me against the wall. With the increased power and strength in his body, he was almost too rough. I hoped he'd learn to gauge his strength better or I'd be in trouble. I tried to catch my breath. 'Ow! A bit heavy handed.'

His brow crinkled. 'I hurt you?'

'No, well, maybe a little. Just letting you know.'

He narrowed his eyes. 'I have something serious to discuss.'

Oh, I didn't like the sound of that.

'I hear you've been a bad girl, Maggie McLaine. A girl lusting after a holy father, I believe. It can't go unpunished.' He caressed my breasts and whispered in my ear, 'You need to confess your sins.' He hoisted up my choir gown and stroked my thighs. 'Tell Father Jason or there will be consequences. Hmm. Feels like you're lusting after this Father too. That definitely can't go unpunished.'

I played along. 'Please don't penalise me, Father.'

'Oh, I'm going to penalise you all right.' He gripped the choir gown and ripped it in two. He stroked my breasts and sucked my nipples. His hand slid between my legs, and he held me up as my knees gave way. Jason took my arm and pulled me across to the bed. He sat on the edge, laid me across his knee and fondled my naked buttocks.

'You must be reprimanded, Maggie.' He slapped hard.

The pain and the shock of the slap radiated through my body. I gasped and cried out.

Jason rubbed my buttocks to soothe the sting, while his other hand squeezed my nipple. His thoughts rattled around in my brain turning me on even more. *Oh my God, she's got a gorgeous arse. Her naked body across my legs … the softness of her breasts … the curve of her waist …*

Slap!

He spanked again and immediately took me with his fingers. I groaned and convulsed as pain and pleasure merged into ecstasy.

Slap!

He repeated the process.

'Count.' He grabbed my hair and pulled back my head. 'Four more.'

'One,' I whispered.

Slap! Pain. Ecstasy.

'Two.'

Slap! Pain. Ecstasy.

'Three.'

Slap! Ecstasy. Pain.

'Four.'

Slap! Ecstasy.

I was delirious — my body tingled and quivered with pain and pleasure, shock and excitement.

Jason laid me gently on the bed and stroked my face. 'Are you okay?'

I nodded mutely.

He ran his hand along the front of my body. 'You didn't confess.'

I quivered at his touch, the sound of his voice; my whole body was on fire. Where was this coming from? He was different — Jason had never done anything like this before.

He picked up the choir gown and tore off four long strips. Tying the material around my wrists and ankles, he secured the ends to the legs of the bed and pulled them tight. He looked down at me, surveying his handiwork.

'You're totally at my mercy. You good with that?'

I nodded. I'd lost all power of speech, taken by lust and anticipation.

He climbed on the bed and straddled me, touching my face and hair. 'You're very quiet.' He kissed me gently, then deeply. I groaned and struggled, pulling against my ties, wanting to hold and enfold him with my arms. He kissed my throat, my neck, my breasts, his hands explored every part of me. He took me with his fingers, his mouth, and I cried out loudly feeling faint with the overwhelming sensations flooding my body. But the best thing of all my head was silent — no thoughts, no images, no visions, no psychic flotsam and jetsam — only pure, unadulterated silence. No wonder I loved sex.

I pulled so hard on my restraints the material ripped. As the bonds around my arms loosened, Jason pushed my thighs apart with his knees and entered me. Passionate, possessed, his face was flushed with power. His eyes devoured mine and I drew on his strength. I tore my arms free, shredding the material and my wrists. I wrapped my arms around him, and we merged in a flash of transcendent sexual energy.

When my power of speech had returned, I whispered, 'Thank you, Father Jason, but I'm sorry. I will always be a bad girl and I will never, ever confess my sins. You'll have to keep trying.'

His body convulsed with silent laughter. Now he'd lost the

power of speech. We were absolutely spent, our bodies hot, melded together. Jason was heavy on top of me. He tried to raise himself but could only manage a couple of inches before dropping back.

I pushed him off me. 'I can't breathe.' I was surprised at my own strength. Maybe I'd been tapping into him.

We lay quietly, enjoying the peace in our bodies and minds. My mind felt vast, like a grand ballroom, huge, expanded. Around the edge of the ballroom were hundreds of ornate doors, and I was standing in the middle of the room. All the doors except for four were closed. In the centre of each open door stood a person. I narrowed my eyes to try to see who they were, and as though I'd focused binoculars, the figures sprang into sudden sharpness.

They were Jason, Ashley, Luca and Drom.

Luca stepped backwards, slamming his door shut. Drom struggled trying to pull his door closed. He appeared to be battling an invisible force, which was trying to keep it open. Jason stood in his doorway looking confused. Ashley stepped through his door and held it open with his boot jammed against the bottom of the door.

The realisation hit me like a brick. 'Jesus! We were in a mind meld!'

In the real world, Jason gasped, obviously realising it too. He leapt to his feet, slammed open the bedroom door and made a beeline for Drom. 'That sick fuck! I'll kill him!'

My legs were still tied to the bed, and I frantically tried to undo the knots. I could see Drom through the door. He held a spray bottle and cloth and shouted at Jason, 'I tried to tell you! I tried to tell you before, but you wouldn't listen! I was trying to close it, but it wouldn't; something kept it open. I'm sorry, I was cleaning the windows. It helps when I clean; I was trying to focus, to close it. I'm sorry, Jason. Maggie, I'm sorry!'

I could sense Jason's burning fury, Drom's absolute feeling

of failure, embarrassment and shame, and Ashley's confusion, combined with blatant, shameless lust and curiosity.

Jason stood in front of Drom, buck naked except for Luca's clerical collar. 'Close it, Drom! Close it now!'

Drom held his head and looked distraught. 'I'm trying. I've been trying. I can't!'

I finally freed my ankles, wrapped myself in the shreds of the choir gown and raced into the lounge.

Jason was behind Drom with his arm around his neck. Drom's neck was jammed in the 'V' between Jason's forearm and bicep. Jason squeezed slowly, applying increasing pressure. I felt the blood and oxygen in Drom's brain being squeezed out, and I … we … collapsed unconscious to the floor.

I looked down at myself from the ceiling, a familiar vantage point these days. Drom floated next to me.

'Hello,' I said.

'That worked,' he said. 'It broke the link.'

'Slightly heavy-handed. How are you?'

'I'm not sure. In case I don't get the chance again, I need to say, I'm so sorry. I didn't realise the link was still open. I only had snippets of you and … look how clean those windows are. I scrubbed them to within an inch of their lives.'

'It's fine, Drom, I believe you. I trust you with my life. I think I know what the problem was.'

'You do?'

'Ashley. He was the one keeping the link open.'

Drom appeared shocked. 'How could he do that? He must have powers.'

'You have to be kidding me. Not Ashley with powers!'

'Whatever I was fighting, it was stronger than me. It was a brute force.'

'Oh Jesus. A dark force?'

'No, a brute force.'

'God help us.'

Below, Jason checked Drom's breathing and rolled him over into the recovery pose. He turned and saw me on the floor.

He vaulted over the couch. 'What? Hell. Maggie!' He checked for a pulse in my neck and listened for breathing. The colour drained from his face as he realised there was none.

'Drom, I'm dead!'

Drom had gone back to his body.

I didn't feel dead.

'I'm still here. Jason, I'm here!'

Bang! The front door slammed open and knocked a picture off the wall. It was Ashley and Luca.

Jason was leaning over my body giving me CPR. I was much whiter than normal, barely distinguishable from the shreds of the choir gown around me. My black hair was splayed across the floor.

Jason pounded out a rhythm on my chest. 'Come back! Don't leave, Maggie.' He stopped, tilted my chin back, pinched my nostrils, opened my mouth, covered it with his and breathed his breath into me. My chest rose and then fell.

Ashley looked desperate. 'Jason, let me.'

Jason ignored him.

I'm here! Jason, I'm not dead. You can stop.

But he didn't stop.

Definitely dead then.

Drom regained consciousness, jumped to his feet, and ran to my body. He looked up at me. 'Come back.'

'I can't! Something's stopping me.'

'Luca! Put your hands on top of Maggie's feet,' Drom said. 'I'll hold her head.'

Jason continued to pound on my chest, his face set in stone. I hoped he wasn't breaking my ribs. Drom held my head and I felt his and Luca's energy connect with me. A blinding light spiraled from the top of their heads and solar plexuses. It collected the threads of my frayed etheric cord and restored it in a web of light, connecting it back to my body.

Slam! I gasped for air as I reentered my body. The heaviness of the physical world crushed down — the pain in my chest. The pain in my brain. The pain in my legs, my wrists — my *everywhere*.

Then there was the lightness of the kiss, the kiss from Jason. The kiss of life.

His voice was husky with emotion. 'Oh, thank God.'

Luca and Drom sat quietly, lit from within, moved by their experience. Ashley stood distraught, pallid and silent, pushing his hands through his hair.

I felt sorry for him. He needed something to do.

'Ashley ... drink ... champagne please,' I croaked.

Ashley charged into the kitchen and had a cork pulled and a glass filled in ten seconds flat.

He passed it to me. 'Here, luv.'

Jason looked shocked. 'You're crazy, Maggie. You shouldn't be having alcohol after what happened.'

I took a sip and the bubbles soothed my parched throat. I lifted my glass in a toast. 'I should. You brought me back from the dead. If that's not worth celebrating, I don't know what is. Thank you all ... so much. Thank you. I love you all.' Tears streamed down my face. I always became emotional after a reentry.

'Your life, it's crazy. These are typical days for you?' Luca asked.

Jason helped me to my feet. 'Pretty much,' he said.

Ashley assisted, taking my arm. He saw my wrists. 'Jesus Christ! You're bleeding!'

I still had remnants of cloth tied around my wrists. I'd pulled so hard against my constraints that when I'd broken free, the material had cut into my flesh and was imbedded in my skin. I hadn't noticed at the time. It appeared as though I had red silk ribbons tied around my wrists.

Ashley sounded horrified. 'You bloody moron, Jason! Look

what you've done to her!' He shoved Jason away.

'Hey! Back off, Ash!'

'It's not Jason's fault. Find me a couple of band aids or something.'

Ashley stroked my face. 'You're going to need more than a couple of band aids to fix this. I'll find a first aid kit.'

Jason took my wrists and examined them. He tried to gently pull away the cloth. 'This isn't good. Bloody hell, I'm sorry.'

'Ow, it's stuck. I need to soak them off. Jeepers, I didn't even realise I'd done that.'

I'd felt no pain at the time, but, boy, was I feeling it now.

Jason looked upset. 'Wait for Ash to come back with the first aid stuff. Maybe I'll have to take you to the clinic.'

'Ash has been, and Luca, so why not me?'

Ashley returned with a first aid kit. He filled a bowl with warm water and Dettol and soaked the cloth off my wrists. It looked worse than it was, with a couple of gashes contributing to all the blood. He gently bathed my black and blue wrists, applied antiseptic cream, and wrapped them in bandages.

I surveyed his work. 'Thank you. It looks like I've tried to top myself.'

Ashley was thin-lipped and stony faced. 'This would not happen on my watch. Red silk ribbons, not blood red ribbons, for fuck's sake.'

'Ashley, please, I know you care, but so does Jason. I did this. Me. Not him.'

'No, that's not how it works. He bound you, he's responsible. It's unforgiveable.'

I held out my arms. 'Shhh. Here, give me a hug.'

We wrapped our arms around each other. I felt his body relax as we took pleasure and comfort in the moment.

Unfortunately, that moment of comfort was to be short-lived.

Chapter 4: Betrayal

'She weeps bitterly in the night with tears on her cheeks; Among all her lovers she has none to comfort her. All her friends have dealt treacherously with her; they have become her enemies.' — Lamentations 1:2

I was tucked up in a wingback chair in the hotel room writing rhymes on a notepad I'd found in a drawer. My head was filled with music from my favourite playlist. Jason had given me Apple AirPods for Christmas, and they were seldom out of my ears. Music helped to block the psychic rubbish. Rhymes helped too. And quotes, somehow. They came to me unbidden, and I had to get them out, scribble them into notebooks I'd purloined from Dad.

Jason removed my AirPods and pulled me from the chair and into the bedroom. 'Come with me. We need to get you into some proper clothes.'

He closed the door and we hugged silently, no words required.

'Do you need to rest?' he asked.

'No, I'm fine. I feel better after getting those rhymes out.'

Jason pulled opened the clothes bags. 'Let's see what Jon chose for you.'

I hoped it wasn't another red silk dress and stiletto shoes.

Jason lay the clothes on the bed. A simple round neck, long sleeved black top, black leggings and a pair of red sneakers. Perfect!

'Oh, bless him!'

Jon had also included a new pair of jeans, black leather jacket, a couple of tops, a new pair of boots, three new sets of underwear — all gorgeous, plus some black leather and silver accessories, makeup, and a new leather, over the shoulder messenger bag.

Jason sat on the bed watching me intently. It was as if he'd never seen me before. I was very happy with all my new things. I wasn't a girl who enjoyed shopping. I liked to look good, but I couldn't be bothered with all the hassle and the crowds. Having someone shop for me and getting it right was such a treat.

I held up three bras. 'Which lingerie set?'

Jason pointed to the Gabriella bra, a sexy slip of material in black and silver.

I slipped off the choir gown, or rather it fell off as there wasn't much left of it, and put on the new bra and knickers. I pulled on the black top and leggings, red sneakers, jewellery, a lick of red lipstick and mascara and I was done.

I smiled and spun around. 'Oh, that feels so good!'

Jason stood and put his arms around me. 'That looks so good. You look even more beautiful in this than in the red silk dress, and that's because it's you and you love it. And I love you.'

'I love you too.'

We both wanted to say so much more, but for now, we didn't need to.

He held my hand. 'Come on, let's get you some champagne.'

'Yes, please!'

Back in the lounge, the guys chilled out, drinking and chatting. Jason moseyed out to the kitchenette to organise our drinks.

'Looking good, Maggie,' Ashley said. 'Happy with everything?'

'Love it! Thanks so much for organising it all, but I'm going to pay you for the clothes.'

Ashley came over, took my hand, and led me to the window. His face was serious. 'I don't want any money. Please, it's a gift and it's the least I can do after all the trouble I've caused. I'm sorry. I can't even begin to tell you how I felt when I saw you lying there, lifeless.'

'It wasn't your fault; it was Jason doing whatever he did to Drom.'

'I taught Jason that. LVNR.'

'What's that?

'Lateral vascular neck restraint. I learned it in the army. It's a neck restraint. Cuts off blood and oxygen to the brain rendering the victim unconscious. It won't do lasting damage if used correctly, but you can kill someone with it, if you want to. And, it was my fault the link wouldn't close. I was sitting in the bar with Luca — oh, and that's another story — when there you were, right in my brain, and there I was, with ringside seats, no, make that in the ring with you and Jason and your insane sex scene. I mean, Jesus Christ, didn't you know I was there?'

'No, I didn't. I was otherwise occupied.'

'You can say that again.'

I blushed and looked at my red sneakers, thinking about what we'd done. My face burned so hot it probably matched the sneakers perfectly.

'I'm sick about this, Ashley. What you did was so wrong. I don't think Jason knows it was you; he thinks it was Drom. He's furious.'

'Have you told him?'

'No, we've barely had time to speak.'

'I'm not making excuses, but one minute I was there minding my own business having a quiet drink, and the next I was in some wild sex scene with you and Jason.' He held up his pinkie finger. 'I don't know if it was because of our previous connection, but not only could I see everything, I could feel everything. I could sense what you were feeling, what Jason was feeling, all combined and at once. What that generated in me, well, let me tell you, I thought I'd have to punch myself out it was so intense.'

Words tumbled out of his mouth. He was completely overwhelmed.

'Take a breath,' I said, softly.

'I couldn't function. I thought someone had spiked my drink and I was tripping out. It felt like my fantasy — you've seen it, you know I'm telling the truth. Honestly, I thought I'd lost it, gone mad. I was trying to process the sensations, emotions and feelings of three people, and it paralysed me. It was the best and worst thing I've ever experienced. Tuning in to you was divine. I'm sorry, but I'll never forget it. And tuning in to Jason. My God, I've never felt emotions like them.

'I still feel raw, out of it, not back in my body or something. I wasn't deliberately keeping the link open, being a mega sleazebag voyeur, I was caught in the tidal wave of your energy and I couldn't get free ... didn't know how to and maybe, to be honest, in the end, didn't want to.'

Ashley gripped my arms, his face a mix of emotions as he awaited my response.

'I believe you and I appreciate your honesty. You're not used to sharing minds so I understand. It still freaks me out. I was so angry, so embarrassed when I realised it was you watching us. But explaining it as you have, I guess I don't feel so bad.' I felt my face match my shoes again. 'I'm still so embarrassed.'

'Please don't be. Don't let this spoil things between us. I love you and you know that. I wish I could undo everything.' He pushed back his hair and clenched his fists in frustration. 'I don't want you to be embarrassed. I don't want things ruined between us.'

I felt his surge of anger as he slammed his fist towards the wall at the side of my head. Without thinking, I stopped his punch cold.

Ashley stared at his fist in my hand. 'Crikey!'

Jason bounded over and pulled me away. 'What the hell are you doing? Did you try to punch her?'

'No! I wanted to hit the wall ... and she ... she ... stopped me. Jesus, she's super woman.'

'What is it with you guys and having to hit things?' I asked. 'Is it testosterone? A lack of verbal ability to express how you're feeling? *What?*'

'Dunno. Just happens,' Ashley replied.

'Make it not happen. You're not a teenager anymore. Act your age.'

'Give me a break, the last few days haven't been easy,' he said.

'You're telling me? Do you think it's been easy for me? Do you see me going around trying to smash walls?'

Ashley grinned at me. 'With your new-found strength, you may find it therapeutic.'

I laughed. It was impossible to stay mad at Ashley no matter how hard I tried.

Jason looked concerned. 'What was all that about, Ash?'

'I think you two have some catching up to do,' I said. 'I'll leave you to it.'

Drom and Luca were sitting in the lounge, eating sushi and drinking red wine.

'Thank you again for bringing me back,' I said. 'You make a dynamic duo.'

'It was amazing,' Luca said. 'The most incredible thing that's ever happened to me. I still feel in another world. All those years in the church and nothing could compare to what I felt connected to ... to you and Drom and ... I don't know, the universe?'

'God?' I suggested.

'Must be.'

'How did you know what to do?'

'I didn't, I held your feet like Drom told me. I didn't consciously do anything.'

'He's a natural,' Drom said. 'Very powerful, naive energy. Luca, you're stronger than me. You don't know what you do, but in time you will, and I think the Dark Force will be quaking in its boots. You'll need to be careful.'

'So, what do I do?' Luca asked.

'Follow your heart and find your own way. It will be unique to you. I can help, but I think in the end you'll end up teaching me.'

'Was it Ashley who kept the link open?' Luca asked.

'Yes,' I said.

'He's powerful too then.'

'It appears so. He feels wretched about it. He was caught in the energy and didn't know how to get out. I saw all four of you in my head when I finally realised what was going on. Drom, you were struggling hard to close the link, and Luca, you slammed the connection shut. How did you do that?'

Luca was silent. I could sense his mind turning. His heavy eyebrows knitted tight over his brown eyes, and his mouth, which at rest kicked up in a slight smile, was straight and serious. He was weighing his response.

Finally, he met my gaze, eyes soft, mouth relaxed. 'It was love.'

I tapped him on each shoulder with an empty champagne glass. 'I dub thee Saint Luca.' I repeated the process for Dromeus. 'I also dub thee Saint Drom. You two are fair dinkum legends.'

Jason joined us on the couch. He looked like he needed a holiday. No wonder, after talking to Ashley.

'Maggie has officially pronounced Drom and me saints,' Luca said.

Jason nodded towards Ashley. 'I'll second that decision, particularly after talking to him.'

'Now, Luca, you don't have to tell if you don't want to, but what happened with you and Ashley on your big night out?' I asked.

Luca blushed.

'I'm such a sticky beak. Sorry, I shouldn't have asked.'

Jason gave me a look. 'No, you shouldn't. It's none of your business.'

Luca laughed. 'It's fine. It seems there was a miscommunication. It's true I've never had a woman, but when Ashley said he was going to take me out and show me a good time, I assumed he meant with him. You see I'm gay.'

'Oh crikey. I'm so sorry, Luca, it's all my fault. You said ... I thought ... oh dear.'

Luca was shaking with laughter, as was Jason and Drom.

'It's a shame because I have a crush on Ashley,' Luca said. 'When I reached across the table and held his hand, he ran out of the room like the devil was after him. I was upset because I thought it was because of me, but later he explained he was caught in the mind meld, and that's why he left.' Luca shrugged his shoulders. 'So anyway, it's all good, I guess.'

I was curious. 'Have you had a boyfriend?'

Jason looked appalled. 'Maggie! It's none of your business!'

Luca laughed. 'It's okay. No, I haven't. I haven't had a sexual relationship with anyone, man or woman. I've felt love, of course, but not physical. Prior to becoming a priest, I trained to be a doctor. I was desperately in love with one of the lecturers, but was too shy and scared to act on it.'

I could feel our minds processing Luca's answer in the context of our own lives. 'Crikey,' we all said.

Ashley sauntered over. 'Maybe you shouldn't have closed your link so fast, Padre. Hung around a bit longer and you could've learned something. Pretty mind-blowing stuff with those two. Even I learnt something.'

Luca didn't glare at him, but Jason, Drom and I certainly did.

What the hell was it with him? Didn't he know how to quit while he was ahead? The guy had a death wish.

That one comment made all his talk with me seem like a big fat lie. I'd stupidly believed him and his hogwash. My stomach turned. I felt betrayed, demeaned and tawdry. I also felt otherworldly strength in my bones and muscles, fuelled by anger and adrenaline. I rose to my feet.

'Maggie, let it go,' Jason said.

'I'll let it go all right!' I jumped over the back of the couch and shirt fronted Ashley. He staggered backwards, arms waving, grasping for something to hold onto before he lost his balance and fell flat on his back.

'You lied to me!' I screamed. 'You take me for a fool? You demean and embarrass me, you ... you disrespect me. Is everything you say and do a lie? Is everything between us ... a joke?'

They say you shouldn't kick a man when he's down, but I kicked him all right. In the ribs. With my boots. Hard. And then again. And once more for good measure.

Jason and Drom yelled, 'Maggie! Stop it!'

I felt the tiny atom cinder of the Dark Force glowing quietly in my being. A breath of anger, an exhale of fury, and it smoldered, drawing on the fuel like oxygen and bursting into a flame of retribution.

'Oh shit,' Jason said. 'Look at her face.'

Ashley gripped my ankle to stop me kicking him. I smashed his wrist with my other boot. He let go and I had my foot on his throat. He rolled forward. I reached across and snatched the gun from his jeans and jumped back.

I checked out the gun. It wasn't a revolver. It was sleek, smooth and black. I couldn't find a safety, and I didn't know how it worked. If I pulled the trigger I'd soon find out if it worked. I stepped back and took aim.

Ashley held out his arms in surrender. 'No, Maggie! No!'

I could sense his mind weighing up options, chances, and opportunities.

I tightened my finger on the trigger. 'Nothing you do will be quicker than this.'

A voice behind me called my name. The tone was soft, gentle ... beautiful.

I turned. Luca held out his hand to me, and I felt his love, his power. The Dark Force roared into flame in response. I pulled the trigger.

Ashley leapt up and wrapped his arm around my throat, locking me in a chokehold. I dropped the gun as I began to lose consciousness. He loosened his grip in response.

I tried to kick backwards and get him in the groin. My leg wasn't long enough, and all I achieved was a massive cramp in the back of my thigh. Not to be deterred, I ran the side of my shoe along his shin and elbowed him in the stomach.

Ashley ramped up the pressure on my neck again. 'Jesus, Maggie. Jason, Drom — some help, please! Sometime soon, would be nice.'

Luckily for Luca the gun hadn't fired. I closed my eyes as he touched my head and doused the flaming dark rage with liquid love. It was instant, a mere touch vanquished the beast, and I felt my knees give way as its strength withdrew. Ashley released his chokehold, and being well attuned to my knees, held me so I wouldn't fall. He picked me up and set me on the couch. 'I'm sorry. I don't know why I said that. It came out all wrong. I'm an idiot. You have every right to hate me. I didn't mean it.' He rubbed his ribs and the front of his shin. 'Christ, you pack a punch.'

'It's not good when I'm angry.'

'That's an understatement.'

'You're a liar, Ashley Beringer. I do hate you. I hate you for betraying me and everything we had. You said I was naive, and I have been, about you anyway. I feel foolish; you've abused my trust and my love. Everything's a game and a joke to you. You've hurt me badly. Honestly, it's the last straw. I can't do this anymore. I want you out of my life. I can't stand to look at you, and I can't stand you looking at me. Everything's ruined. Thanks for that.'

Ashley seemed shocked. 'Come on, you're overreacting. It's not like that. You've taken one comment out of context. Oh Jesus, I'm digging myself a bigger hole. I meant it not in a bad way; I meant it in a way that if Luca had stayed in the link, he would have experienced a true love relationship, a love that would have sustained him for the rest of his friggin' life. Forget the sex, I wasn't talking about that. I was talking about the love, Maggie, the love.'

'Luca knows what love is, more than you could ever conceive.'

'Maybe so, but that's what I meant. I know, the tone was wrong, it came out wrong, but I meant that if he'd stayed ... oh, fuck. I'm going to shut up now. I'll go, you're right. I don't want this either. I'm outta here.'

'Good decision, Ashley. You've crossed too many lines for my liking.'

He picked up his jacket, tucked the gun in his pants and strode along the hallway and out the door, closing it softly behind him.

'Are you sure you want him to go?' Jason asked.

I closed my eyes and shrugged my shoulders.

'He's nothing but trouble. He does my head in. How can you not see it? You don't know the half of it.'

'But he means well. He told me what happened, his side of the story and believe me, I was angrier than you, more upset than you. What we have is precious, is sacrosanct. I was so enraged at the thought of him violating that, violating you, us. That's what it felt like to me too. But he's our friend. He has his faults, granted, but we all do. He feels more devastated than we do at the thought of losing us, and our friendship, especially after everything we've been through together. He said we have to stick together, the three musketeers, well, we have five now, but we can't let him go. What's he going to do? Can't you find it in your heart to forgive him?'

'He'll be waiting outside the door, won't he?'

'Probably.'

I got off the couch. 'For you Jason. I only do this for you.'

'No, it has to be right for you. If you don't want him around, then I'll respect that.'

Drom and Luca had been sitting there quietly and somewhat uncomfortably, during our discussion. I looked at them for guidance.

'Go with your heart,' Luca said. Drom nodded.

'What if it's the wrong decision?'

'It could be wrong, but it will always be right,' Luca said.

I stood. 'Makes sense to me.'

Jason looked confused.

'I'm forgiving him,' I said, heading along the hallway.

I opened the door. Ashley was leaning against the wall near the lifts, pretending to wait for it, even though I'd just heard the lift doors close.

'Ashley?'

'Yes, luv?' His expression was sunken and distraught.

Reaching out to him exposed my neatly bandaged wrists, that had been so lovingly tended to by him. I touched his arm. 'You did a good job on my wrists.'

His sarcastic reply registered in my mind, but he didn't voice it. He was too afraid to speak.

'Don't go. Please. Stay.'

'You're sure?' he croaked, his eyes meeting mine. 'No. You're doing this for Jason. I know. What we had is broken. I've ruined everything. You won't get past it. I can't be around you feeling this way.'

He jammed his finger on the down button, then he squared his shoulders and tapped his foot as he watched the illuminated lift numbers.

Should I stay or should I go? Would he stay or would he go?

We were at that point in a relationship where the fragile, delicate dance could go either way, leaving us both feeling broken and betrayed, wanting vengeance, wanting the other to want them, but also wanting what was right and true for the heart and soul. Maybe space would be good, some time out. We'd been trapped in a pressure cooker, so no wonder we were nuts. But where would he go? If it was me, where would I go? No one would understand or be able to relate. He'd be so much more than alone. He would also be in danger. We were his family now, his crazy, dysfunctional family, and we needed each other to survive. What was I thinking? There was only one choice.

'I mean it. Please stay. We're family.'

He pivoted on his heel, threw his jacket on the ground and gripped my arms.

'Family?'

'Yes, family. Musketeers.'

His voice broke. 'I wasn't lying to you. I swear.'

'I believe you. I'm sorry.'

'Don't say sorry, you don't need to be sorry. Are you sure?'

'More than sure.'

'Really sure?'

'Yes. Sure.'

'Absolutely sure?'

I laughed. 'I'm really, really, really sure. Please, come home with me.'

His breath caught in his throat and he looked like he might cry, but instead he pulled me into his arms and held me tight. I could hear his heart pounding.

'You won't regret this. I won't let you down.' Ashley offered me his pinkie finger, and as I connected with it, I felt a rush of electricity surge through me. It tingled in my body and set my hair on end. Ashley stared at me. 'Bloody hell, did you feel that?'

'Gave me goosebumps.'

'Darn carpet static,' he said.

We opened the door to our suite, entered the lounge and were welcomed back by an enthusiastic round of applause.

Jason slapped Ashley on the back and gave him a man hug. 'Good job, glad you decided to stay.' Jason hugged me tight, kissed me and whispered, 'Good job, too. I know it wasn't easy for you. I appreciate it.'

Ashley heard him and gave me a flinty look. He nodded and mouthed the words 'for Jason.'

'For you,' I mouthed back. 'Don't start.'

He held out his pinkie finger in acknowledgement.

It was getting late and everyone was tired. The rollaway bed had arrived, so Luca and Drom opted for that, Ashley took the couch, and Jason and I would have the bed.

Ashley barricaded the suite door and set out his beer can early warning system. He volunteered to be the first line of defense, along with Drom, who only slept for three hours anyway. Drom had placed holy hand grenades around the room, and his big tower buster pointed at the door. Ashley made mugs of hot chocolate for everyone before we turned in.

'Luca, I've been meaning to ask you something.'

'Yes, Maggie?'

'There was a weird little kid at the cathedral. He would've been about seven, with thick black hair, hacked into the worst bowl cut I've ever seen. He had big, wide set eyes and a spindly body. He reminded me of the cartoon character, Prince Planet. He was the one who led me into the church. He had a strange name … um …Tapakah, that's it! He said you were his father. What's with that?'

'I know the child you mean. He had a very powerful dark energy — I could feel it seeping into me. He was hanging around the church prior to your arrival, obviously charged with the task of bringing you to us.

'Fair dinkum? So the roach entity is recruiting children now.'

'There's a worrying thought,' Jason said.

'It's terrible! The poor kid. I wonder where he is now?' I said.

I felt a prickling sensation in my brain, and the image of Tapakah's face flashed into my mind. I was in a warm, yet dank and enclosed space. The light was dim, and my eyes strained to make sense of the surroundings. A shadowy blur, a waft of damp air and Tapakah was in front of me, smiling a soulless smile. I jumped in fright.

He was small, almost skeletal, but he pushed me so hard I was on the ground before I knew it. He crawled on top of me, and I felt his cold spindly fingers on my skin. His psychic power was such that I couldn't move. Black glistening eyes stared into mine. His body quivered, and his head moved backwards and forwards as though he wanted to vomit. And he did — regurgitating a thick fluid over my face. The smell hit me and I dry retched.

Anal glands. The stink reminded me of anal glands. Boo once had a case of blocked glands, and the vet had taught me how to unblock them. Her "bum juice", as Jason disgustingly called it, smelt like *Chanel No. 5* compared to this.

I wanted to scream, but there was no way in hell I was going to open my mouth. I screwed my face up tight. I couldn't breathe through the thick slime.

He whispered in my ear, 'I'm coming for you. Not now, but soon. Very soon.'

I couldn't hold my breath for much longer. but I'd rather die than open my mouth. My body had ideas of its own. My mouth flew open, and I sucked in air and slime and I screamed and screamed and screamed.

I heard Jason's voice in the distance. My head started to bounce back and forth; he was shaking me. The hideous vision left as quickly as it came.

'Maggie! Wake up! What's wrong?' His fingers tapped sharply against my cheek. I gasped.

Ashley rubbed my back. 'You're whiter than a ghost. What the hell happened?'

Jason stared into my face. I knew he was looking for signs of the Dark Force.

'It's okay. I had a vision. A creepy, hideous vision of Tapakah.'

'What happened?'

I trembled. The power of the vision had been so real. I'd had many visions in the past, but mastered blocking them out. Not this one. I felt traumatised. I touched my face. I could still feel the residue.

'Maggie?'

'Oh, I … I … forget it. It was nothing. Must be stress, from the church.'

Jason and Ashley gave me knowing looks. I was no good at lying. I knew they didn't believe me, but they decided not to push it.

Thank God. I didn't want to reinforce the vision by speaking about it.

Ashley took out his phone. 'Tapakah's a weird name. How do you spell it?'

Hearing the name sent a shudder along my spine. 'He said his name was Tapi for short. I don't know, *T a p a k a*?'

'Here it is. It's Russian, spelt T a p a k a h. One guess as to what it means.'

'What?'

'Cockroach!'

'Eww.' I rubbed my face. Why could I still feel the awful slime?

'Bloody hell!' Drom said. 'We need a list of foreign words meaning cockroach. The next time someone introduces themselves, we'll be one step ahead. Leave it to me, I'm onto it.'

Luca turned on the television to see the news. 'Look, Maggie, here's the riot you were caught in today — a number of different gangs, apparently, Sudanese, Pacific Islander and others. You were lucky to get out of there without being injured.'

'Sure was, and then right into the arms of the church,' I replied.

'Have you noticed the sudden spike in all kinds of violence?' Drom asked. 'It was never like this before. Now we have riots, car jackings, road rage, stabbings, home invasions, pensioners getting mugged for their cars and money, every kind of sick and crazy thing dominates the news. After the all-important sport, that is. Even sport is filled with violence, by players and spectators alike. The Dark Force is generating this. We need to pull our fingers out and find those crystals.'

'Yep, we sure do,' I said, hearing the lack of enthusiasm in my own voice.

'Hey, Maggie, it was lucky you didn't know how to use my gun,' Ashley said. 'Lucky for Luca.'

Luca nodded in agreement.

'Yeah, okay. I was wondering when you were going to bring that up.'

'Was I right, or was I right?'

Ashley was going to persist. He wanted to hear me say he was right and I was wrong.

'If I'd been facing an enemy, I would've been screwed, not knowing how to work the thing. I still need to know how to use a gun, and if you don't teach me, I'll find someone else, at a gun club or something.'

'But in this instance, it was a good thing, wasn't it?'

I screwed up my nose at him. 'Yes, Ashley. You were right. Happy now?'

Ashley leapt out of the chair and began tickling me in the ribs. 'Yep! It's not often I'm wrong. I thought I was once, but I was mistaken. Finally, gotcha!'

He made me laugh until I couldn't breathe and his touch turned me on. I gasped and made big eyes at him. 'Ash, stop, please!'

'I will teach you how to use a gun, because I promised, but it's going against my better judgment. If you'd known how to use it, Luca would be dead.'

'Yes, I know already. Don't remind me.'

'Let it go,' Luca said. 'She needs to be able to protect herself, despite the risks. You'll have to learn not to antagonise her.'

Ashley looked chastened. 'Point taken.'

'So, what's the plan, the next step?' Drom asked.

'Tomorrow after breakfast, Jason, Ashley and I are going home to clean our trashed house and hopefully find Boo and give her a big roast chicken dinner,' I said. 'Then we need to debrief and see where we're at. My dad, the Prof, has notebooks with information about the crystals, so we'll have to study them and follow our noses as to finding … how many crystals did you say, Drom? Twelve?'

'Eleven.'

'Hopefully we still have a crystal at home, one here and one in Ashley's truck. Eight to go. How and where do we find them? And what do we do with them once we have them?'

'The crystals will guide you,' Drom said.

I nodded. 'I hope it's that easy. 'Drom, you and Luca are welcome to stay in the self-contained bungalow we have out the back of our place rather than be on your own. I keep thinking about you and what's going to happen to you, Luca.'

'Here it is on the news!' Drom said. 'Hoodlums gatecrash cathedral. They're blaming it on the rioters.'

'Have they said anything about the missing priests?' I asked. 'Inspector Johnston will probably call us in for more interviews.'

Luca looked distressed. 'I'm going to have to lie.'

'For the greater good, I think you will,' I said. 'You're needed as warrior against the Dark Force. It was meant to be. You can't let yourself be locked away or tied up in red tape.'

I noticed Ashley's mouth twitch at the mention of red tape, and I rolled my eyes at him.

'You're right. I'll have to lie. But I think my days as a priest are numbered,' he said sadly.

'Can I keep the crucifix?'

'Maggie!' Jason scolded. 'It belongs to the church.'

'You can have it. I don't want it. It's stained with the blood of my brothers.'

'Are you sure you don't want it? There's incredible power in it.'

'It's yours.'

'Thanks, Luca.' I felt very attached to that crucifix. 'I'll add it to my tool kit along with the stiletto.'

'Stiletto?'

'God, that seems a million years ago,' Jason said. 'It's only twenty-four hours. I'll tell you later, Luca. I'm sure Maggie doesn't want to go through it again.'

'Actually, I'm fine. I can tell them. They need to know what's happened.'

'Tell them everything? Boo? Maestro? The Prof? Everything?'

'Yep. They're Team Musketeers now. Guardians of Light.'

'Well, do you mind if I have a shower and go to bed? I'm beat,' Jason said.

'No worries. Ashley and I will bring them up to speed.'

Luca and Drom gave the thumbs up.

'More red?' Ashley asked.

I nodded as Luca and Drom settled back in their chairs like a couple of kid's ready to hear a bedtime story. This one would probably give them nightmares.

---

[4] *Maggies' Playlist: Deception — Christina Grimmie*

Chapter 5: Truth be Told

Drom and Luca were wide-eyed and silent by the time I'd finished. Finally, Luca said, 'So we're dealing with two evil creatures. The Dark Force, which is the materialisation of eons of negative human energy, and the roach creature, a new entity bent on destroying humanity.'

I nodded.

'And you, Jason, Ashley, Drom and your dog Boo were dragged into this because of the crystal sphere?'

'Yes, the crystals are the weapon to defeat the Dark Force, and apparently we're Crystal Keepers charged with finding the crystals and bringing them together. We've only just met Drom. He's a spiritual intuitive with similar skills to me.'

Drom gave me the thumbs up. 'I was drawn to Maggie to help her fight for the light.'

I looked at Luca. 'We're currently four musketeers fighting the good fight — three blokes, a psychic chick and a beagle cocker-spaniel cross. Perhaps we'll be adding a priest to our crew?'

Luca's expression seemed grim. 'Do I have a choice?'

'Probably not.'

He sighed. 'And the roach creature? You think it's after the crystals because it wants ultimate power and control over everything, Dark Force included?'

'We reckon so.'

Luca shook his head. 'I can't believe these entities can digest matter, similar to a black hole. I'm in an episode of *Doctor Who*.'

'Tell me about it,' I agreed. 'One good thing, I guess, is contact with the crystal has enhanced our abilities. Jason's physically more powerful, and my psychic abilities are stronger. I'm not happy about that bit, particularly. I've been trying to switch the bloody things off for years.'

'I'm with you there,' Drom agreed.

'Did anything happen to Boo?' Luca asked.

I laughed. 'Absolutely. Boo now has the ability to levitate and can communicate with us telepathically.'

Luca and Drom looked at each other.

I nodded. 'Amazing, hey?'

'Any further news about your father?' Luca asked.

'Still missing. The only recent development we had was the appearance of the Maestro, the weird woman I mentioned. She gave us the heads up about Dad bringing the irradiated cockroach back from the Hadron Collider.'

Drom nodded. 'I remember reading about your dad in the paper when he vanished. The scientific community was devastated.'

'Yes, his genius in astrophysics is a huge loss.'

'I'd love to meet the Maestro,' Drom said. 'She sounds amazing.'

'You'll probably fall in love with her, like Dad did. She has that effect on men, and maybe even women. I still don't trust her, but Jason thinks she's the bee's knees.'

Ashley had dozed off and was snoring softly. I lowered my voice and nodded towards him. 'In case you were wondering, Ashley and I were an item about five years ago.'

Drom nodded. 'I thought you two were close. How'd you

hook up with his best friend then?'

'Fate, I guess. Jason and I weren't even aware of the Ashley connection until Ash came home from Iraq and turned up on Jason's doorstep. I answered the door! It was a shock for everyone and awkward for a while, but now we're the best of friends.'

'The three of you are like brothers and sisters,' Luca said. 'You can feel the love.'

A bit too much love from some quarters. I paused to take a swig of red wine, and the movement must have stirred Ashley because he opened his eyes and stared at me. I felt hot and flustered under his gaze. That's all I needed. Feelings reactivated. As if things weren't complicated enough.

Ashley put his arms behind his head and closed his eyes again. His biceps bulged against the sleeves of his T-shirt, and the couch seemed diminutive against his frame.

I couldn't be in love with two men … could I?

Drom looked at me knowingly.

I sighed.

Luca rubbed the back of his neck and tilted his head from side to side. His bones cracked. 'So what now, Maggie?'

'The cockroach has bred, creating an army of clones under its control. We're being hunted by them. This new breed of roach has the ability to infest humans and use them for their own purposes. It's what you experienced in the cathedral and what happened to your brothers. You managed to defeat it, but your brothers weren't so lucky. Failed hosts are destroyed, leaving no evidence.'

'Roached humans are hunting you and the crystals? Luca asked.

'A number of roached humans have already attacked us. They've slaughtered innocent people in the process. I was attacked right here in this suite, by a hotel employee—'

I had to stop talking. My heart raced and the room began to

close in. I took long, slow breaths. I could do this. I could talk about it. I wouldn't be held hostage by that creep, Dylan. I wouldn't.

Luca leant forward and put his hand on my arm. 'What's going on? You're as white as a ghost.'

I could do this. I could do this. I could do this. Breathe.

The couch squeaked as Ashley leapt up. He took one look at my face, sat next to me and put a protective arm around my shoulder. 'Keep breathing. You shouldn't do this to yourself. You have to stop reminding yourself of this shit.'

'No. I won't let him win.' I took another deep breath and continued. 'So ... with this waiter, D ... Dylan, the guys were in the restaurant, and I was here on my own. He attacked me ...' *breathe* ... 'but I managed to dispatch him by shoving the heel of my stiletto through his eyeball and into his brain.'

There, I'd done it!

My hands trembled. Ashley wrapped a strong, warm hand around them. I stared into the concerned faces of Drom and Luca. 'I have post-traumatic stress disorder. It gets triggered by that ... experience.'

'Perhaps we should stop now?' Luca suggested.

Ashley nodded.

'I want to ask one more thing,' Drom interjected.

I nodded.

'What's the roach's ultimate goal?'

'Not sure yet, but it can't be good; it hates humans. When I had the vision and it possessed me, I felt it. We're stuck in the middle of two evil entities, and sometimes it's difficult to tell who the hell's who.'

A bottle of Dom Bénédictine and crystal glasses sat on the coffee table. Ashley lined up four glasses and poured out a heavy-handed measure into each one. 'Get that into you,' he said, pushing the glasses our way.

'It's way too much,' I said, raising my glass.

'Trust me, that's the minimum you'll need if you want to get any sleep tonight.'

We did a simultaneous scull and staggered off to bed. I felt the warmth of the liqueur wrapping its arms around my brain. Ashley was right. Dom was the new Diazepam.

---

5 *Maggie's Playlist: Storm in My Heart — Colin Hay*

Chapter 6: Home

'By wisdom a house is built, and by understanding it is established; by knowledge the rooms are filled with all precious and pleasant riches.' — Proverbs 24:3-4

I pulled back the hotel curtains to reveal a grey and dismal morning. Clouds hung black and heavy over the city. The wind's fierce grip rattled the trees in the park and dislodged flurries of autumn leaves. The room was warm, but I felt cold.

Jason yawned and stretched. 'Close the curtains and put some clothes on. There's probably someone training a pair of binos on you as we speak, or worse, trying to take a bead on you.'

I hastily drew the curtains and threw on a robe. 'Happy Monday to you too.' I sat on the edge of the bed and gave him a kiss.

He smiled. 'Time to go home, Mags.'

'Why doesn't it stress you out ... going back to all that?'

'It'll be fine. Drom and Luca have accepted our offer to stay and to help clean up. It'll be done in a flash.'

'Great, many hands an' all that. I'm glad they're staying. You don't mind?'

He stroked my hair and his hawk eyes searched mine. 'No, not at all, we're going to need them.' His eyes were dark and troubled, mirroring the gloom of the morning outside.

Showered and dressed, I entered the lounge. The guys were up, and Ashley had ordered coffee for everyone. He passed one to me. 'Here you go, luv. Flat white, no sugar.'

'Thanks, Ashley, you're always looking after us.' I glanced around the hotel suite. 'Boy, this place feels almost like a home now. So much has happened in such a short time. It's nuts.'

'Yeah, good stuff and bad,' Ashley said.

'Some good stuff thanks to you,' I said.

Jason slapped Ashley on the back. 'And some bad stuff thanks to you.'

Ashley looked hurt.

'Just kidding!' Jason said in response.

I had the feeling he wasn't.

* * * * *

When we pulled into the driveway of our home I was surprised at how neat the garden was. Normally, if left unattended for only a couple of days, the paths would be littered with eucalyptus leaves, bark, twigs, small branches and possum poo.

Our property was next to a nature reserve in a leafy green suburb on the outskirts of the city. The joys of that found their downside in the fact that nature was messy, and yard duty was pretty much a daily task. Lorikeets and rosellas constantly tip pruned the trees and bushes, and when the eucalypts were in blossom, clouds of pollen filled the air littering the ground with snow-like drifts.

Ashley switched off the motor and we sat there. I dreaded walking through the front door. I dreaded the carnage and congealed blood, the memories of murder and mayhem, and the sense my home would never feel like home again.

Jason opened the truck door and helped me out. 'Let's get this over with.'

'Give me the keys,' Ashley said. 'I'll go in first.'

I handed them over. 'Go right ahead.'

Ashley gave Jason a look as he unlocked the door.

Jason pulled his gun out from back of his jeans. 'You seriously think someone's in there?'

Ashley pushed open the door. 'Can't be too sure.'

'Hey!' he yelled, as one very happy, excited dog landed on his shoulders before bouncing off and landing in my arms. Boo madly licked my face and snuffled my ear with her nose.

A voice similar to Prince Charles echoed in my brain. *Thank heavens you're back, Maggie!*

Boo, we have comms! I can hear you in my head. You still sound like Prince Charles, but that's great. Are you okay? I was worried about you.

Couldn't be better!

I thought you'd be starving. We've brought you a roast chicken.

Marvelous, my favourite! Thank you, indeed. But I've been doing very nicely.

Yes, you look amazing. Your coat is so shiny. Is that rose essence I can smell?

Boo pushed off from me and floated across to Jason giving him a similar treatment. It was obvious Boo had completely mastered gravity as she bounced around between us like an astronaut inside a spaceship.

'Check out Boo!' Jason said, watching her do a 360-degree barrel roll and then push off the wall of the courtyard, bounce off the other side, and come to a gentle landing at his feet. 'Amazing!'

Boo had a big grin on her face, pink tongue hanging out to one side. *The possums aren't safe from me now. I can sit in the trees with them if I want!*

Jason gave Boo a good scratch. She closed her eyes in bliss.

I'd imagine not much is safe from you now, Boo.

Bit more to the right, Jace.

Jason looked at me and rolled his eyes.

Ashley stood in the doorway and gave me a look, motioning

with his gun that I should go in. I took a deep breath and entered.

The first thing to hit me was the smell.

The scent of bee's wax, lavender and furniture polish filled my nostrils. And what was that? Something was baking! I inhaled and smelt ... cinnamon. I stared in amazement at the scene before me.

Not a thing was out of place. Nothing was smashed or broken, and the wooden floorboards gleamed like honey in the sunlight. Vases of fresh flowers sat on tables and sideboards. It felt as though someone had put our house up for sale, and it was open for inspection day.

I took a few steps forward. The venetian blinds hung in perfect condition, and my favourite lamp, which had been a smashed mess, was without a dint or tear. Everything was perfect. More than perfect. Mozart played softly on the Bose machine. In the kitchen, two vanilla candles flickered softly on the table, and my fine china cups, plates and crockery were set out for a tea party. Looking through the glass window of the oven, I saw two cakes baking; they were nearly ready to come out.

I ran from one room to the other — all of them perfect — while Boo floated beside me, grinning crazily and wagging her tail. It was weird to have her at eye level all the time.

In our bedroom, everything was faultless, and the ensuite was sparkling, no blood, no water. I emerged from the room to see the four musketeers standing in the threshold, their faces sporting huge grins.

'Surprise!' they yelled.

I burst into tears.

Jason wrapped his arms around me. 'Don't cry, you should be happy.'

I buried my face in his chest. 'Am happy. Am so happy,' I snuffled. I was happy beyond measure. I couldn't believe it.

What a thoughtful, beautiful thing to do. I looked around in awe. 'How ... who did all this?'

'Come into the kitchen,' Ashley said. 'The oven bell's gone off.'

In the kitchen, I examined things I knew had been broken. I couldn't see a scratch. I ran my hands over walls and cupboard doors previously covered in dents and holes but now perfectly smooth. 'Tell me, how is this possible?'

'The Maestro,' Jason said.

'The Maestro! What?'

'I rang her, as you know, and she offered. She said she has 'cleaners', so while we were away, the Maestro and her cleaners did all this. Whatever couldn't be fixed was replaced. And you probably won't be happy about this, but she won't accept any money for it. When I asked for her help to organise this, I said I would pay for everything, but she refused. She wanted to do something to help us ... you, and in honour of the Prof.' Jason lifted my chin and searched my expression. 'I hope you don't mind.'

I had mixed feelings about it. I hated being in someone's debt, and this made me very much in her debt. Looking around though, I was so grateful and realised she'd saved me from losing my home. Because it did feel like home again. Even the energy felt right — warm, peaceful and safe.

'Maggie?'

'I don't mind at all. It feels like home again.'

Jason smiled and hugged me tight. 'It does, doesn't it?'

'Even the vibe is good again.'

'She brought in someone who does house cleansing on an etheric level. Awesome, huh!'

'Perfect.'

Ashley had oven mitts on and was pulling cakes out of the oven. 'Come on, guys. I'm taking orders. Tea, coffee, beer?'

There was a sharp knock at the front door, followed by the

familiar sweep of a cape. It was the Maestro.

I ran to greet her.

'Welcome home.' She encircled me in her arms, and I was wrapped in folds of purple velvet and fur. I smelt the familiar scent of lavender and something else, spicy like cedar. I stepped back and gazed into her violet eyes.

'I don't know how to thank you.' I spread out my arms to indicate the whole house. 'I can't tell you how wonderful it is to come home to this … and etheric cleansing too.'

She put her arm around my shoulder and walked me to the kitchen. 'It's important for you, my love, I know.' Her boots clicked loudly on the floorboards. I hoped the stilettos wouldn't ruin them.

She flashed a huge smile displaying her perfect teeth. '*Hello,* boys. My, my, what a fine group of men we have here. Maggie, I see you've added a couple more to your collection.' She extended her hand to Luca. 'And you are?'

He took her gloved hand and kissed it. 'Luca.'

'Impressive.'

She turned to Drom. 'And you?'

He gave a small bow. 'Dromeus.'

What was it with these guys? They were acting as if she was the queen or something.

'Ah, Dromeus. The runner. It's lovely to meet you both. I am the Maestro.'

She turned to Ashley and extended her hand, palm down. 'And of course, the ever-handsome Ashley. Lovely to see you again.'

Instead of kissing her hand, he took it, turned it sideways and shook it firmly. 'Lovely to see you too.'

Ashley had dabbled in sales at one time, and I knew he hated power handshakes and all variations thereof. Catching his eye, I grinned and he winked at me.

Boo was floating right behind the Maestro. Luca and Drom

watched her in amazement.

So, the Maestro knows you float, Boo? I said, in my mind.

Yes, I hope that's okay? She brought me more power feathers, hence the rapid increase in my abilities.

She wasn't fazed by an anti-gravity beagle cross?

Not in the slightest. In fact, she didn't appear to register my behavior was strange at all. It was almost as if she thought all dogs did this. I firmly believe there is more to the Maestro than meets the eye, and I, for one, want to get to the bottom of it.

Boo was just getting started. *Can I stop you there, Boo? Can she hear you too?*

No, only you and Jason can at this stage. I think we should be able to loop her in. Do you want to try?

Maybe hold off for a bit.

Boo decided on a slow vertical barrel roll, before pausing upside down so that her ears flopped groundward. She was showing off.

Of course. I await your command. This headstand is excellent for getting blood to the brain, with no strain on the neck. Simply marvelous.

Oh my. Puppy school hadn't covered this in their curriculum.

Ashley stacked on the politeness. 'Maestro, some refreshments?'

'Green tea would be lovely, thank you.'

'Can I take your cloak, Maestro?' I asked.

She undid the gold clasp that secured it around her long neck. 'Sure, thank you.'

I lifted the cloak from her shoulders and pulled it away from her body. The velvet felt soft and luxurious under my fingers. It was so goddamn heavy. The Maestro wore her sprayed on black leather pants, black over the knee boots with stiletto heels and black long sleeved shirt with a low V-neck, buttoned at the front.

The guys couldn't help themselves. Even Luca was staring, seemingly entranced.

'Mmmm, the cakes look divine. Did you make them,

Maestro?' I asked.

The guys started slightly and awakened from their trance.

'Yes, I enjoy a spot of baking on occasion; it helps me relax. I made a cinnamon teacake and a banana and walnut cake. Ashley, the icing for the banana cake is in the fridge, ready to go. I also make the most divine hash cookies. I'll bring some around next time.'

'Hash cookies? Jeez, I haven't had a hash cookie in twenty years, I reckon,' Ashley said.

'You have to make your own cannabis butter and use it in whatever you make; it's the only way. Maggie, here's a story. I made a batch of garlic bread using cannabis butter and froze one of the leftover loaves. Your dad had a key to my apartment, and one day he let himself in whilst waiting for me to finish rehearsals. He was peckish so defrosted the garlic bread, toasted it in the oven and ate the lot. The high kicked in after a couple of hours, and he was very stoned indeed. It took about eight hours to wear off. He thought he was losing his mind until I checked the freezer and realised what had happened.'

'Crikey, the Prof on drugs. Was he okay?'

The Maestro smiled. 'Oh yes, we had a lovely time.'

Ashley raised his eyebrows. 'I'll bet you did.'

Oh, for God's sake. I still can't get my head around her and Dad.

We sat around our wooden refectory table enjoying afternoon tea. The sun streamed in through the windows and felt warm on my back. Aromas of coffee, cinnamon, and banana cake filled the room, and the gentle patter of conversation overlaid the mellifluous sounds of Mozart playing softly in the background. It was wonderful to be home, surrounded by familiar things.

Boo was eye level with the table hovering near the food. She was also a cake hound.

Boo, move away from the cake! I'm watching you.

She floated away, alighted gently in front of the sliding door, and lay in the sun. The sound of gentle snoring was immediate. I always envied her ability to fall asleep in an instant.

Jason sat next to me and took my hand, giving it a gentle squeeze. 'Happy?'

I smiled. 'Very.'

'It's great to be home,' he said. 'It feels as if we've been gone for weeks. I can't wait to sleep in our own bed.'

'Ditto to that.'

---

6 *Maggie's Playlist: Home — Simply Red*

Chapter 7: Fox

'Behold, I am sending you out as sheep in the midst of wolves; so be shrewd as serpents and innocent as doves.' — *Matthew 10:16*

Knock. Knock. Knock.

Boo leapt to her feet barking madly. She raced across the floor to the front door. Good. She had remembered not to float in front of strangers.

Jason eyed Ashley. 'I'll get it.' Ashley stood and pulled his gun from the back of his jeans.

'Oh, dear,' the Maestro said. 'Expecting unpleasant company?'

'Not sure,' Jason said.

'Please, let me,' the Maestro said. It was a command, not a request.

She stood, reached a perfectly manicured hand into the top of her boot and pulled out a small silver, pearl handled pistol. She tucked it into the side of her pants and strode like a panther, lithe and fluid, towards the front door.

'Phew,' Drom said, echoing the exhaled breaths of all the men in the room.

Oh, for goodness sake.

Luca laughed. 'Heaven help the person on the other side of the door.'

The Maestro peered through the glass and opened the door.

'Well, I never. Detective Inspector Johnston. What a pleasure.'

The announcement of this visitor elicited a chain of responses:

'Shizen.'

'Oh no.'

'Fuck.'

'Damn it.'

'Bugger.'

We heard the detective say, 'I was hoping to catch up with Jason and Maggie. Are they home?'

'Yes, do come in,' the Maestro said. 'Follow me.'

Inspector Johnston seemed only too happy to follow the Maestro. We could all see that as he loosened his tie, brushed his hair back from his face and tried to keep his eyes off her derrière. He looked tired and in need of a good night's sleep. I hadn't taken much notice before, but he did have rugged good looks. He must've been around fifty, I guess. A five o'clock shadow covered his broad angular chin and jaw. His mouth was reasonably full and wide, but his lips were dry and cracked. He had a scar on his top lip, and one above his eyebrow. His eyebrows were thick and sat low over brown, almond shaped eyes framed by laugh lines. His forehead had three deep creases, and two lines ran between his eyebrows. Must have been from frowning over difficult cases. Probably ours. His brown hair had one lock which tended to flop across his face. He reminded me a bit of Ashley.

He surveyed the faces around table. 'Well, well. Seems like I've hit the jackpot. Everyone I want to see, all in the one place.'

The Maestro stroked his shoulder and moved in close. 'Can I get you something to drink?'

I'll bet he could smell the lavender and spice in her hair.

'Tea, coffee, something stronger?' she asked.

'Coffee thanks. Long black, strong and hot.'

Ashley sat up straight in his chair, staring at the man who

shared his coffee preference.

'I'm interrupting your tea party,' Inspector Johnston said.

Jason pushed out a chair for him. 'No, we've just arrived home and are settling back in.'

Inspector Johnston scrutinised the surrounds. 'The place looks better than when I last saw it. Good clean up job. I keep finding places which are too clean — a morgue, a crypt, a swimming pool, a bathroom, prison cells — all too clean.'

'Really?' I said. 'Surely that's a good thing? Who doesn't love a clean swimming pool and bathroom?'

'Not when you're trying to find evidence.'

'So how can we help you?' Jason asked.

'We still haven't located the thugs who attacked you — they've vanished, as you know. You haven't had any unwelcome visitors, have you?'

'We've been at the Hyatt,' Jason said.

'Yes. I believe there was a strange malfunction with the swimming pool. And the twenty-four-hour clinic had a visit from Ashley and Luca. What was that about?'

'Only a scratch, cut my arm on a piece of metal at the gym,' Ashley said.

'And why were you being resuscitated next to an empty swimming pool?'

'Ashley gets asthma. He had an attack and I was giving him CPR,' Jason said.

Inspector Johnston didn't look convinced. 'Apparently, he vomited a truck load of water.'

Ashley nodded. 'That's 'cause I drank a truck load. I do every morning, water, that is.'

'Uh-huh. And Luca, you needed medical attention too?'

'Yes, my back was injured during all the chaos in the church.'

'How?'

Luca shifted uncomfortably in his chair. 'I'm not sure.'

Having the police here made me apprehensive. Food always

settled me, so I reached across for a piece of calming teacake. Inspector Johnston's eagle eyes picked up on my bandaged wrist.

Damn it. Damn it. Damn it. I forgot about the bandages.

He nodded at them. 'You've sustained an injury too. What happened there?'

I pulled my jumper over the bandage and felt my face turn as red as my sneakers.

Jason put his arm around me. 'She was caught up in the city riot, right in the middle of it. Managed to get out, but sustained a few cuts and bruises. She's been traumatised by the experience.'

'Why are you blushing?'

I felt my face burn even more. 'I always blush.'

His mouth twitched, and his eyes wouldn't let go of mine.

Staring match it was then. I met his gaze, determined to win. Your lips are very dry. I have something to fix that. Your nose dips slightly at the end. I wonder how you got those scars. I'm sorry for you, Inspector Johnston; you don't know what you're dealing with. I want to tell you the truth, we all would, but you wouldn't believe us. I wonder if he drinks. He'd have to, with his job, dealing with murder and mayhem every single day. No ring on his finger. Probably was married, now divorced.

'Maggie?'

'Yes?'

'You win.'

'Win what?'

'You were staring me out,' he said.

'You started.'

'You're very good.'

'I know. I'm used to staring out my dog.'

Inspector Johnston's mouth twitched and broke into a smile, stretching the skin on his cracked lips. He touched his bottom lip and winced.

'I've got something to fix that,' I said, racing off to the bathroom. I came back and handed him my tube of super-duper, no fail, lip balm — results guaranteed in twenty-four hours.

'What's this?'

'Lip balm. Results guaranteed in one day. Keep it. You'll have kissable lips in twenty-four hours. I mean, not that they aren't now, but they're very dry and...' Oh dear, I was babbling. 'Anyway, it'll help.'

Jason and Ashley rolled their eyes.

He unscrewed the top and applied it to his lips. 'Thanks. Feels better already.' He pressed a button on his watch, and it beeped.

'What's that?'

He smiled and locked onto me with eyes again. 'A timer. Twenty-four hours, you said? Twenty-four hours to kissable lips.'

The Maestro stroked his face and flicked her long black hair back over her shoulder. 'You're welcome to test them out on me.'

Now, it was Detective Inspector Johnston who was a little red in the face. But only a little. Thank God, it took the heat off me. He was valiantly trying to keep his eyes above her plunging neckline, but that only left her violet eyes and luscious mouth to focus on. He pulled at his tie and looked away.

I giggled and he shot me a look.

I held out the plate of banana walnut loaf. 'Cake?'

He helped himself to a large slice. 'Thanks. Breakfast, and probably lunch too.'

'I'm assuming you have a first name, or do we have to call you Detective Inspector Johnston?' the Maestro asked.

'My name is Elliot Fox Johnston, but people call me Fox. Fox was my grandfather's name.'

'And people call you Fox because you're a cunning and wily detective?' I asked.

'One of my commanders was a military history boffin. When he learned my middle name was Fox, he felt it was more apt than Elliot. Apparently, I reminded him of The Swamp Fox, Francis

Marion, a partisan leader of the American Revolutionary War. He was one of the pioneers of guerrilla style tactics, a gun at gathering intelligence. According to records, he didn't fight like "a gentleman and a Christian".

Fox paused and met our eyes one by one with a penetrating stare. I couldn't help but shift in my chair under the intensity of his gaze.

'The commander didn't elaborate on the particular quality he thought was relevant to me — whether I was good at gathering intelligence or a dirty fighter. Maybe it was both. Anyway, like it or not, the name's stuck.'

'Sounds interesting,' Ashley said. Fox had definitely caught his attention.

'Is it all right if we call you Fox?' I asked.

'Sure.'

'Are you married?' the Maestro asked.

'Was,' he said. 'Married to the job now.'

She nodded. 'Kids?'

'No. I have a dog. Schmoo.'

I laughed. 'Boo & Schmoo! What sort of dog?'

'English bull terrier.'

'Oh, I love them. They're called "a kid in a dog suit". Great dogs, but they don't like to be alone.'

'That's why he comes with me wherever I go. He's a bit of a mascot at work too.'

'Is he here now?'

'Yep. In the car.'

'You can bring him in — we're a dog friendly house. We'll introduce Boo to Schmoo outside first, so Boo doesn't get territorial.'

Fox pushed back his chair. 'Sure, let's do it.'

'I love bull terriers. I'll come too,' Luca said.

Boo raced ahead, pushing in front of us as I opened the front door. Outside, we saw Schmoo sitting in the driver's seat of the grey Holden Commodore.

Luca laughed. 'He looks as if he's ready to drive off. What a funny dog.'

Fox opened the car door. 'Come on, boy. Out you get.'

Boo was ready and waiting, excited to meet someone new.

Oh, very handsome. So strong and muscular.

Schmoo was an impressive dog, with the typical egg-shaped head and white gladiator body of the English bull terrier. He was all white, with black tipped ears, and he had a black nose with an uneven edge, as though the colour had run and soaked into the pinky white on his snout. His eyes were dark and shaped like two large commas — they punctuated his face with intelligence and wit.

Boo's four feet lifted off the ground. *Boo! Feet on the ground!* She dropped instantly to the path.

'They're getting on like best buddies,' Fox said.

'Good, let's go back in. Appears it might rain,' I said.

Boo and Schmoo disappeared through the dog flap and out into the garden.

'Boo's doing the tour of garden and house. It's a ritual,' Jason said, as we entered the kitchen.

'No news on your six colleagues, Luca?' Fox asked.

'No, I was hoping you'd have some.'

'Do you think they've been abducted?' Fox asked.

Luca stared at his shoes. 'I'm not sure what happened to them.'

Fox leaned against a kitchen chair and turned his attention to me. 'What do you think, Maggie?'

'How would I know?'

'Aren't you supposed to be psychic?'

'Yes.'

'Well?'

'I've got nothing.'

'Have you tried?'

'I don't like to try. Trying is bad for me. If things come, then all well and good. I don't want to go looking for trouble.'

'How can it be trouble?'

'You can open yourself to bad influences.'

'What sort of bad influences?'

'Demons. Devils. Every kind of universal scum if you don't keep your vibration high and positive.'

'Really?'

'Really.'

'You've had bad experiences?'

'Yes. That's why I try to shut it off.'

'What sort of bad experiences?'

'I don't want to talk about it. It's like saying don't think about an elephant. You can't help but imagine one, and I don't want to go there in any way, shape or form.'

'I understand. Would you ever consider using your skills to help solve these crimes?'

'Only if things come to me unbidden.'

'You'd let me know?'

'Of course.'

Boo and Schmoo blasted in through the dog flap, nearly knocking it off its hinges.

'Bloody hell!' Ashley said.

Jason jumped out of his chair at the noise.

The dogs hightailed it along the corridor, Schmoo in hot pursuit of Boo. Their nails scrabbled wildly on the wooden floorboards. Schmoo missed the turn and slammed into a door, bounced back off and continued his pursuit.

'I think I should take Schmoo to the car,' Fox said. 'He's getting too excited.'

'They'll settle,' I said. I could imagine that out of sight Boo would be having some serious floaty fun with Schmoo. 'I'll check things out.' I tiptoed up the hallway and peeked around the bedroom door. Boo floated just out of reach of Schmoo who was balanced on his hind legs, hopping across the floor.

Boo, play fair and play on the ground. Are you two okay?

Indeed. Nothing for you to concern yourself with whatsoever. Schmoo is the perfect gentleman.

Is that right? Keep things calm and on the ground please.

Boo floated back to the floor and greeted Schmoo with a big lick. The two followed me out of the bedroom looking like butter wouldn't melt in their mouths. They made a beeline to the rug in front of the open fire, snuggled together, and lay quietly staring into the flames.

Fox's brow was furrowed as he stood, hands on hips, watching them. 'I don't believe it. Schmoo's never settled anywhere so quickly. He's made himself right at home.'

'They love each other.'

Fox pushed back his recalcitrant hair. 'Appears so.'

'When's the last time you had a holiday, Fox?' I asked.

'Can't remember.'

'Not even a long weekend?'

'Nope.'

'What do you do to relax?'

'I work out at the gym, that's it. I used to walk the dog, but I get a dog walker in now.'

'We have some beautiful walks around here; along the river is Boo's favourite. Fresh air, tall trees. Pretty much off lead the whole way.'

'Sounds fantastic. I could use some fresh air.'

'Let's go now. Boo and Schmoo would love it.'

'Now?'

'Yes, right now. Why not? Forty minutes of fresh air and exercise. You'll feel like a new Fox.'

'Nup.'

'Oh, come on! Be spontaneous. It'll do you the world of good.

'It's tempting, but I've too much to do.'

'But you're not getting anywhere. A change of scenery will refresh you, recharge your batteries. You'll be more open to new insights.'

He flashed me a smile. 'Let's walk.'

'We'll go in five. I'll let Jason know.'

Fox sat on the floor in front of the fire with the dogs, stretched out his long legs, and leaned back against the couch. The three of them sat mesmerised, gazing into the flames, chilling out in the soft flickering light. Wood fires were always so therapeutic and relaxing.

'I could stay here all night,' Fox muttered. Boo gave a groan of agreement.

Back in the kitchen, the guys had made good work of the Maestro's cakes.

'It's nearly beer o'clock,' Jason said.

'Not quite,' I said. 'Fox and I are taking the dogs out for a walk. We'll do the river circuit.'

'Yeah, I heard. I don't think it's a good idea. We should come with you. Protection an' all,' Jason said.

'You said you were going to make dinner for everyone. You'll have enough to do.'

'I'll go,' Ashley said.

'I'll be with the Swamp Fox, so I'll have protection. He's a copper and he's got a gun. That's enough for me.'

'Be careful what you say to him,' Jason said. 'He's probably going to pump you for information.'

The Maestro smiled at me. 'I think it may be the other way around.'

'Ain't that the truth,' Ashley said.

'See, Jason, they know me better than you do.'

I grabbed Boo's lead and collar from the coat stand. Jason followed me and wrapped his arms around my waist and pulled me close. I felt the heat from his body and the angst in his mind. 'Please be careful. With everything that's happened, I hate letting you out of my sight.'

'I'll be fine. Can Fox stay for dinner? He probably won't, but I'd like to offer.'

'We won't be able to speak freely, and we need to make plans,' Jason whispered.

'I know. He probably won't stay, but I think we would benefit from getting to know him better. Having a sympathetic, high-level contact in the police force would be good for us. If he learns more about us, it could help take the heat off.'

Jason looked to the others for confirmation. They nodded in the affirmative.

'Ask away,' he said.

---

[7] *Maggie's Playlist: Fox — Toby Johnson*

Chapter 8: The Ranger

'Be sober-minded; be watchful. Your adversary the devil prowls around like a roaring lion, seeking someone to devour.' — 1 Peter 5:8

Fox hadn't moved when I went back into the lounge. He was a million miles away, his elbows balanced on his knees, his fingers interlocked and his chin resting on his knuckles. It was a shame to interrupt his reverie.

'Ready to go?' I asked.

He jumped to his feet in one fluid movement. 'Sure.'

Jeepers, he was fit. I couldn't get off the floor as easily as that.

'I thought we'd drive to the start of the walk to save time,' I said.

'Sounds like a plan. Anyone else coming?'

'Jason's making dinner and the others have things they need to get organised. You're welcome to stay. I'm sure you could use some home cooking.'

'Sounds tempting, but I'd better head off after the walk.'

'You can always change your mind. Jason's making Thai green curry, with chicken, so we can send you off with some to go.'

'Sounds good. Come on Schmoo, we're going for a walk!' Fox laughed at Schmoo's stunned expression. 'Check him out, he can't believe his ears.'

*****

Me, Fox, Boo and Schmoo were a twelve-legged entity. Boo loved this forest walk. Schmoo couldn't believe his luck and kept staring into the tree tops.

'He's a city dog,' Fox said. 'This is such a treat for him.'

I laughed. 'Same goes for you, I reckon.'

We walked on as the dogs lagged behind, stopping to fill their noses with new and exciting scents. Eight pairs of paws thundered across the boardwalk as they ran to catch up. The dog's faces were split with wide grins, pink tongues hanging out to one side, eyes bright with delight, ears pinned back in the breeze. Their whole beings exuded happiness.

'Check 'em out,' Fox said. 'They know how to enjoy the moment.'

'Different from the joyless faces of the joggers running past,' I said.

We continued along the track, past grand eucalypts and the green snake of the river. The dogs looked around in alarm as an unfamiliar sound echoed through the trees.

Boom! Boom! Boom!

The sound of drums, loud and monotonous, disturbed our peaceful expedition.

'What the hell?' Fox said. 'Sounds like war drums. It's as if a tribe of warriors are going to attack. Let's get to the top of the hill and find out what's happening.'

He raced ahead while I struggled to keep pace. My lungs burned. I so needed to get fit. He was twenty years older than me. Feeling pathetic, I stopped to catch my breath and looked up to the hilltop.

Sheltering under the Cypress pine trees were a group of people in brightly coloured clothing. They were banging the hell out of huge drums — Boom! Boom! Boom! It was relentless. No wonder they used drums for war in the old days; it sounded so intimidating.

Fox was waiting for me at the top. I ran to him trying to suppress my heavy breathing. I'm sure he could see my pulse throbbing in my neck. Oh, look at him — no change in his breathing and his pulse rate was probably exactly the same.

'Oh, I love those saris!' I gasped, checking out the circle of people. 'The guy in red silk even has a huge scabbard on his belt.'

'Look at the size of those drums,' Fox said. 'They're nearly as big as the people. Hell, the noise will be echoing across the 'burbs.'

A sound of screeching tires made us jump.

'Park ranger,' Fox said. 'This'll be interesting.'

A very large ranger shoehorned herself out of her ute and strode towards the drummers.

'Jeez,' Fox said. 'How tall is she? Got a beer gut to rival any bloke I know. Seriously scary.'

'Yeah, wouldn't want to mess with her!' I agreed. 'Wonder how this will go?'

A harsh Aussie twang rang out. 'Do youse realise you need a permit? You can't start drumming wherever the hell you want, you know. Hey! Shut it! I'm trying to talk!'

The drummers fell silent in their circle.

'You can't drum here! It's not on. Have some bloody respect! You can't come to this country and carry on like frigging idiots. Pack up your crap and get the hell out of here.'

Fox looked angry. 'She shouldn't speak to them like that.'

Red silk man left the circle and moved towards the ranger. The ornate silver scabbard bounced against his leg as he walked. The scabbard was secured to his belt by a beautiful filigree gold clasp and chain. He gripped the hilt of the sword to steady it. He reached the ranger, stood in front of her and stared directly into her eyes. His sword flashed in a silver arc through the air. It sparkled, reflecting the colours of the sky and surrounds.

'Bloody awesome,' the ranger murmured.

It was the ranger's last thought as her head left her shoulders and landed with a thud at her feet. The headless body stood for a second before falling backwards. A cloud of pine needles flew skyward as the body hit the ground with a thump. It reminded me of a felled tree hitting the deck. The severed head began a slow roll along the slope. Schmoo leapt forward to grab what he thought was the ultimate prize — a bloody soccer ball.

'Schmoo! *No!*' Fox shouted.

We watched in horror as Schmoo seized the head and hightailed it down the hill dragging his trophy along by the hair. Schmoo's jaunty air indicated he thought it was the best thing he'd found — *ever*.

A collective gasp of shock reverberated around the group. Everyone froze, except for red silk man, who raised his sword and turned slowly on the spot. He stared at each person as though they were strangers. His eyes aligned with mine and he stopped. Lifting his sword higher, he advanced towards me.

The red silk sleeves of his tunic rippled away from his wrists and fell in gentle folds around his elbows. Intricate designs of Catherine wheel tattoos danced on his forearms.

'Everybody, *run*! Now!' I shouted.

Twenty screaming people ran for their lives. As they did I reflected how beautiful their clothing was. Multi-coloured flowing silk scattered like flowers thrown to the wind. It was all the more beautiful set against the grey day and overshadowed by the imposing Cypress pine trees surrounding us.

'Maggie! Get back!' Fox shouted. His gun was drawn and directed at red silk man who was now only a few feet away from me.

'Stop! Police. Drop the sword. Now!'

'You'll have to shoot him, Fox. He won't stop.'

'Put the sword down. Now! This is your last warning!'

I stepped backwards as red silk man advanced. We still had

about six feet between us. Fox retreated, keeping a similar distance.

My eyes were fixed on the dark eyes of red silk man. He halted his approach and held his sword high. It glinted in the light. Trickles of the ranger's blood ran along the blade and onto his hands.

I appealed to him. 'You don't want to do this. You know you don't. Fight it! You don't want to kill me. Please. Fight it! You have a choice. You can beat it. You can win!'

Emotions rippled across his face. His arms jerked. His knees jumped and quaked, and in that moment his eyes softened to reveal for an instant the kind man he was.

'Fight it,' I whispered, as despair filled his eyes, and then he was gone, lost to the dark.

He leapt into action, a ninja warrior springing skywards. I gazed up at him as he hovered above me, his sword ready to strike. His face had the visage of a demon from hell.

Blood and red silk. Blood and red silk. The story of my life.

I marvelled at the red silk fluttering like a flag of death in the air. The blood from the sword splashed across my face.

My ears imploded, shattered by the rending noise of gunfire. Blood rained over me as his head came apart. He hit the ground with a thump, his crumpled body bent and broken on a bed of rust coloured pine needles. They soaked his blood into their dry embrace.

Fox stood stone faced and spread legged, arms stretched out, both hands wrapped around the butt of his gun. A slight haze escaped from the barrel, and my nostrils were filled with the scent of chemicals — sulphur, copper, blood, pine, grass and mud.

My knees crumpled and I sank to the ground, feeling the roughness of the needles through my jeans. Boo bounded over and tried to lick the blood from my face. I pushed her away. 'Don't, Boo, you don't want to drink that.'

Maggie, we should get the hell out of here. It was Boo in my brain.

Oh, hell yes. But where was Schmoo? Where was the head? We didn't want another missing person.

I grabbed one arm of the headless corpse and attempted to pull it towards a big tree. 'Fox! Help me with the ranger's body.'

I tried not to look at the bloodied, headless shoulders. The body barely moved. Jesus. I needed some of Jason's strength. I locked onto him in my mind and pulled again. The body shifted.

'Fox! Help me!'

What the hell was he doing? I looked at him. He was examining the body of red silk man.

'Fox! Get away from it! Listen, you have to help me. Now!'

He jumped back from the body. 'What the?'

A very large black cockroach sat on red silk man's chin. It rose up and hissed at Fox.

He stepped back in horror. 'What the *fuck*?'

'Fox! You need to help me. *NOW!*' I screamed. Christ, I needed a frigging megaphone to get his attention.

Finally, he came over and grabbed the other arm.

'Quickly, help me drag her behind the tree. Red silk man is going to self-destruct.'

'What?'

'Don't ask questions; do what I say, *please*. Behind this tree. It should be wide enough to provide cover. Where's Schmoo? Where's the head?'

We scanned the park, but it was deserted, and neither Boo nor Schmoo were anywhere to be seen.

Fox tried to shake hair out of his eyes as it whipped across his face. 'Hell, the wind's sprung up.'

If only he knew this was no ordinary wind.

He pulled out his mobile and hit a speed dial number. I snatched it from him, disconnected the call, switched off the phone and put it in my pocket. Before he could protest, I said, 'Listen to me now. We only have seconds left. You can call your buddies in a minute.'

The ranger had fallen over from her sitting position behind the Cypress pine, so I pulled her back upright. I dragged Fox across to the next Cypress pine. It had two intertwined trunks, with a small hole at eye level where one person could see through to the other side. I shouted over the noise of the wind. 'Whatever you do, don't move from behind this tree. Look!'

Fox put his face to the peephole and I felt his body go rigid with shock. I peeked out from the side of the tree and saw the shimmering swirl of the black hole rising from red silk man's body. The carpet of rusty red pine needles had come to life and flowed like a tide of insects into the jaws of the black hole. The whirlpool gained momentum, ripping autumn leaves from the trees. A kaleidoscope of colours — orange, red, yellow, purple, black, orange, pink, magenta, blue and brown — swirled insanely against the charcoal grey sky. A wooden picnic bench juddered slowly forward leaving tracks in the grass behind it. Branches, litter and dog poo all scuttled along, heading for their new home in an alternate universe. Wherever this stuff ended up, it must have been starting to look like one big rubbish dump by now.

A three-foot-thick black tendril unwound itself from the main body of the whirling black hole. It stretched straight up, unravelling to the height of the Cypress trees. There it hovered, flexing in the wind while the base of the whirlpool continued to spin around it. Jeepers, I hadn't seen it do that before.

The top of the tendril widened and spread. It bent forward and fluttered, seeming to taste the air. The tendril swayed hypnotically from side to side, drawing itself higher, stretching and pulling back slightly. The stance registered in my subconscious and came screaming into my frontal lobes.

A cobra! A Big Mother of a Cobra in Strike Mode.

I gripped Fox's jacket collar and pulled him away from the hole. He simultaneously hooked onto my belt and yanked me back behind the tree. He dragged me in front of him and squatted. I was wedged between his legs as he jammed his boots into the roots of the tree, pushing back into a hollow at the base. He wrapped one arm around me, while his other gripped a loop in a tree root.

The strike was like being hit by a grenade. The earth jolted, the tree groaned and cracked, green pine needles rained down on us, and a branch crashed to the ground just missing our feet. My ears — which were still ringing from Fox's gunshot—were shattered as the cobra struck again.

Slam! The tree cracked, bark exploded around us, and a sinewy black tendril poked through the hole in the tree. More tendrils appeared around the sides of the tree, trying to gain purchase on the tree — and us.

The wind force was at maximum frenzy. I knew from previous experience the hole had to close soon. Didn't it? My mind was spinning. What to do? The tree shuddered and groaned behind us. The tendril was trying to rip the tree out of the ground.

We were screwed. It'd evolved. It had us. We weren't far enough away. We couldn't make a run for it. Please tree, please tree, hold on!

'What do we do?' Fox yelled in my ear.

I could barely hear him over the wind, the cracking of the tree and the ringing in my ears. The tendrils were only inches from us, digging into the bark of the tree, clawing like fingers as they gripped and pulled. The tree groaned and cracked further, the soil rose around us, and we tipped backwards as its roots let go of the earth. The tree slammed into the ground and shuddered along the grass towards its new home — and we accompanied it.

Something on the horizon caught my eye. It resembled a little black bumblebee, zigzagging crazily towards us. I narrowed my eyes, trying to see through the flying debris.

'It's ... Boo!'

Sorry I took so long. I was trying to find Schmoo.

Boo flew in and hit the upturned tree root like a scud missile. Her lead was in her mouth, but it flapped madly out of reach. Her voice was clear in my head.

Grab the lead. I'll tow you to safety.

What about Fox? We can't leave him.

Tell him to hang onto you. I can pull you both. Quick! It's in its final phase.

I launched myself at the lead. *Got it!* I wrapped it around my wrist and watched as Boo hovered, moving slowly backwards, teeth clenched around the lead, lips curled back.

I hope her teeth don't break.

I heard you! My teeth are fine.

I stretched towards Fox, and he managed to grip my wrist.

Oh, my poor wrists. Can you do this, Boo?

Of course I can! It's tug of war, my favourite game, and you know how good I am at that.

True, you'd never let go of a shoe or towel unless we prized it out of your mouth.

Boo was floating in a full-fledged tug of war stance.

The tree slid away from us, and the massive root tipped upwards and over into the black hole. Boo was nearly on the ground, neck stretched as she hovered, pulling us slowly away from the vortex.

The lead had cut off the circulation in my hand. It had turned a peculiar shade of purply pink. Hopefully it wouldn't fall off, so I could hold on for another couple of seconds.

Fox was still attached to my left arm, which felt like it was being subjected to a medieval rack treatment. I figured he must weigh at least eighty-five kilos and wondered how long my shoulder joint could hold out.

We floated horizontal to the ground, caught in the slipstream of the black hole. Boo had her eyes closed, concentrating, teeth clenched on the lead. She was growling.

Fox dug his feet and spare hand into the ground, trying to take the pressure off Boo and help inch us forward. A loud *thunk,* which reminded me of the noise our vacuum hose made when I yanked it out of the wall outlet without turning the power off first, echoed through the air as the hole slammed shut. The slipstream stopped instantly, and the ground slammed into me expelling the air from my lungs. Ow! I hated being winded. I curled into a fetal position, wheezing and trying to get my breath. We'd made it!

The tree was gone. Everything not tied down was gone, including the ranger. Boo and Fox lay sprawled in the mud.

I pulled Fox's phone from my back pocket and tossed it to him. He picked it up, staggered to his feet, and surveyed the situation.

'Is it safe now?' he croaked.

'As safe as it can get for the meantime.'

Fox turned on the spot — a three-hundred-and-sixty-degree rotation. 'Everything's gone. Ranger's gone. Car's gone. Head's gone. Sword man's gone. Tree's gone. Every. Fucking. Thing. Has. Gone.'

Fox stared at his phone, thumb poised. He looked at it for a good sixty seconds before he snapped the cover shut and put it back in his pocket. His head twitched back and forth. 'Who the hell do I tell? There's no one. They'll think I've lost it,' he muttered to no one in particular. 'I have lost it. I must've. A flying dog for fuck's sake?'

The sound of sirens broke the silence.

'I think your buddies are on the way. Also, we don't know for sure the head's gone,' I said, trying to be helpful.

He dragged his hands through his hair and did another three-hundred-and-sixty-degree slow turn. 'What was that?'

'The cause of your high crime rate.'

'Is Boo all right?'

Boo? Are you okay?

Definitely. It was the best tug of war ever. I won!
You sure did, Boo. You saved the day.
'She's fine.'

'Then let's get the hell out of here. I need to find Schmoo. And I need a drink.' Fox seized my hand and we staggered back towards the river path. He seemed to have developed a constant headshake.

I rubbed my wrists. 'A drink? That's the best thing you've said all day. Oh Jesus, I'm sore. It's going to take a bucket load of Arnica to fix this.'

Fox stared at my wrists and bit his bottom lip, which made him look pensive and vulnerable. He needed to urgently reapply his lip balm. The lines between his eyes and along his forehead seemed deeper.

The light was falling fast. We needed to move quickly or we wouldn't be able to see our feet. The path was muddy and slippery in places. I strode ahead as I was more familiar with the route. Boo skipped along in front of me, and her tan coloured bum reflected the light, so all I had to do was follow the bouncing ball.

The forest was redolent with the scent of eucalyptus. Currawongs' calls echoed eerily through the treetops. I couldn't wait to get home — the temperature had dropped with the sun, and I felt cold and damp. The adrenaline had gone, and I became aware of my body and how much it ached.

I needed a big glass of red wine. Shiraz.
Paracetamol. Lots.
Food. Green Curry and Rice.
A hot bath with Epsom salts, candles, steaming, soothing hot water and—

Something slammed into me.
'Oomph!'
The air left my lungs in a rush.
What the?

80

I fell flat on my back and slid down a steep embankment. It was similar to a ride at Wet 'n' Wild — apart from the sharp rocks, branches and tree roots that bruised and scratched me en route.

I plunged into the sticky mud and silt at the river's edge. At least the ride had a soft landing. I sank deep into the sludge as a weight on top of me pushed me under. It was pitch black. I could feel the suction of the mud against my skin. The mud felt alive as it tried to pull me into its murky depths. I gasped for the breath to scream. I wheezed and coughed. A hand pressed hard across my mouth. I froze. The sound of a thousand mosquitos buzzed in my ears. I felt disorientated. My body shuddered as a wave of icy water splashed over me. I wanted to scream. I needed to — *scream!*

I inhaled sharply and felt my breath flow more easily. I expanded my lungs, raised my shoulders and sucked in as much air as I could. The hand pressed harder. A voice in my ear hissed, '*Shhh*. It's Fox. Shut up. Keep still.' The hand released.

'What the *hell?*'

'Someone's after us.'

'I can't hear anything except mosquitos.'

'It's your ears. The gun. Trust me. Be quiet.'

'I'm sinking. You're too heavy.'

I was completely submerged in mud with only my face sticking out. I seriously needed to work on my visualisation techniques. I had wanted a bath bath, not a mud bath. This felt horrible, as if I was encased in wet cement. Maybe I was. Maybe he was trying to kill me. Get rid of evidence. Yes, it had to be. He might think that way. I didn't know him. I didn't know him at all. He was giving me concrete boots. He was going to push my face down into the mud at any minute. Never trust anyone who says, "trust me". He'd be home and hosed. No witnesses. No reports. He probably couldn't handle what happened. He'd snapped. Gone loco. Non compos mentis. He could shoot out the tires on his squad car and retire with a big fat pension. Call it quits right now. He needed to get rid of the evidence — me. I was the only thing standing in his way. Jesus.

Panic stirred in my gut. I tried to move. I took a breath and forced out a smidgeon of a scream before his hand cut it off.

I tried to scream through his hand. 'Mmmmm. Mmmmm.'

He pressed even harder.

'Shut up.'

Along with the mud and Fox, claustrophobia now had me in its grip.

My arms and legs were immobilised by mud. I wriggled and squirmed, trying to break free. Strange slurping, sucking noises arose in response, and the mud released odours of mushrooms and decay. The mud held me even tighter in its sticky embrace.

'Stop it,' Fox whispered. 'I'll move my hand. Promise. No sound.'

I nodded and he slowly released the pressure.

He was heavy on top of me. I tried to get a breath and felt myself sink even deeper into the mud. It flowed into my ears and magnified the sound of the buzzing. I was trapped in a sensory deprivation tank with a swarm of bees. A sense of dread, anxiety and panic overwhelmed me. I was going to die. I felt my anatomy shift into survival mode. My brain fired, and there was a moan as I sucked air into my lungs. My mouth stretched open to emit a final primal scream.

'No,' Fox whispered sharply.

His mouth closed over mine and captured the scream so not a peep escaped my lips. The air set to explode through my mouth escaped through my nose as he kissed me with intent. He held my head and his thumbs brushed my cheeks.

Oh my. Oh my. Oh. My.

The spreading panic and claustrophobia withdrew their tentacles from my mind and body and made a rapid retreat back into their shell. In the depths of my body a new sensation blossomed, warm and sensual. I lay entombed in the embrace of mud and one muddy detective, who kissed me as if our lives depended on it. And indeed, they did.

I felt the vibration of approaching footsteps, and above the sound of the buzzing in my ears I finally heard the tread of a multitude of feet. Flashlights beamed through the trees, swathes of light cut through the undergrowth. A crack of thunder exploded overhead, and I jumped. Fox jumped too and broke his kiss. He pressed one finger across my lips.

The rain came. Illuminated by the torch light, it fell in showers of crystal rainbows. A torch beam cut along the river right next to us, and in the reflected light, the bright eyes of a possum stared out of a nearby bush. I could just make out Fox's face as he scanned the surrounds. The whites of his eyes glowed in his mud streaked face. He looked like Rambo.

'Cops are coming,' a male voice said.

It had an accent that sounded vaguely familiar. Other voices barked orders at each other.

'Hurry, we must get her!' a woman said. 'Check by the river.'

'It's too dangerous.'

'I'll do it.'

The undergrowth rustled on the bank above us. The torchlight moved erratically as someone made their way down the bank.

The water rose rapidly with the rain, which fell in glistening sheets on the river surface. Raindrops bounced and rattled noisily next to us, and I gasped as a wave of water flowed over my face. Fox grasped my hair and pulled my face above the water.

The beam of a torch came to rest inches away from my face. No doubt in response to my horrified expression, Fox shielded me with his body and resumed the business of kissing me.

Could be worse ways to go. It certainly helped to take one's mind off things. It actually felt quite warm in the mud. Almost cozy. That's it, Maggie. Relax. Let go. Oh. Dear. Me.

The sound of police radios crackled in the distance.

'Let's go. It's too late!' the man's voice said. His footsteps scrambled back up the bank and splashed away hastily. The rain was teeming. Lightning ripped the cloak of darkness from the forest and thunder rumbled overhead. I poked my finger into the side of Fox's leg.

He broke the kiss. 'Yes?'

'Is it safe?'

'As safe as it can get I suppose. It pays to be sure,' he said, kissing me gently again. After a moment he hauled himself off me and tried to stand in the mud and silt. 'I think the coast is clear now.' He located my hands in the mud.

'Oh, please, not my wrists.'

'Sorry.' He stepped around behind me and gripped me under the armpits. 'Will this be okay?'

'Yes.' I let him heave me into a sitting position.

I tried to move my legs, to get up, to squat, but the mud had me firmly in its grasp. Fox held the top of my jeans and tried to yank me out. My jeans tore, and he slipped and fell into the river.

I latched onto his jacket to stop him being swept away.

A sharp bark echoed next to my ear.

It's me, Boo. To the rescue again. Take the lead.

I can't see it.

The lead dangled across my face.

Got it.

Hang on; I'll haul you up the bank.

'Fox, can you hold onto my waist? Boo's here. She's going to pull us out.'

He gripped my ankles. I heard the splash of water and the sucking of mud as Fox hauled himself up and wrapped an arm around my waist.

'Go, Boo,' Fox said.

God, she was strong.

The slack on the lead tightened. I held on, hoping I could maintain my grip. The mud released its hold on my legs as Boo moved straight up like a rescue helicopter.

I'm on my feet now, Boo.

I'll keep pulling. Don't let go.

My feet finally contacted grass and scrub, and the weight lessened on my waist as Fox made purchase with solid ground.

Nearly there, Boo. Keep going!

Our feet slipped, the rain making it difficult. We slipped and cursed, but Boo pulled us upwards until finally we felt and heard gravel under our feet.

'Thanks, Boo. Again,' Fox said.

My pleasure.

I slowly collapsed to the ground. Huh. Delayed weak knee reaction. I'd never had that before. 'Far out. What a day.'

Fox must have felt me go, and he took my arm and helped me up. 'Put your arm across my shoulder. Do you need me to carry you?'

'No, I can walk, except my jeans are around my ankles.' I pulled them up.

Damn it. Another pair of jeans gone. I needed Ashley's clothes dude around full time at this rate. I clutched my jeans with one hand. 'Let's go.'

Fox switched on his mobile and a flood of beeps responded. He flicked it to mute and turned on the torch app. 'Excellent, we can see. How far to the car?'

'Ten-minute fast walk.'

'Let's go. Keep your eyes and ears peeled.'

'Do you have your gun?'

He patted his side. 'Yep. Boo, go on girl, you first. Maggie in the middle. I'll cover your behind. I mean back.'

'I'm sure you will.'

'I owe you an apology. For before.'

'Save it.'

'We need to talk.'

'Of course. Later.'

'Over a drink?'

'Make that drinks. Lots. I take it you'll be staying for dinner?'

'If it's still okay with you?'

'Sure. We have a spare bed. Stay the night.'

Fox heaved a huge sigh. 'Thanks. I will.'

We reached the end of the path with no further trouble, but no sign of Schmoo. Fox's face was tight with worry.

The car was parked outside the tennis courts, as we had left it. Good street lighting illuminated the area. The place was deserted.

'Give me the keys,' Fox said. 'You wait here. I'll walk over alone.'

I gave him the keys and he pulled out his gun, holding it under his jacket. He moved quickly to the car, scanning the surrounds as he went.

Boo and I waited quietly in the shadows.

All was quiet on the western front. Too quiet.

In the shadows of the tennis court car park, a motorbike revved into life. Smoke plumed from its screaming back wheel as it rocketed out of the dark and headed straight towards me. *Shit!*

I was standing behind a solid post and rail fence. I stepped back further and hid in the bushes as the bike screeched to a halt on the other side of the fence.

The rider wore black leathers and a helmet. He kicked out the stand, leaving the bike idling. Maybe it was one of the park rangers. He dismounted and vaulted the fence.

Black leather guy stood quietly for a second checking out the path. I held my breath. A thousand volts of adrenaline coursed through my body as he sprang into life. His legs propelled him high into the air in a massive leap. For a moment he was suspended in space, like a silhouette of a Japanese Ninja. His legs were folded underneath him in a flying squat. His neck was craned forward, his arms stretched out to each side. He clutched a long dagger. I could sense his condensed power and anger. He was bursting at the seams, ready to inflict maximum carnage.

I ducked and rolled under the fence. Boo barked and growled madly, buzzing like a bee around his helmet, a whirlwind of furious fangs.

Black leather guy vaulted back over the fence.

He had to be a parkour guy. Only a parkour guy would vault a fence which had a perfectly good opening in it. Either that or he was a Ninja.

He reached the graceful apex of his vault and his chest exploded. He fell across his bike and the motor roared as his gloved hand caught on the accelerator.

Fox stood under the street light, silhouetted against the rain, legs spread, arms stretched, both hands wrapped around his gun.

Adrenaline coursed through my body as I raced towards him. 'What have you done? You're crazy. How...'

Fox gripped my arm and dragged me towards the bike. He flipped up the visor of the man's helmet with the barrel of his gun.

I had a terrible feeling.

Oh God. Please. Please don't let it be Drom.

The girl was beautiful. Her eyes were wide and blue. Dark lashes, perfect skin and rosy lips. Couldn't have been more than nineteen. The beauty of her face was such that it was only slightly diminished by the crush of the helmet and the cockroach crawling out of her mouth.

Fox pointed to the petrol tank with his gun. White tank, black Catherine wheel.

'Oh,' I said, as Fox raced back to the car.

'Come on!' he yelled. 'Hurry!'

Something caught my eye on the body draped across the bike. A familiar silhouette on the back of her leather pants. You beauty! Reaching in, I pulled out a pistol and quickly stashed it inside my jacket. Noticing a satchel, I took that too, looping it over my shoulder.

I reached the car and Fox said, 'I'll drive.'

'It's my car. I'll drive.'

He tossed me the keys, and we jumped in and I took off. I opened all four car windows. Fox stared at me, puzzled. Boo flew in through the back window and I closed them again. I saw a twitch of a smile on Fox's face as he looked at Boo and back at me. He scratched his head and furrowed his brow. *That's only adding to your wrinkles, Fox.*

I drove through the streets at the maximum speed limit, maybe a tad over, and travelled a convoluted way home. I stopped about a block from our house and turned off the engine.

'What's up?' Fox asked.

'Waiting to see if we were followed.'

'Good plan.'

'You look like Rambo,' I said, 'All I can see are the whites of your eyes.'

Fox grinned.

'And your teeth.'

'You look like a commando yourself. Christ, have a look at us!' he said. 'Oh, and Maggie, I have to apologise.'

'For what? Saving my life?'

'Actually, you saved mine. As did Boo. Let's call it even. I wanted to apologise for kissing you. I was out of line.'

'Desperate times, desperate measures, Fox. I get it. You had to shut me up somehow and, the kiss worked a treat. It stopped my panic and claustrophobia and calmed me. Good strategy. Anyways, I pretended you were Jason.'

'You did?'

'Yes,' I said, lying. He seemed so concerned about his behaviour that I wanted to make him feel better.

'It was a strategy,' he said. 'It was the only thing I could think of. You were freaking out, and I had to do something to keep you calm. I hoped it wouldn't freak you out more — I took a calculated risk. So, I don't have to apologise then?'

'No.'

Fox was quiet for a moment and then said, 'I do want to apologise for the second kiss.'

'You kissed me *three* times, but who's counting,' I said, grinning.

Fox crinkled his brow, and the mud on his face cracked. 'Jesus. I did too. That's even worse. It was totally unnecessary. I took advantage of the situation … of you. I'm not sure what got into me. I'm sorry. I was totally unprofessional.'

'I didn't mind. Except the time wasn't up.'

'What time?'

'The twenty-four hours — you know, to kissable lips.'

Fox threw back his head and laughed. I hadn't heard him laugh before. It was deep and dirty. 'So, even though the time wasn't up, was I kissable?' he asked with a cheeky smile.

'Oh, my word yes. No problems whatsoever. Listen, Fox, you probably already know it, but this is war. War makes you live on the edge. It makes you crazy. It makes you do stuff you normally wouldn't do — things you thought you would, could, never do. Believe me, I know. So don't beat yourself up about it. It's nice you're even concerned. Thank you. I appreciate it.'

'Thanks. And may I say you're very kissable too.'

I felt myself blush underneath all the mud. 'Thank you.'

We sat in silence and I heard the thoughts whirring in his brain.

I started the engine. 'Let's go home and drink.'

Fox gave me the thumbs up.

---

8 *Maggie's Playlist: Don't Lose Your Head — Andy Carhart*

Chapter 9: The Trophy

The porch light was on as I pulled into the drive. We exited the car and Fox scanned the surrounds. He was always "on".

The front door opened to reveal five anxious faces.

Jason stared at us in horror. 'Holy shit! What the hell happened? Boo said you were fine. How is this fine?' He glared at Boo.

'We are fine,' I said. 'Don't have a go at Boo. Boo is the heroine of the day.'

'Jesus, what's going on?' Ashley asked. 'Looks as if you've gone ten rounds in championship mud wrestling.'

'Long story. Later. We need a drink. Oh, it's so good to be home,' I said, reaching out to Jason. My jeans tumbled down around my ankles.

Damn it! I'd forgotten.

Ashley gave a throaty chuckle.

'Oh, shut up, Ashley.' I hoisted my pants back up with as much dignity as I could muster. Given the situation, it wasn't very much. The Maestro had a big grin on her face.

Jason stared at me with laser beam eyes. 'Just great. I don't even want to ask. What is it with you and your pants?'

'She has trouble kee—

I shot Ashley a vicious look, and he shut up mid-sentence.

'Has anyone seen Schmoo?' Fox asked. 'We've lost him. I thought he may have come back here.'

Drom shook his head. 'No sign of him I'm afraid.'

Boo's voice shouted in my mind. *He's here. He's here! Coming along the path.*

We heard the ticking of claws racing on concrete and a muffled, excited bark.

'Huff, Ruff, Huff, Huff, Ruff.'

'It has to be Schmoo!' I said.

The gladiator raced into the courtyard with his prize clamped in his mouth.

'Holy hell!' Ashley exclaimed.

Luca crossed himself. 'Jesus, Lord!'

The Maestro covered her mouth. 'Oh, my God!'

Drom turned white. 'Not good.'

Jason and Fox looked horrified and took a step back.

Schmoo was beside himself with joy. He bounced around Fox with the ranger's head dangling from his mouth, her long hair between his teeth. The ponytail poked out from one side of his face, like some crazy moustache, and the head bobbed around on the other side. The ranger's jaw clanked up and down with each exuberant bounce.

'Oh, that's so wrong,' the Maestro said, now holding both hands over her mouth.

'Fox, here's the head,' I said, stating the bleeding obvious.

'Get a bag or something, someone, please,' he replied.

Ashley dashed away and came back with an empty plastic Tontine pillow bag.

'Who the hell is ... was it?' Jason asked.

'Park ranger,' I said.

'Jesus, I know you've had runs-ins with rangers before about Boo being off lead, but ... but ... how could you do this?'

Fox's head snapped around. I sensed he was wondering why

Jason would say such a thing if I didn't have priors.

'I didn't do it! For Christ's sake, Jason, give me some credit. It was someone else.'

'Drop it, Schmoo,' Fox growled. 'Drop it! Drrrop it! Give! Give it to me! Now!' Fox put the bag over the ranger's head and held it. 'Drop it, Schmoo, so help me, I'll—'

Schmoo was way too happy with his prize to give it up. A deep warning growl rumbled from the depths of his big chest.

Fox stood and brushed back his hair. He appeared stressed and exhausted. 'For fuck's sake!'

Boo, can you help here? We need to get the head off Schmoo.

Leave it to me. Get everyone inside. He won't give it up with you lot around. Leave the front door open.

'Boo'll get it, Fox. Come on, let's go inside.'

Fox looked at me. He had a slightly deranged appearance about him. No wonder.

Three minutes later the two dogs trotted back inside. Schmoo was sans head, but looked pretty happy nevertheless. Boo dropped the bag with the head at Fox's feet.

Fox wearily scratched her ears. 'Thanks, Boo.'

Ashley picked up the bag. 'I'll put it in the fridge in the basement. We'll think about this later. First, we have to get you two cleaned up, fed and watered.' He gave me a look and then a wink. I poked my tongue out at him.

How'd you get it off him? I asked Boo.

Easy. Feminine wiles. Schmoo's gorgeous, but a bit dense at times. Reminds me of Ashley.

I laughed out loud.

'What?' Ashley asked.

'Nothing.'

Jason grinned, privy to the conversation.

'Fox is staying tonight, if that's all right, Jason?'

'No worries. What about the Maestro?'

'Oh, sorry, I forgot. Maestro, you can stay too. We have a

fold down double bed in the study. It's very comfortable.'

'That would be lovely.'

'Hey, we have a full house,' Jason said. 'We'll be setting up barracks soon.'

'Yeah, command central — Light Force!' I said.

'HUA!' Ashley yelled out from the kitchen.

Luca looked puzzled. 'Hua?'

'Heard, understood and acknowledged. Army speak,' Jason explained.

'You obviously haven't watched many action movies, Luca,' I said.

He smiled. 'Only religious action movies. My one indulgence is *The Simpsons*. I love that show.'

Ashley chuckled. 'That explains the Homer Simpson jocks. Who would've thought? By the way, Maggie, Fox, you need a shower, your mud is starting to crack. Here's a garbage bag each for your muddy clothes. I'll throw 'em in the wash later.'

'Hey, Fox, you can borrow some of my clothes if you want,' Jason offered.

'Thanks, but I always keep a bag packed in the car. I'll go get it.'

* * * * *

I stripped off my muddy clothes and stashed them in the bag from Ashley. Good old Ashley. He always looked out for everyone, taking care of things. You never had to tell him what to do.

I picked up the jacket and pulled the pistol out from its interior pocket. Wow. What a ripper. It was bright and shiny — I could see myself in the finish — all silver except for the black grip and sights. It was huge too. I turned it over and read the inscription.

Desert Eagle Pistol. Made in the USA.

Desert Eagle. I liked the sound of that. I held the gun. It was heavy. Maybe about three kilos. The grip was extremely wide. You could blow away a few zombies with this thing. I was glad Suzuki girl didn't get the chance to use it on me. I couldn't even fathom how she could get her hand around it, it was so big. I made sure the safety was on and tucked the gun away under some towels. I stashed the satchel in the wardrobe, planning to check on the contents later.

I turned on the shower and rested my forehead against the shower wall, letting the steaming water run over my back. I couldn't live without a hot shower. A track of muddy water ran along the white tiles and pooled at my feet. My hair was caked in mud, and I had to shampoo three times before the water ran clean.

'Are you right in there?' Jason yelled through the door. 'You've been ages.'

'All good. Come in.'

'Feeling better?' he asked. 'I would've come in there with you, but you were one muddy puppy. What happened out there?' Jason came to the shower door and gasped. 'Jesus! Look at your wrists, they're black and blue, worse than before.'

'Don't fuss. I just need a pile of paracetamol and ibuprofen.'

Jason gave me a look. 'Is there something you need to tell me in private?'

Uh-oh. Don't tell me Fox told him about the kissing business. 'Um, what do you mean?'

'Anything you don't want the others to hear?'

'I don't think so. It was a roach attack again. Two attacks actually.'

Jason's face crumpled with concern. 'I knew I shouldn't have let you go without me.'

Phew. It appeared Fox had kept quiet after all. The last thing I needed was more angst over nothing.

'Fox looked after me. He saw everything. The roaches, the

black hole. We haven't debriefed yet. He didn't even call the police. The whole thing must be messing with his mind.'

'What do we do? Tell him everything? Trust him?'

'I think we have to. What's the worst that can happen? If he talks, they'll think he's crazy. It'll take the pressure off us if we have a police ally.'

Jason nodded. 'I'll talk to the guys. See what they think. And what about the Maestro? Should we tell her everything, too?'

'I guess. Oh, the trunk! Where the hell is Dad's trunk?'

'Relax. Ash put in in the back of his truck when we left for the hospital. Everything's safe. Shall I give the Maestro her baton back?'

'No, don't. Not yet. I don't want her near the trunk. Not sure why.'

'There's a drink waiting for you, and dinner is ready.'

I opened the shower door and gave him a watery kiss. 'Thank you.'

He kissed me back, hard. 'I look forward to seeing *you*, later.'

* * * * *

When I entered the lounge, Fox was sitting in front of the fire with the dogs. He'd found his favourite place, but he'd have to fight me for it, 'cause it was mine too. He held a glass of amber fluid and ice up to the firelight and admired the colour.

'Scotch on the rocks?' I asked.

He raised the glass in acknowledgement. 'You look better.'

'Ditto to you, too.'

He'd changed into jeans and a black T-shirt. It accentuated his muscular arms and torso. Nice guns. He'd definitely put work into those.

'You look more relaxed, Fox.'

He rubbed his forehead. 'I wish my head was. We need to talk.'

'I thought your head would be giving you trouble.'

'That's an understatement. Plus, I have to respond to one thousand and twenty-four emails, and forty-seven voice mail messages.'

'Jesus. Is that normal?'

Fox's foot started to bounce up and down on the spot. 'Probably slightly more than.'

'Crikey.'

'Yup.'

'I'm plating up,' Jason called out from the kitchen. 'We're going to eat out of bowls, around the fire. Stay where you are if you like, Fox. That's if Maggie hasn't turfed you out already.'

'I've taken your spot, haven't I?'

'Yes, but stay there. You've earned it.'

Fox indicated a glass of champagne on the coffee table. 'Jason left that for you.'

I took a sip and smelt citrus and apples. 'Mmmm. This is going to go down like the first cold tinnie at a butcher's picnic.'

'Cheers, Maggie.'

We clinked glasses.

'Cheers, Fox. Thanks for saving me.'

'Ditto. You kind of zoned out there with the red silk man.'

'I do that sometimes. Get caught in the beauty of the moment.'

Fox stared at me with a concerned expression. 'What?'

'Sounds mad, I know. But things are beautiful even when they're awful. That man, he looked magnificent silhouetted against the dark sky, red silk flowing, sword shining, lustrous dark skin, flashing eyes. It was a moment of beauty.'

Fox rolled his eyes. 'Yeah, just before your beautiful head was going to be sliced apart with that beautiful sword.'

'I would've ducked.'

'I don't think so.'

'I would've. I felt every atom of every passing second, like still frames. I was in perfect awareness.'

'Really?'

'Yes. But you definitely saved me. Without you there, I would've been history, eventually.'

Fox stroked Boo's silky ears. 'Big thanks to Boo, too.'

Boo closed her eyes and made heavy breathing noises. *I like Fox. I like Schmoo too. Fox knows exactly where to scratch.*

'You know you've hit the right spot when she breathes that way,' I said.

'Yeah. Schmoo does it too.'

Jason came in and handed us bowls of curry and rice. 'Here you go, you two mud commandos. Get that into yah.'

The aroma of coriander and spices filled the room as everyone came in with their bowls and found a seat. Maestro sat next to us, near the fire.

'Doesn't get any better than this,' she said. 'Good food, good wine, good people. When are you going to tell us what happened?'

'Soon as we've finished eating,' I mumbled through a mouthful of curry.

Ashley turned on the TV to check the news, which Fox looked pleased about. He was obviously worried but feeling powerless. Everyone chatted quietly while Fox and I ate as if we hadn't had food for a month.

'My God, this is good,' Fox said. 'Jason, this is perfect, not too spicy.'

'My signature dish. There's plenty more if you want.'

'I won't say no.'

Ashley took his bowl. 'I'll get it for you.'

I offered him my bowl. 'Me too?'

'Jesus, you're good on the tooth.'

'I've had a busy day.'

He grinned. 'Then every day must be busy for you, luv.'

'Lately, yes, and mind your own beeswax, Mister Food

Police. I have a secret. I was going to tell you, but now I'm not.'

Ashley was such a sticky beak. This would do his head in.

'Extra curry for your secret?'

'Maybe. It's an A1 secret, worth a lot. At the moment though, it's in the vault.'

Everyone was looking at me, Fox in particular. His eyes bored into me.

'What? Stop it, you guys, all will be revealed sometime. Later.'

'You're a tease,' Ashley said huffily. He stomped off with our bowls.

Drom turned up the TV volume. 'I think this is it on the news.' The banner read, *Missing Park Ranger – Feared Dead.*

Fox punched his fist gently and repeatedly against the carpet. 'There's a police hunt for the red silk man. What a waste of resources.'

A photo flashed onto the screen. It was of a smiling man with dark hair, skin and eyes. The photo had been taken in his backyard. He was a family man with a wife and three children. His name was Avinash, he loved music and he was thirty-two years old.

The ranger's name was Geraldine and she had been forty-five, single, and had lived with four dogs and two cats. Geraldine's friend, a tiny slip of a girl, was shown surrounded by the animals.

Another missing person was profiled. Samantha. She was twenty-one years old, had a Suzuki motorcycle, and was recently engaged to be married. Her partner, Jeremy, and her distraught mother and father appealed for information.

I burst into tears, and Drom switched the TV off. Fox slid across the floor and put his arm around me. I sobbed into his T-shirt. The two dogs leapt on me, and with paws planted on my chest, they licked the tears off my cheeks. Their concerned eyes scanned mine.

I laughed despite myself and moved them gently away. 'It's

okay, doggies. Come on now, down you get.'

Fox relinquished his hold as Jason sat next to me and put his arm around my shoulder and hugged me. He knew how deeply I was affected any time I heard about missing persons.

Those poor families of Avinash, Geraldine and Samantha. They'd never know what happened. They'd keep hoping. They'd never have closure. At least by handing in the ranger's head, that'd be *something*.

Fox stared at me, concerned.

'Missing persons upset me, given my dad an' all. The worst thing is, I'm the one involved in creating an endless stream of missing persons.' I wiped my eyes. 'It's a cruel joke. Adam, Marlon, Dylan, Mike, Gaetano, Francesco, Luigi, Roberto, Giovanni, Leon, Avinash, Geraldine and Samantha. Thirteen families in ruin. How many more before this all ends? Will it ever end?'

Fox looked horrified. 'Jesus, I'm sorry. But it's hardly your fault.' I heard his thought … *is it her fault?*

'You're keeping count?' Ashley said. 'You know all their names?'

'She loves, which is why she's one of the chosen,' Drom said.

Ashley looked grim. 'Hardly seems fair then.'

The Maestro offered me a silk hanky. 'Here, take this.' It smelt of lavender and spice. Her face was filled with emotion. I blew into it with my signature trumpet noise. 'Thank you.'

She smiled gently. 'You can keep it.'

Jason kissed my forehead. 'Fox, are you up to telling us what happened?'

Fox looked at me. 'Is that okay?'

I nodded.

'I'll get you both another drink,' Ashley said.

I was grateful for Ashley's attentiveness. 'Glass of red, paracetamol and ibuprofen, please.'

He took orders and came back with my drugs and a tray of

drinks. When we were settled, Fox began. 'Can I record this on my phone? Just what I say, for my use only?'

'I don't know,' I said. 'What are the implications for us? What are you going to do with the information and the recording?'

'As much as it pains me to say this, I'm not going to do anything. What can I do? No one would believe me.'

'I could give evidence,' I suggested.

'Do you want to?'

'No, then they'd think we were both mad.'

'Exactly. Look, it's fine. I won't record anything.'

'I think it's better not to.'

Fox reported the day's events like a cop on TV, in police speak, as if he was preparing a statement. It was a very thorough and accurate account, with no detail spared, except for one.

He looked at me. 'How did I do? Did I miss anything?'

'No,' I said.

'Bloody hell, you two were lucky,' Ashley said. 'It's evolved and grown stronger. We're going to have to allow more distance, and with the tentacles ... it puts us at a whole new level of danger.'

Fox looked exasperated. 'Can someone please tell me what the hell is going on. What is that thing? And what's with the roaches? And a friggin' flying dog?'

Jason leaned across and whispered in my ear. 'I talked to the guys and they're fine with us telling him. Are you?'

I nodded.

Fox watched me intently. He was as bad as the dogs, always staring.

'After what happened today, I'm sure you've already put two and two together, particularly with some of the strange crimes you've been investigating and the lack of evidence, an' all,' I said.

'Correct. I'm assuming bugs and black holes were involved at the Hyatt, the morgue, the church and the incident here.'

'There are other crimes too,' the Maestro said.

Fox pushed back his hair and rested his head on his knees. 'Jesus.'

'We want to trust you, Fox,' I said, as he looked up at me. 'You need us and we need you. If you involve the police it will only slow us down, and that would be a disaster. I think we've, well, I know we've all been brought together for a purpose. To fight this thing. You must promise us, on Schmoo's life, you'll keep what we tell you confidential, not share this information with anyone, unless we give you permission. You have to promise not to arrest us or involve the police in any way unless we all agree. Do you promise?'

Fox clenched his fists. 'I promise. On Schmoo's life.' He took his glass of scotch and drained it.

Ashley held out his hand. 'Give me your phone. I'm going to put it in the other room, for peace of mind.

Fox relinquished his phone. When Ashley returned he said, 'Who's going to do the talking? Maybe I should record this for the next recruit. It'd save us going over the same ground each time.'

'No,' Jason said. 'I'll go first, if that's okay, Maggie?'

'Yes. I don't want to talk about it anymore.'

'Anyone, please jump in whenever.'

It took two hours to bring Fox up to speed with everything. By the look on his face, I knew his sense of place and his understanding of the universe had been pulled out from under him. He was in free-fall — mind, body and soul.

Fox reached across and took my hands. He turned them over and examined the black, blue and purple striations running in thick bands around my wrists. He ran his thumbs gently across them. 'What you've been through ... what you've all been through. And, Luca, your brothers—'

Luca nodded, his eyes full of tears. Ashley slapped an arm around him, and I whipped out a clean tissue and passed it to

Luca.

'Back to business,' Ashley said. 'We need to decide what to do with the ranger's head.'

Everybody groaned.

'I want to cleanse and bless it,' Luca said.

'We have to give it back, don't we?' Drom said. 'Or will it make it worse for them to get back just a head?'.

I couldn't get my mind around the dilemma. 'Jesus, I don't know. What do you think, Jason? If it was me, would you want my head back?'

'I don't know. Would you want mine?'

'I ... I'm not sure! It's awful. We have to hand it in; we can't get rid of it. And if we did dispose of it, how? It's too horrible to contemplate.'

Ashley rubbed his chin. 'We could keep it until the next encounter and pitch it into the black hole. It might get reunited with its body. Who knows what goes on in there? She could be a headless zombie and we would be doing her a favour.'

Jason made a face. 'Yeah, so what? We have to carry a head around in an Eski, 24-7? That's practical. Not.'

'The way things are going, something else could happen before the night's out,' Drom said. 'Could be another black hole around the corner.'

Fox sounded shocked. 'Seriously?'

'Seriously.'

'Hell,' Fox said, 'I think I'm going to have to resign. This is insane.'

I shook my head. 'Don't make any hasty decisions. We need you in the police force.'

'We could leave it outside a police station with a note saying, "Beware, severed head enclosed",' Ashley suggested. 'We wouldn't want to freak out some poor young constable. It would give them the heads up.' Ashley chuckled at his joke. I rolled my eyes at him.

'It's gonna freak somebody out no matter what we do,' Fox replied.

'Could they trace it back to us forensically?' I asked.

'We'd have to be careful,' Fox said. 'There'd be CCTV and potential witnesses. You'd have to be in disguise. No car.'

'I have an idea!' I said.

'What?' Fox asked.

'Boo could drop it off. We could park a block away and she could fly it in. Keep to the bushes and out of sight. We could disguise her. Put her in a black T-shirt and wrap something around her head.'

'Yeah. That could work,' Jason said.

Would you do it, Boo?

Indeed. I enjoy having a mission to accomplish. Do I get a say in my disguise?

Of course. What were you thinking?

Maybe a cape?

Um, perhaps bit too ostentatious. We need to have you look like a Rambo dog, camouflaged.

Oh, indeed. Excellent. I love the idea. I'll leave it to you.

No worries, Boo. I'll make sure you look the part.

'Boo's up for it,' I said. 'Are you really going to clean the head, Luca? It's an awful task to undertake.'

'I've had experience with the preparation of bodies with a funeral director. It doesn't faze me although this is particularly gruesome. It's the right and respectful thing to do.'

'You can use the laundry downstairs,' Jason suggested.

'I can supervise,' Fox said. 'Make sure you don't leave any incriminating evidence.'

'So, when do we make the drop?' Ashley asked.

'I don't think we'd be up for it tonight,' Jason said. 'Tomorrow night.'

'I have a concert tomorrow night,' the Maestro said. 'I'll need to leave early in the morning. I may even leave tonight. I haven't done any preparation.'

'No worries, Maestro,' I said. 'Thank you so much for everything you've done for us.'

'It's my pleasure. I think I may take my leave. I have a lot to prepare for. I'll be in touch day after tomorrow. Good luck with the plan. Don't hesitate to call if you need me.'

She stood and stretched, reaching to the ceiling, her hips moving to and fro. The eyes of the room were upon her magnificent body. She flicked her head, and her long locks swayed and glistened in the light, like she was in some shampoo ad. The Maestro seized Fox's face and kissed him, right on the lips. 'Mmmm. It's not twenty-four hours, but the lip balm is a winner. He's divinely kissable. I'll be back to try again.' She flashed him a big, sexy smile. 'Keep up the good work, Fox.'

It was the first time I'd seen Fox lost for words.

The doorbell rang. Ashley jumped to his feet.

'Relax, Ashley. It's my driver. Cape?'

'Of course,' Luca said. He stood and draped her cloak around her shoulders, securing the gold clasp.

She kissed him on the cheek. 'You're divine too.' Luca blushed.

'Keep your chins up, darlings. The fuckers don't stand a chance against us. You won't have time, I know, but in case, I've left free concert tickets on the table for you. Ciao.'

And she was gone.

---

[9] *Maggie's Playlist: Collect the Trophy — 10Ft. Ganja Plant*

Chapter 10: The Arsenal

'For the weapons of our warfare are not of the flesh but have divine power to destroy strongholds.' — 2 Corinthians 10:4

'Look at Fox,' Ashley said, chuckling. 'He's been Maestroed. Here's a tip, mate. If she brings out any red silk ribbons, run for the hills.'

'On that note, I think we should turn in for the night,' Jason said. 'We've a big day tomorrow. Bacon and eggs at 7.30 am.'

Everyone gave the thumbs up.

'What about security?' Fox asked.

'I've checked. All the windows and doors are secure. External alarms and floodlights are working,' Ashley said.

Fox still looked uncertain. 'Do you have weapons? Other than what you're already carrying?'

We all looked at one another in silence.

'You noticed?' Ashley said.

'Of course.'

'Um, a couple of things may have fallen into our hands along the way. Do we have your assurance—'

'Yeah, yeah. It goes without saying. I won't dob you in for anything.' Fox sounded annoyed.

'Just checking. We need to be sure,' I said, equally annoyed he was annoyed.

'Now's as good a time as any to take stock,' Jason said. 'Let's lay out what we have on the table.'

Ashley plonked down a gun. 'Here's mine. Beretta 92FS 9mm.'

'That was Adam's,' I said.

'Here's mine. A SIG-Sauer P229R 9mm,' Jason said.

'That was Marlon's. You said you'd give it to me, Ashley.'

He rolled his eyes.

Jason opened a nearby cabinet drawer and took out two more guns. He placed them on the table. 'We also have two Smith & Wesson .357 revolvers.'

I shuddered. 'It was Dylan's. Whose is the other?'

'The guy who jumped me in the hospital corridor,' Jason said.

Fox looked at the table and raised his eyebrows. 'So, you have four handguns.'

'Wait a mo,' I said, scooting off to the bathroom. I returned and placed a bundled-up towel on the table. 'Here's my secret, Ashley.' I unfolded the towel.

'Holy hand gun!' Ashley said. 'It's a frigging .50 caliber Desert Eagle!' He picked it up and it sparkled in the light. 'Phew. Where the hell did you get this?'

'It was Samantha's. Bike girl.'

'There's no way this is a girl's gun. It's huge. Great if you want to shoot blocks of concrete to smithereens.'

'Or zombies?'

'Maybe, but these guns are known to jam more than the Citilink freeway,' he said. 'But folks probably don't use good ammo.'

'Oh, I forgot!' I raced back to the bedroom and returned with the black satchel. 'I also have this, but I don't know what's in it yet.'

'Where's that from?' Fox asked.

'Samantha's bike.'

Jason stared at me in horror. 'You brought it into the house without knowing what the hell was in it?'

I suddenly felt very stupid. 'Um … obviously. Yes.'

'Jesus, Maggie,' Ashley said.

I unzipped the satchel. 'Oh, for heaven's sake, settle down.'

Jason, Ashley and Fox grabbed guns off the table and sprang back, pointing their pistols at the satchel.

'Talk about jumpy.' I reached into the bag and felt cold metal. I was going to play a cockroach joke on them, but thought better of it. 'It's another gun. Relax.' I pulled out the heavy bit of kit and placed it on the table.

Ashley examined the gun. He had strong, beautiful hands and he ran them over the handgun as if caressing a woman. He looked at me while he was doing it, and I felt myself flush. 'Crikey, you've hit the jackpot. It's a Heckler & Koch MP5A3 submachine gun!'

'Jesus,' Fox said.

'Wait. There's more.' I felt in the bottom of the bag and pulled out another bit of metal. 'What's this?'

Ashley took it shaking his head in wonderment. 'It's a grenade launcher, which fits on the Heckler.'

I ferreted around and fished out multiple boxes of ammunition.

'Bloody hell,' Fox said. 'What were they planning to use these on?'

Jason looked worried. 'Probably us. We're screwed.'

I felt sick. 'Locked windows and doors aren't going to help us, are they?'

No one answered.

'Ashley, can you get dad's trunk?'

He picked up the Desert Eagle. 'Sure, luv.' Once he'd checked to see it was loaded, he dashed outside. He returned and plonked the trunk on the table.

I unlocked it with the key I kept around my neck. 'My dad

gave this to me, Fox. We found a secret compartment, which had this stuff in it.'

I placed the items on the table, one at a time. 'We have a Smith & Wesson Carbon Steel Pocket Baton, one UZI Tactical Defender Pen with DNA catcher and built-in handcuff key, one Cold Steel Torpedo fifteen inch throwing knife, and three Cold Steel Sure Balance nine inch throwing knives. Oh, and a twelve-inch Mollard Lancio Conducting Baton, which I guess you could stab someone with, at a pinch.'

Drom took a nine-inch knife and weighed it in his hand. 'Hey, awesome! I'm good with throwing knives.'

'Yeah, yeah, sure, city boy,' Ashley said. 'As if.'

Drom stood. 'Pick a target.'

'Not in the house,' I said.

Jason brought a large wooden chopping board from the kitchen and pressed a bit of Blu Tack in the middle of it. 'Here, use this.'

'Ash, walk away about fifteen feet and hold up the board,' Drom said.

'You're kidding, mate. No way.'

I snatched the board and marched across the room. 'I'll do it.'

'No, don't!' Jason said.

'It's fine. What's the worst that can happen?'

Jason's eyes blazed. 'Don't even go there.'

'I think this is a bad idea,' Fox said.

Drom moved to the other side of the table. 'Stop there, Maggie. Ready?'

'Yep.'

Before Jason could move or say another word, the knife flew through the air. I knew because I was watching, my face at the side of the board. The guys buried their faces in their hands.

Thunk! Bullseye.

I ran back to Drom, put the board on the table and gave him

a hug. 'That was fantastic!'

'You're fantastic for trusting me.'

'I trust you with my life, always.'

Jason, Ashley and Fox looked sheepish to say the least. Luca gave me the thumbs up. He trusted Drom too.

'Good work, mate,' Ashley muttered. 'Impressive.'

'Real good, but Christ, Maggie, you're taking years off my life, I swear,' Jason said.

'Drom, you can have these knives,' I offered. 'No one here can throw them. I don't know why Dad had them. Maybe you could teach me?'

'Sure, no worries. Thanks, the knives are awesome.' Drom seemed happy and gave me peck on the cheek.

'You garner a lot of kisses,' Jason said.

Fox looked away and picked up one of the guns. Ashley fiddled with the sleeve of his T-shirt. I wrapped my arms around Jason. 'I know, I'm a lucky girl. None as sweet as yours, but.'

Ashley laughed. 'Aw, shucks. Well, we have quite an arsenal here. Not bad.'

'Wait, there's more,' I said, racing off to the bedroom. I returned with a bundle of velvet, and placed it on the table. 'Here are the most important weapons.' I unfolded the velvet, to reveal two dull crystals.

'These are the crystals?' Fox asked. 'They don't look very impressive.'

'Here's the other one.' I unfolded the rest of the velvet to reveal the glittering crystal.

'Wow. It's beautiful. So, the others are dead?'

'They'll recharge eventually, or there's things you can do to help them regain power faster, such as putting them next to a live crystal. We need to find another eight of these little beauties.'

'Let's charge 'em up,' Ashley said. 'It may help to protect us.'

'Would the extra power be a beacon to the Dark Force?' Luca asked.

Drom shook his head. 'I don't think so.'

'Me neither,' I agreed. 'Let's do it. What should I do, Drom? Put it next to the other two?'

'Yep.'

I took the velvet cloth and spread it out on the table. I placed the two dull crystals on the cloth, leaving a space between them. After blessing each of the crystals, I took the live crystal and positioned it carefully between the inert ones.

The room disappeared in a blaze of white light. I felt my atoms shake as the light penetrated them. The dark cinder in my being quivered and hardened against the onslaught. It pulsed out darkness in retaliation. I floated in space, in light. The shimmering outline of a door appeared. I pushed against it and found myself in the middle of the huge ballroom again. This time all the doors were closed.

A gust of wind raced around the ballroom like a mini tornado, and doors began to open in front of me.

Boo, Jason, Ashley, Drom, Luca, Fox and the Maestro stood in each doorway. Another door opened and out stepped — Dad!

'Dad!' I screamed. 'Is it really you?'

'Yes, it's me! I've been trying to—' He moved forward, his arms outstretched, and I ran towards him.

Bang! The Maestro disappeared and her door slammed shut.

Dad's body jerked as he was dragged backwards through his door. The door slammed closed. He shouted something through it, but his voice was muffled.

'Dad!' I ran across to his door and pulled on the handle. I banged on the door. I slammed my shoulder against it. I kicked it, trying to break it down. Boo and the guys came to help.

Drom held the handle. 'Everyone hold onto me, and when I say go, use your psychic force. One, two, three, *go!*'

We focused on the door and it rippled, quivered and stretched outwards as if it was made of rubber. Light sparkled around its edges. It felt as if it was going to give way. A piercing noise shattered our concentration. The sound of a million fingernails dragging across a chalkboard screeched in our minds. It was impossible to focus through the pain. We collapsed to the floor in agony holding our heads.

Dad's door solidified.

The noise stopped.

The ballroom filled with light, and we floated to the ceiling suspended in webs of shimmering, pulsing colour. The ballroom began to fade, and gradually the kitchen appeared again, coming into focus like a Polaroid photograph.

It was as if we'd ingested high wattage light bulbs — everyone was illuminated. Jason's eyes glowed and his skin was radiant. He looked stunning. I hoped I looked as good.

Nobody spoke. We sat. In the moment. In the now.

Thought was nonexistent as peace and bliss coursed through our veins. Eventually, Jason stood, ambled slowly into the kitchen and put the kettle on.

Boo lay on her back on top of a kitchen cabinet, her legs propped against the ceiling. Luca had his elbows on the table, hands in prayer, eyes closed. Fox had his head on the table, resting on his arms.

'It's like kissing God,' Ashley whispered. 'Better than drugs.'

'Tea anyone?' Jason asked softly.

'Yes please,' we muttered, starting to come back to "reality" as our brains and egos kicked into gear.

'How are you, Fox?' I asked.

'Other than feeling amazing, I'm not sure. I've never believed in God. In anything. Now, I don't know what I believe in. It was, is, so incredible. You could shoot me now and I wouldn't care. There are no words.'

'Check out the crystals now,' Ashley said.

The three crystals radiated so much light it was hard to look at them.

Drom fished around in his satchel. 'I've more velvet. Here

you go.' He handed me two pieces, along with a drawstring bag.

I felt the live crystal's power tingling in my arms as I wrapped it in the velvet cloth. By the time I'd wrapped the other two and placed them in the drawstring bag, the bruises around my wrists had completely disappeared, along with all my aches and pains.

I held out my wrists. 'Hey, everyone, check this out!'

'Wow! Completely healed. That's incredible,' Fox said.

'The crystals have strong regenerative powers,' I said.

'Before, when you told me you grew back body parts, I couldn't believe it. But now, I think I do,' he said.

'The crystals truly are a miracle,' Luca said.

'Fox, the crystals don't heal everyone,' Drom said. 'They protect the keepers of the crystals — the life forces who have travelled with them since the dawn of time. The crystals only heal entities who share the same crystal energy.'

Fox looked flabbergasted. 'So ... I'm one of the keepers?'

'Appears so. Otherwise you wouldn't have been able to share our experience.'

Fox pulled off his T-shirt and examined his chest, stomach and arms. He unzipped his jeans, dropped them to his knees and pulled down a corner of his jocks on the right-hand side.

'You right there?' Jason asked.

Fox ran his hands over his body. 'Everything's healed. Even my appendix scar has vanished. It's bloody impossible!'

I wished he'd stop doing that. He looked so hot. I noticed Luca staring at him with appreciation too.

Fox turned around. 'Maggie, have a look. Are there any scars on my back?'

'Not a one.'

'Not a big one running across my right shoulder? Or a bullet wound, top of my right arm, and another left side of my waist?'

'No. Nothing.'

He pulled the back of his jocks down. 'What about a four-inch scar on top of my right buttock?'

Luca's eyes were nearly falling out of his head. Ashley rolled his. 'Now you're showing off. No, no scars.'

'Will you miss them?' I asked.

'Maybe. They're battle scars, hard earned.'

'You'll get over it,' Ashley said. 'And now you have room for a whole lot more that you'll probably end up with before all this is over.'

'True.' Fox zipped his pants and put his T-shirt back on.

The expression on Luca's face almost made me laugh out loud. He looked like a kid who'd had his candy taken away.

'What about the scars on my face?' Fox asked.

'Huh. They're still there. That's weird. What caused them?' I asked.

'Someone I loved,' he said, quietly.

'There's your answer,' Drom said. 'The crystal is part of you, and you're part of the crystal. It won't do anything you don't want. It knows you better than you know yourself. You want to keep those scars; that's why it didn't take them.'

Fox nodded slightly but didn't say anything. He seemed to want to change the subject.

'Want some cake, Fox?' I asked. 'Jason found a spare one in the pantry.'

He smiled. 'Great, thanks.'

'My dad's still out there. You all heard him, right? I didn't imagine it?'

Everyone nodded.

'He was there all right, and he was trying to tell us something,' Jason said.

'And something was trying to stop him.'

'What was that sound?' Ashley asked. 'I thought my skull was going to explode.'

'I don't know.'

'Me neither,' Drom said. 'Whatever it was, it was a powerful deterrent.'

'So many strange things,' Luca said, examining the trunk. He pressed and prodded, trying to find more secret compartments.

Fox picked up the Maestro's baton. 'What's with this? It has *Maestro* inscribed on it. Is it hers?'

'We think so.'

'Why's it in your dad's trunk?'

'They were an item,' Ashley said.

Fox sounded surprised. 'Really?'

'Yes. Really,' I said, dryly. 'Who knew?'

'The Maestro disappeared from our mind meld pretty quickly,' Ashley said. 'Maybe she dragged the Prof back behind the scenes for a bit of horizontal mind meld tango.'

I glared at him. 'Is that all you think about?'

'No. I think about other stuff. Beer, food, guns, and how to keep you safe.'

'In that order?'

He laughed. 'Probably.'

Fox fiddled with the baton. 'It's telescopic. Look, if you twist it, it retracts to the size of a pen. Very handy.' He extended the baton again and clinked it on the rim of the drinking glasses, listening to the different tones it produced.

'Are all the crystals exactly the same?' Ashley asked.

'I think so.'

'Can I have a look at them for a sec?'

I pushed the bag across.

Ashley opened the bag and took out the crystals. He unwrapped them from the velvet and carefully examined each one.

He held one out. 'You see where the three finger indents are? Near one of the indentations is a tiny mark. Two on this one, four on this one.'

Fox pointed to the remaining crystal with the baton. 'How many on that one?' The baton flew out of his hand like a scud missile and stuck to the top of the crystal.

'Jesus!' He reached out to retrieve the baton, but the tip of it was stuck fast to the crystal. He tried again to gently prize them apart, but they were welded together. An orange glow emanated from the end of the baton, radiating back into the crystal. 'It appears to have embedded itself in the crystal,' he said.

'This isn't good. I don't think the crystal's happy,' I said.

'How would you know?'

'I feel it.'

Drom looked worried. 'I feel it too.'

'Let me try.' Ashley gripped the baton in one hand and the crystal in the other, and attempted to pull them apart. His biceps quivered as he increased the pressure.

'Stop it. You might break something,' I said.

He put the crystal back on the table. 'Yep. Stuck fast.'

We sat staring at the blinking orange light.

'Maybe it's going to explode,' Jason said. 'Could it be a bomb?'

Ashley looked alarmed. 'Jesus, Jace. You reckon?'

'Who knows? Maybe the light is a timer. It's in countdown mode. The baton was in a collection of weapons after all.'

'Perhaps we should put it outside,' I said. 'Maybe that's why the crystal isn't happy. Hell, we can't afford to lose a crystal.'

Ashley nodded. 'I'll put it out on the deck. We can keep an eye on it, but have some distance between us. Not sure how much distance we need, but. What if it goes off like an atom bomb?'

'Then we're history, obviously.'

When Ashley moved to pick it up, the orange light flickered faster and turned to flashing green.

'Get down!' Ashley yelled, pulling me under the table. He pushed me to the floor and covered me with his body. Luca flung himself on top of Ashley, Jason covered me on the left, and Fox was on my right. Boo licked my ear — at least I thought it was Boo.

It was stacks on Maggie under the table. We had our arms over our heads ready to kiss our bums' goodbye.

'I love you,' Jason whispered.

'Love you, too.'

'Love youse all,' Ashley said.

We waited. Nothing.

There was a short whoosh, a click, and the sound of something hitting the top of the table.

I'll check it. Stay put. Boo floated out.

The coast is clear. It's transmogrified into ... something ... some type of artifact.

'Um ... Luca, you can get off me now,' Ashley said.

'Yes, please,' I said. 'I'm crushed under here.'

We clambered out from under the table. Ashley, always the gentleman, sort of, helped me up.

Drom hadn't moved. He sat there, feet on the table, leaning back in his chair, a big smile on his face.

'You knew!' I said. 'You mongrel!'

Ashley clipped him across the head. 'Very funny, Drom. That's something I'd do.'

Drom laughed. 'You all disappeared before I could say anything. I figured it was a simple charger. The baton charges itself from the crystal. Check out the baton now.'

On the table lay the most beautiful piece of jewellery, or artifact, I'd ever seen.

---

[10] *Maggie's Playlist: 21 Guns — Green Day*

Chapter 11: The Baton

'The most powerful weapon on earth is the human soul on fire.' — *Ferdinand Foch*

It still resembled a baton, but the handle was gold and inscribed with intricate symbols next to a row of four, small sparkling crystals. Imbedded at the top of the baton was a larger crystal, which glowed an iridescent green.

Next to the gold segment was a silver band, around which ran a row of eight crystals. Gold strands wound around the baton joining with each stone, making eight crystal rings.

The next section was made of a clear, glass like substance. It was divided into four segments, each separated by a band of gold. Each of the segments was packed with tiny coloured crystals, green in one section, blue, red and clear in the others. As the baton narrowed to a point, the material changed to a strange, multicoloured metal, ringed with the finest threads of gold. The very tip of the baton, which was about two inches long, appeared to be made of copper covered in fine horizontal grooves.

'What the hell is it?' Ashley asked.

'See all those characters?' I said. 'It's an inscription.'

Jason took a magnifying glass from a drawer and gave it to me. 'Try this.'

'It's incredibly detailed. There's heaps of writing and

symbols. This is the largest. It says *Sonus Ignis Mortem Radium*.'

Luca took the magnifier. 'It's Latin. Yes … *Sonus Ignis Mortem Radium*.'

'Which means?' Jason asked.

'Basically, it translates as Sound Fire Death Ray.'

'That explains why it was in the weapons trunk,' Jason said.

'On the other side it says *Libido Virgula*. That's odd,' Luca said.

'What's it mean?' I asked. 'Sounds sexual.'

'Yes, essentially it means *pleasure wand or rod*. There's a setting for *Mas* — male, and *Femina* — female.'

'Crikey. I like the sound of that!' Ashley said. 'A sex toy that'll literally blow your brains out if you press the wrong button! No wonder this is the Maestro's.'

'I can't understand the symbols, but some of the other words, I can,' Luca said.

No one was game to touch the thing. Luca pointed at it with a pencil. 'The top here says *Vis*, which means power, or strength. The end crystal is labeled *Altum*, *Tener*, *Ignis* and *Mutatio*, which roughly means High, Low, Fire and Change.

The second crystal says *Accantus*, which means intensity, the third crystal says *Musica*, which means music and the forth says *Scutum* which means shield. I can't decipher anything else.'

Ashley slapped Luca on the back. 'Fantastic! How handy is it to have a padre in our midst?' Luca beamed with pleasure.

Jason gave him a notebook and pen. 'Can you write it down for us?'

'Sure thing.'

Gingerly picking up the baton, I kept my fingers away from anything resembling a button. 'It appears the first crystal is multi-functional — High, Low, Fire and Change.' I poised my finger over the first crystal. 'Here we go.'

'No!' everyone shouted.

I pressed the top crystal firmly and quickly. One — two —

118

three — four.

A whoosh, click, and the device transmogrified back into a baton. I held out it out. 'Ta-dah!'

The guys cowered around the table, hands covering their faces. When they realised everything was fine they pretended they were fixing their hair, scratching, adjusting clothes or brushing dog hair away.

I laughed and pressed the top of the baton with my thumb. It whooshed, clicked, folded inside out and changed back to the device. 'How nifty!'

I checked Luca's notes. 'What if I press it twice for low — *Tenor?*'

Ashley screwed up his face. 'Don't muck around with it!'

I winked at him and pressed it. The crystal button glowed blue. The blue section of crystal further along the baton began to flash. 'And now if I press *Accantus*, intensity, just once—'

Jason held up his hands. 'Hey, point that thing away from me!'

'Whoops, sorry!' I pointed it at the wall and pressed *Accantus* — the light changed from blue to pink. 'Anything happening?'

'Nope,' Fox said. The others shook their heads.

I slowly increased the intensity.

Luca crossed himself, Ashley turned grey, Jason became pallid and Drom looked like he was going to vomit. I felt suddenly anxious and couldn't focus properly. I clicked the top of the baton and the crystal lights turned off.

Ashley rubbed his eyes. 'Phew! Low frequency sound waves. Did your eyeballs vibrate?'

'I couldn't see properly,' Jason said. 'And I felt unreasonably terrified.'

Luca crossed himself again. 'It felt as if the devil was in the room.'

Ashley put his hand on Luca's shoulder. 'It's okay. Don't stress. Infrasound can cause fear, or sometimes awe, in humans and you don't generally perceive any sound. It's a sonic weapon, and judging by that little demo, we'd better be very careful indeed. Particularly using the *Altum* setting, which I'm betting is ultrasonic sound. It could make your brain explode or severely incapacitate you.'

Fox rubbed his temples. 'My brain already feels like it's going to explode.'

I ferreted through the trunk, pulled out the Prof's field notebooks and flicked through them. 'Here! There's a drawing of the thing. Dad's already decoded heaps of it. You're right, Ashley, it's a sonic weapon with a laser function. You turn the end to adjust the radius of the sound blast.'

Ashley raised his eyebrows to the max. 'This technology's way too advanced for earth. Our sound weapon technology is still the size of a room.' He grinned at me. 'Why don't you press the *Libido* button?'

'I'm actually more scared of pressing that than the weapon buttons.'

'Here, I'll do it then.' He pressed the *Libido* crystal and the *Mas*, male button, together. Like some transformer creature, the baton assembled itself into a silver device which appeared soft and flexible.

Ashley peered into the hole at the end of the device. It fluttered invitingly at him. 'Oh, sweet mamma.'

Jason was laughing his head off. 'Are you going to try it? I dare you to stick your old fella in there.'

Ashley held the device away from himself. 'Yeah right, Jace. I'd try a carrot first. It'd have to be a big one of course. If it comes out in one piece, I may consider it.'

'What if it's tuned to a specific user? I wouldn't imagine you would share this thing around?' I said.

'Who knows?' Ashley pressed the button and it reassembled into the weapon. 'Maybe let's focus on the weapon bit. Don't want to put the meat and veg at risk for no good reason.'

120

Luca nodded in agreement. 'Definitely.'

I flicked through more pages of the notebook. 'Check this out! The Prof has done another diagram, which looks similar to the Maestro's watch. It's defined as a "Multiverse Accelerator Energising Space Time Relativity Order", or *Maestro* for short.

'Well, well, well,' Jason said. 'Things are starting to add up.'

'Dad's notes say it has a dual function which enables an individual to travel to alternate universes and, get this, through time.'

'Impossible!' Luca said. 'That's science fiction.'

'I knew she wasn't from around here,' Drom said.

'Me too,' I agreed. 'I always thought there was something weird about her. Listen to this. Dad goes onto say more about its functions. It has an *Auto Memory Link,* so if you activate that function, it'll automatically take you to the place and time you hold in your mind. There's an *Atmospheric Analyser*, a needle you stick into your body which programs the device to only jump to universes and places which have an atmosphere and environment that won't harm you.

It has eight extension rings which allow others to travel with you, and a *Probability Analyser* which gives you an indication of the severity of disruption to the space time continuum, which ranges from negligible to catastrophic.'

'Sounds as if the Maestro has some explaining to do,' Ashley said.

'You're saying we should confront her?' I asked.

'I'm not sure what I'm saying. Yet. We have the upper hand while she doesn't know we know.'

'Do you think her intentions are good or bad?' Jason asked.

'Maybe a bit of both. But probably on our side?' I said.

Fox ran his fingers through his hair. 'I think we should sit tight for a while until we get our heads around the implications, if that's possible. Christ, how things change from one second to the next. Apologies, Luca.'

'Please don't censor yourself because of me. I don't mind.'

'We do take the Lord's name in vain a lot, don't we?' Ashley said.

'I think we should all turn in for the night. I don't know about anyone else, but my head's spinning,' Jason said.

Ashley smiled to himself. 'We've got five handguns. Fox has his own, so one for each of the guys and one left over.'

I took the bait. 'Oh, so I don't get one?'

'Don't let's go through this again. Not until you've had lessons, and it's too late tonight.'

'You're deliberately trying to annoy me. Since I can't have a gun, I'll take this then.' I put the baton in the back pocket of my jeans. 'Any problems, Mister Gun Police?'

'I know which function you'll be trying out tonight, sweetheart,' Ashley said.

Everyone's smiles quickly vanished when they caught the look of fury on my face.

'Shut up, Ashley. Try and think about something else for once in your life.'

'Obviously hit a nerve there. Pot kettle black, Maggie.'

I rolled my eyes at him. 'Oh, for heaven's sake.'

Bloody Ashley Beringer. He drove me crazy.

---

11 *Maggie's Playlist: Baton — Junip*

122

Chapter 12: The Nightmare

'When I say, 'My bed will comfort me, my couch will ease my complaint,' then you scare me with dreams and terrify me with visions.' — Job 7:13-14

I stripped off my clothes and flopped into bed, tucking the baton under my pillow. Jason had a quick shower and climbed in next to me. My mind whirled with a million thoughts.

'You awake?' he whispered.

'Yep.'

'Come over here.'

I moved over and nestled into his outstretched arm, put my leg over his, and snuggled up tight. He stroked my back.

'Head spinning?' he asked.

'Yep.'

'Want me to make it spin some more?' He caressed my breast and squeezed my nipple. My body quivered in response.

'Never fails,' he whispered into my ear. His breath was sweet and hot on my face. He kissed my neck and along the inside of my arm. Oh, he knew just what I needed. My mind willingly gave way to the pleasures of the body, as his strong hands touched me in all the places which made me tremble. He was on top of me, inside me, taking me, slowly, deeply, rhythmically, wanting to make it last, and I was lost in him, surrendering everything to him — until the screaming made us stop.

Jason jumped out of bed. He stood frozen, fists clenched.

'What the hell?'

'It's Ashley!' I snatched something from the laundry basket, threw it on and raced out the door to his bedroom. Fox was already in the hallway hopping on one foot, dragging on some jocks. I tried not to look, but too late. I got an eye full. Impressive.

The sound of a grown man screaming his guts out is truly terrifying. He was being murdered; I had to save him. That was my only thought as I pushed open the door, sans gun, sans baton. Damn it! I had nothing. Idiot!

'Maggie, stop!' Fox shouted.

Jason and Fox were right behind me; Jason pushed past, the force knocking me against the wall. The plaster cracked and a heavy picture fell off the wall, right above my head. Fox caught it before it brained me. Ashley was on the bed screaming his lungs out, his arms and legs thrashed in desperation. He was caught in a nightmare.

The bedside lamp glowed softly, illuminating his tortured face; his naked body glistened, drenched in sweat, his muscles flexed as his body writhed and twisted. The bedding lay in tangled heaps. His mouth was stretched wide open, and the sound filling the room was primeval and shattering. The hairs on my body stood on end.

I moved towards the bed. 'Ashley, wake up! Wake up!'

Jason shoved me back. 'Get away!'

'Ow, you arsehole! That hurt.'

'Fox, hold her. Don't let her go anywhere near him,' Jason growled. 'Both of you, stay away from him! I'll be back in five seconds.'

'Damn you.' I jerked myself free of Fox and made a break for Ashley. Fox gripped my arm and twisted it up my back. He wrapped his other arm around my neck. 'If you don't move, it won't hurt. Please, stay put. I don't want to hurt you.'

Tears ran over my face and onto Fox's arm. I couldn't bear

124

to see Ashley suffer so.

Luca and Drom must've heard the screaming from out back. They stood at the door, guns in hand, staring at me in Fox's choke hold. Their gazes flashed back and forth, from Ashley, to Fox, to me, unsure as to what was going on. Jason yelled down the hallway for them to stay out. When he returned to the room he pushed past everyone and yelled, 'I said stay out!'

He was holding a broom. Everyone exchanged puzzled glances. Surely now was not the time to sweep up dust bunnies? I knew he was neat and tidy, but this was ridiculous.

'Wake up, mate!' He yelled as loud as he could.

No response.

Jason widened his stance on the floor before leaning forward and poking Ashley in the shoulder with the broom. Ashley responded in less than a split second, plunging a twelve-inch serrated dagger into the head of the broom and pinning it to the bedhead. The screaming stopped.

'Shit,' everyone said.

'Oh, Jesus,' Ashley croaked. 'Thank God, a nightmare, only a nightmare.' He let go of the dagger, collapsed back on the bed and rubbed his face. He was covered in sweat.

Jason gave me a look as he strode towards the door. 'I'll go make you some special chamomile tea, Ash. You can thank me later, Maggie. You need to learn to do as you're told.'

'Screw you!' I was furious. He had no right to speak to me that way, but it also niggled me that he was right. 'How about letting me go now, Fox? Or do you have to wait to be told too?' I said, icily.

Fox released me. 'Settle, Maggie.'

I glared at him, rubbed my arm and raced across to Ashley. I sat on the bed and gently touched his shoulder. I was ready to jump back if I needed to. He noted my reaction.

'It's okay. I'm only dangerous when I'm asleep.'

'I don't know; I think you're pretty dangerous while you're

awake too.' He smiled, and I held his hand. 'That was one helluva nightmare.'

'Yeah, combat nightmares. They're so real. Generally, war stuff, but now it's roaches too. Fucking millions of them. Dead set does my head in. It's from the mind meld, when they were all over you. I don't know how you cope,' he said, looking at me with concern.

'I don't know either. Red wine?'

'There's help for what you're suffering,' Drom said. 'You have Trauma Associated Sleep Disorder. It's different from PTSD. There's a drug called Prazosin which blocks the nervous system rush that makes you fight in your sleep. You should check it out.'

'The only thing that'll help me, mate, is to have the friggin' memory erased. Maggie, isn't that my T-shirt you're wearing?'

'Huh. So it is.'

'It's my favourite. Take it off. Now!' He tickled me under the arms.

'Oh. Ha. Ha. You wish.'

'There's a setting on the baton called *Memoriae*, which means memory or recall. Maybe it could help?' Luca suggested. 'We could investigate it more.'

'Then we're going to have to get the Maestro to help us,' Ashley said. 'It's too dangerous. We might erase all our memories with the touch of a button.' His jaw clenched so hard the muscles flexed. 'If Maggie has to live with the memory, I will too.'

I squeezed his hand. 'Please, for me. Think about what Drom said about the drug. I can't bear for you to suffer like this. Please?'

He met my gaze. 'Oh, jeez.' He was silent, thinking, staring into my eyes. I could hear the cogs turning.

'Please?'

'For you, I'll do it.'

126

I knew he meant what he said.

'Thank you.'

'I'll hook you up with someone tomorrow,' Drom said.

Jason returned and put a mug of chamomile tea on the bedside table. 'You okay now, mate?'

'Yeah. Can I borrow Maggie? I need a hug. Something to ground me. Five minutes.'

'Five minutes. No monkey business. Not under the blankets either. Fox, keep an eye on them in case they both fall asleep.'

Fox nodded agreement.

I glared daggers at them. 'Do I get to have a say in this? I'm not a piece of property to be handed hither and thither. Or do I have to do as I'm told?' I was already furious and getting more so by the second.

Luca and Drom disappeared, probably retreating to their rooms. Fox sat on the chair in the corner and watched.

'*Whatever*, Maggie.' Jason glared back at me and clomped out of the room. I felt my eyes prick with tears.

Ashley held out an arm and said softly, 'Come here, luv.'

I tucked myself into his arm and he pulled me against his sweaty body, which now felt icy. I screwed up my nose. 'You're in a muck lather of sweat and you're getting cold.' Against orders, I pulled a coverlet over the top of us.

'I hope I don't stink.'

'No, you're just wet.'

He grinned. 'That's normally y—,' he said, and cut himself off, realising Fox was in the room.

'Here, let me sit up,' he said. 'I don't want to fall sleep with you here. It's good to hold you.'

A wave of sadness flooded over me. 'Now I understand. That's why you said you have to sleep alone.'

'Sleeping next to me is … was a death sentence.'

'You mean you—'

'I put my girlfriend in hospital with serious injuries and … and

... I killed my dog,' he said, his voice breaking.

'Oh, my God. Kippy?'

His chest heaved with sorrow as he blinked back tears. 'Yep.'

Over in the corner Fox whispered, 'Jesus.'

'Don't be too hard on Jason. He knew. He only wanted to keep you safe, and he gets frustrated when you don't listen.'

'It's the way he says things. He can be so rude and disrespectful.'

'I know, luv, cut him some slack. He doesn't mean it.'

Ashley held me close and kissed the top of my head. He felt warmer and I sensed his body relaxing.

He whispered in my ear so Fox couldn't hear and linked my little finger with his. 'I wish I could hold you all night.' I felt energy spark between us.

Reaching across me, he pulled the knife out of the bedhead. 'Sorry about that.' The broom fell on the bed, its plastic casing split in two.

'Don't worry about it. There must be ways to help you. Maybe the baton has a force field. We can fix you...' I trailed off as sleepiness overtook me.

I must have been dozing when Jason came back him. I half heard Ashley say, 'You can have her back now, she's starting to snore.'

'Feel better, mate?

'Yeah. Sorry for all the palaver. Not easy to get a good night's sleep these days, is it?'

'Want a sleeping pill?'

'No, thanks. Special tea's kicking in and Maggie's my sleeping pill.'

'I wish she was mine,' Jason said. 'She keeps me awake.'

'With worry?'

'Yep.' Jason scooped me up in his arms. 'Come on, Mags.'

'Night, Ash,' I mumbled, still holding onto his pinky finger.

'Night, Fox. Thanks for your help,' Jason said.

Fox stood and stretched. 'My pleasure.'

Jason mumbled something under his breath I couldn't hear.

I felt a million miles away. 'I can walk,' I muttered.

He kissed my forehead. 'I love carrying you.'

'I'm sorry, Jace, I didn't know. You should've told me. How awful. Poor Ash. Poor Kippy.'

I'm sorry too. I shouldn't have spoken to you that way.'

'Jason?'

'Yes?'

'How come you let Ashley in our bed at the Hyatt?'

'I didn't know he was still having combat nightmares. I don't even want to think about it. When it happened, with Kippy an' all, Ashley didn't want you to know. He was ashamed beyond words.'

Jason put me on the bed and cuddled up to my back, tucking the blankets in around me. We slept in each other's arms, and I knew we were both giving thanks we could.

---

12 *Maggie's Playlist: Bad Dream (Live) — The Angels*

Chapter 13: The Map

'Not all treasure is silver and gold, mate.' — Jack Sparrow, Pirates of The Caribbean: The Curse of The Black Pearl

The night passed without further event. I awoke to the smell of brewing coffee and frying bacon. Jason wasn't in bed, so it must've been him cooking up a storm.

I threw on some clothes and wandered out to the kitchen. Sunlight flooded the room and my spirits lifted. Thank God it wasn't another grey day.

Someone had put the crystals on the table in the sunshine and they sparkled, creating a kaleidoscope of reflections on the tabletop. Ashley and Drom sat by them reading the paper. Fox was checking his phone, and Luca was out on the deck sitting in the sun, his feet propped on the railing.

Ashley looked up. 'Morning, Mags.'

'Morning, everyone. How'd you go, Ashley?'

'All good. After you left, I had the best night's sleep in ages.'

Jason passed me a cup of coffee. 'Morning, sweet pea.'

Luca came in from the deck. 'What's the plan for today?'

'We're going to do the head drop tonight,' Ashley said. 'Other than that, I've got to collect my old Harley from the mechanic and do some grocery shopping.'

'My business partner, Fraser's, coming over this arvo,' Jason said. 'We seriously have to catch up on work.'

Drom flicked through his phone. 'I'm meeting with some parkour buddies and then I'll do some stock trading.'

'What book are you reading today?' I asked Drom.

'Make that books. *Rules for Radicals: A Pragmatic Primer for Realistic Radicals*, by Saul D. Alinsky, and *The 33 Strategies of War* by Robert Greene. I need to improve my strategic mind.'

'Can you give us a summary of the most important bits when you've read them?' Ashley asked.

'Sure. It's better to read knowing you have to pass on information. Makes you pay more attention.'

'What are you going to do, Luca?' Jason asked.

Luca wrinkled his nose. 'I have a meeting with the archbishop.'

'Ooh, the head honcho. About the missing priests?' I asked.

Luca looked gloomy. 'Yes.'

'We can get the train in together,' Ashley said. 'And if you're not too long, I can give you a lift back on the Harley.'

'I'd love that! Imagine what the archbishop would think seeing me ride off on the back of a motor bike.'

I laughed at the image in my mind — Luca's clerical robes flapping in the breeze, his white collar peeking out from underneath his helmet, crucifix flipped over against his back, arms wrapped tightly around Ashley. Ashley must have had the same image in his mind, and he laughed out loud.

'What about you, Mags?' Jason asked.

'I have to finish some programming for an assignment due today.'

'What about you, Mister Fox?' I asked.

His mouth tightened. 'Into headquarters. I've all these strange cases and disappearances to deal with.'

'I don't envy you. You can leave Schmoo here, if you want.'

'Thanks, but Schmoo likes to go to work with me.'

'Now, to reiterate,' Jason said, 'you're all welcome to stay here at command central while we sort this thing. Come and go as you please, but if you're not staying overnight or here for dinner please call me or Maggie so we know you're all right.

'No worries, Dad,' Ashley said. Everyone gave the thumbs up.

After breakfast, we sat around the table drinking coffee and chatting. I held a crystal to my eye and stared into its translucent depths. As I moved it to catch the light, the interior transformed into a three-dimensional universe. Clouds of soft violet and blue swirled around points of light, translucent air-bubble planets floated inside a Catherine wheel of sparkling stars, all set against a pitch black background, which seemed to stretch to infinity. I gasped. It was an eyeglass to the universe.

I rotated the crystal and the vantage point changed, revealing ever more aspects of breathtaking beauty. It was as if I were looking out the window of a spaceship.

'I don't think that's safe,' Jason said. 'Could burn out your eyeballs.'

I passed him the crystal. 'It's the most beautiful thing I've ever seen. It's a peephole into the galaxy.' He held it to his eye and his jaw dropped.

I picked up another crystal and stared into it. This time, it was an atomic universe. Strange organisms, creatures, formations similar to what you'd see under an electron microscope, appeared and disappeared as I rotated the crystal. Some were truly beautiful, others hideous and frightening. The indescribable, phantasmagorical images held me spellbound. I was on a voyage into the very nature of matter.

I slid the crystal across to Jason. 'Have a look at this one.'

'Wow! It's like looking out a porthole of the Starship Enterprise. Bloody mind boggling.'

After a couple of minutes Jason rubbed his eyes and put the crystal down. The sunlight shone through it, casting bright shapes and outlines on the table. 'Check out this reflection. It looks exactly like a map of Australia.' I traced around it with my finger, and the reflection expanded with my touch.

'Whoah!' Ashley said. 'Did you see that?'

I touched the edge of the reflection again and pulled my finger outwards across the tabletop. The image expanded. 'It *is* a map of Australia!'

Everyone gathered around as I enlarged the map further. It was a topographic, glowing three-dimensional image. At various locations, sharp points of brighter light pulsed rhythmically. I placed my finger on a section with three pulsing points of light, and the map moved rapidly to a close-up view.

'It's similar to using Google Earth,' Luca said.

I suddenly understood what we were looking at. 'It's a crystal location map! This is our place, right here, with the three crystals.'

Jason clapped his hands. 'Oh hallelujah! Finally, a lucky break. This will help speed things up.'

'The closest crystals are here, in Gippsland,' Ashley said. 'About three and a half hours away. Wonder if the Prof discovered this too?'

'He didn't say anything about this map function specifically, but he has notes on locations. One he mentioned is called The Den of Nargun.'

'That's in Gippsland,' Ashley said.

Drom's face split into a smile. He pumped his fist. 'Yes! This helps us create a strategic plan.'

Jason looked cheerier than I'd seen him for ages. 'I love to have a plan with action steps.' He stood and gave me a hug. 'Good work. Sometimes, it's good when you don't listen to what I say.'

Ashley gave me a wink and a smile.

'True,' I said. 'I have to learn to distinguish between what I should and shouldn't ignore.' I poked him in the side. 'Maybe ninety-five percent ignore?'

He mussed up my hair and smiled. 'Sounds about right.'

* * * * *

After the mass exodus of people, the house was quiet. Boo was in front of the fire snoring, her legs twitching and flapping around. She was probably dreaming of chasing bunnies or playing tug of war against a black hole. I was at the sink washing the frying pans. Jason came behind me and wrapped his arms around my waist. He kissed my neck. 'Love you.'

'Ditto.'

'It's great with everyone around, but it's nice to have the place to ourselves again.' He ran his hands over my body. 'Maybe if we have some spare time? Finish what we didn't last night?'

'I'll check my diary. I hope Ashley gets help.'

'I talked to him about it this morning. He promised.'

'That's good news. Otherwise it'll cost us a fortune in brooms and bedheads. Let me go. I need to do some work.'

He turned me around, stroked the inside of my thighs and pressed into me against the sink. 'What about right here in the kitchen?'

I felt a rush of erotic sensations pulse through my body. 'I would like nothing better, but please stop.' I caught his hands and held them away from me. 'I have to do this work. I promised, and it's going to give us a nice fat paycheck.'

'Later then?'

'Later,' I said, walking away to the office. I wished he hadn't done that. Now I'd be in a state of arousal all day. I had to get my head into C++ programming.

'I'll be out front with Boo sweeping up the storm of leaves that fell last night,' he shouted out to me.

I worked solidly for five hours, focused and oblivious to anything else. The time passed in a flash. By the time I stood and staggered to the door my legs were stiff and I felt like a rusty rifle. I should've set a timer and got off my chair every fifteen minutes. I'd end up with a DVT.

Jason was at the kitchen table with paper and pen, looking at the crystal map reflection. 'I'm finding the location of the closest crystals and making a list. How'd you go? Didn't hear a peep out of you. Betcha you have a sore neck now.'

I tried to rub the stiffness out of it. 'Maybe, and yeah, all done. I don't have any more projects now.'

'Take a break until this is sorted. We have enough money coming in from the business.'

I made us ham and Swiss cheese sandwiches with hot English mustard, mayo, lettuce and tomato. Jason loved potato chips, so I put some on the side and poured out a snifter of Sauvignon Blanc, with ice, for us both.

'Here you go. A snifter to keep us going.'

'Thanks.' He slid a piece of paper across to me. 'Here's the list so far. Some crystals are close, two involve going interstate. The site at Uluru shows one crystal, but it's not flashing like the others, it's glowing solid. When I put my finger on the crystals at the other locations, I can move them before they snap back to their location. The one at Uluru doesn't move.'

I perused Jason's list:

Den of Nargun (Two Crystals) — Three hours
Buchan Caves (One Crystal) — Four hours
Hanging Rock National Park (One Crystal) — One hour, twenty
Grampians – (One Crystal) — Five hours
Beechworth (Asylum) — (One Crystal) — Three and a half hours
Murchison WA — (One Crystal) (plane trip)
Uluru NT — (One Crystal) (plane trip)

I wanted to test the map myself, so I put a finger on the point of light at Murchinson. I could slide it out a couple of inches before it snapped back. I tried it with Uluru, and as Jason had said it wouldn't budge. 'Huh. Maybe it can't be moved. Perhaps it's buried under the rock.'

'Maybe it is the rock,' Jason suggested.

'So, what? We'd have to take all the crystals to it?'

Jason tapped his pen on the table. 'Maybe. Otherwise how will it work?'

'That could be it, you know. Uluru is a major energy point in the earth's meridians. It corresponds to the earth's solar plexus chakra. Uluru might be one huge, whacking crystal.'

Jason had a big smile on his face. 'If we bring all the crystals to the chakra, it would be the most logical way to send crystal light energy throughout the planet. It would blast the Dark Force to smithereens.'

'Yes! It's a direct channel to the rainbow serpent running across the earth. It would restore the balance of dark and light, yin and yang.'

Jason banged his fist on the table, making Boo and I jump. 'By George, I think we've got it! I can't wait to tell the others. It's all falling into place.'

I didn't think it was going to be so easy, but I kept my feelings to myself. I didn't want to burst Jason's happy bubble.

---

13 *Maggie's Playlist: Maps — Maroon 5*

Chapter 14: Trial Run

'Curiosity killed the cat, but satisfaction brought it back.'
— Unknown

The doorbell rang and we both started.

Jason checked his watch. 'It's probably Fraser.' He tucked his pistol in the back of his pants anyway.

'It's me,' a voice yelled from the front door.

'Yep. It's Fraser.' Jason raced to the door and let him in.

They man-hugged and slapped each other on the back.

'Mate! It's been awhile,' Fraser said. 'Hi, Mags. You're looking good.'

'Thanks, you look pretty good yourself.'

'Yep, been on a health kick and working out at the gym.'

'You've cut your hair too. Look's great.'

'Yeah, thought it would be better for business if I didn't look so wild and woolly.'

Fraser's mop of ginger hair had gone, replaced with short hair, brushed back off his face. An extended goatee framed his square jaw and covered his cleft chin. He had intense, deep blue eyes, with eyebrows coming in low towards his nose and rising at the outer corners of his eyes giving him a questioning, serious look. It was a softer version of how Jason looked when he raised an eyebrow. Fraser was taller than Ashley, maybe six foot four and, as Ashley would say, built like a brick shithouse.

'Let me make you both a coffee,' I offered. 'I'll bring it to the office. You two get started.'

The two of them set off along the corridor joking and laughing.

They'd started their plumbing and roofing business six years ago and never looked back. Both perfectionists, their high standards and old-fashioned work ethic ensured work kept coming through the door.

After I'd taken them coffee and cake and closed the office door, I poured myself a glass of water and sat at the kitchen table to check Jason's list. Leaning back against the chair, I felt the baton in my back pocket dig into me. I pulled it out and pressed the button. It turned inside out and transformed into the weapon device.

Amazing. I'd never get tired of watching it do that. I turned it off and on a few more times. Baton. Weapon. Baton. Weapon. Baton. Weapon.

Maybe I'd explore the sonic functions.

I took my water and wandered out to the deck wanting to try the *Altum* function. The thought of using ultrasonic sound waves scared me. How far would they travel? I didn't want to blow the eardrums of the whole neighborhood, including all the poor animals. Perhaps the laser function would be safer. The *Ignis* function it was then.

I pressed the crystal three times and the button glowed red, along with the band of crystals on the body of the device. I set the intensity to medium and pointed the device at my glass of water. A blue light beam reflected on the centre of the glass. I pressed the *Emitto* button and the glass vanished. No sound, no flash, no nothing. Gone.

Where had it gone? Had it been destroyed? Vapourised? Had it been sent somewhere else? Jeepers.

I strolled through the garden. Lots of weeds were poking up their heads. Ah-ha. You are so history, weeds.

138

Setting the intensity to low, I pointed the blue beam on a weed and pressed the *Emitto* button. Gone. No hole in the ground, no damage, just the weed — gone.

Fantastic! Would they grow back? Maybe they were gone forever. How good would that be?

I'd always disliked the bougainvillea creeping across our fence from next door. It was strangling our trees. This was a bit further away, so I increased the intensity, pointed it at the bush and fired. A large hole appeared in the bush. What would happen if I held down the fire button? I pressed it and aimed and fired again. Another patch of bush disappeared, and as I moved the device backwards and forwards across the shrub, more bits vanished. It was like using a Photoshop tool — it rubbed things from existence. Awesome!

In an hour I'd weeded the entire garden, trimmed back the bougainvillea to a shadow of its former self and removed a dead tree from the neighbour's back yard. Maybe I'd got a bit carried away. An assortment of small holes decorated the brick wall opposite the deck, accidental damage from me trying to get the hang of things. The holes let the light through and it looked cool, anyway.

The baton had a myriad of uses. I wanted to emit an evil laugh; I could get rid of anything I wanted. Would it work on a building? If it removed a tree, I guessed it could. Would it get rid of a roach black hole? Jesus, one could only hope.

I was pretty pleased with myself. Not only did I have a better understanding of our weapon, the garden looked a picture. I felt confident enough to have a look at the *Libido Virgula* sex toy bit.

Returning to the house, I hurried into the bedroom and closed the door. Sitting on the bed, I pressed the *Libido Virgula* button and then the *Femina* button. The device transformed into a shimmering silver rod. It appeared metallic, but felt soft and flexible. Amazing!

The thing resembled an upmarket vibrator. It was probably

slimmer than a standard vibrator, had a loop at one end, three crystal buttons at the top and two protrusions about three inches long sat under the loop on opposite sides of the shaft. Six slim gold rings, with a tiny crystal in each, wrapped around the shaft.

I held up the device and the rings fell off onto the bed. I poked at them with a finger. What the hell were they for? Better leave 'em alone.

The three crystal buttons on the device were inscribed with *Auto*, *Modus*, and *Asperitas*. I used the Google Latin translator on my phone. *Auto* was automatic, *Modus* was mode, and rather than *Accantus* for intensity, they used *Asperitas*, which seemed to me to mean pretty much the same thing. They needed to improve the consistency of their labeling, whoever *they* were. That was a question that bothered me. Who had made this thing? Some Latin speaking, alien super race?

Had someone used it before? *Ew*. How would you sterilise it? It probably had self-sterilisation built in — it seemed to have everything else. Okay, here went nothing. I didn't want to press the *Inserto* button, so I pressed *Auto*.

The device hummed and vibrated slightly, rainbows of colours swirled through the silver, and a laser-light beamed out of the end. A thin ray of light hit my chest and expanded to engulf me in pulsing, multicoloured light. The hairs on my body stood on end as a wave of electrical impulses surged through me. A sensation of heat on my legs. A slight burning and prickling at my waist that travelled slowly to my ankles. I gasped as my jeans evaporated.

Damn it. Another pair of good jeans gone. I lifted my T-shirt to see my underwear had evaporated too. Oh, hell. I'd better turn this thing off. But which button? I couldn't find an on/off switch.

I felt a flash of heat in my hand and the whole device vanished. Bloody hell. It'd gone. But where?

Oooh! Jesus. It was inside me.

The device started to gently vibrate and expand until it filled every bit of me and then, it began.

Oh, dear. Oh. Oh my. Oh. My. God! This was the best thing — ever. I lay back on the bed totally under its control. It teased me; it did everything to me I loved. It gave me erotic sensations not only down there, but everywhere, and in places I'd never felt them before.

Holy hell. What if I couldn't turn it off? How did I turn it off?

I felt for a loop to pull it out. There wasn't one. There wasn't anything to grab hold of. A rising sense of panic mingled with the erotic sensations.

Jason was ... so going ... oooh ... to kill me. What was that noise?

Damn — the doorbell! It rang urgently and insistently.

'Come on, it's only me!' Ashley yelled.

I'd have to get it. Couldn't let Jason come up here.

Sliding off the bed, I barely managed to walk. I yelled along the corridor. 'I've got ... the ... door!' I had nothing on but a long T-shirt. Ashley was used to seeing me walk around in just a tee, so I staggered to let him in.

'H ... Hi, Ashley. J ... just ... going to ... have a ... shower,' I stuttered, trying to control the erotic convulsions coursing through my body. I gripped the doorframe until my knuckles turned white. *Breathe. Breathe.*

He eyed me intently. 'Everything all right?'

'Y ... yeah ... f ... fine and ... dandy.' I clutched my stomach as another orgasmic convulsion shuddered through my body. 'Ohhhh! I ... I have ... ss ... stomach crampsss,' I croaked, as I felt my knees buckle.

Ashley ran his eyes over me. 'Bullshit. I know you. You're using the device!'

'Oh, Ashley. Ohhhh. I ... I ... can't ... get ... it ... out! ... Ahhhh ... I'm ... g ... going ... to ... d ... die. Ja ... Jason's going to k … kill me.'

Ashley laughed.

'Ohhhhhhhh. So … n … not funny.' I staggered back into the bedroom. Ashley followed me in and shut the door. I lay on the bed and gasped, trying to catch my breath as the sensations intensified.

Ashley grinned. 'Can't you pull it out?'

'No! I c ... can't.'

'Let me have a look. I'll see if I can get at it.'

'Ashley! N ... no way... I ... can't ... let ... you ... Ah ... Ahh ... Ah...'

Ashley saw the rings on the bed and slipped one on his finger. 'What are these for?'

A laser light beam jumped across from the ring to my head, bounced back to Ashley, and engulfed him in green light. The effect was instantaneous — he buckled at the knees and bent over clutching his groin. He turned around and leant his head against the wall.

'Fuck me!' He banged his fists against the wall, as his body convulsed. 'It's like the friggin' mind meld!' he croaked. 'Bloody hell!'

I couldn't speak because my brain and body were busy trying to process two sets of erotic sensations. I seriously was going to die from this. No wonder Ashley lost it in the mind meld, trying to process *three* people. This was insane.

The door flew open and hit Ashley square on the back.

'What the hell's going on?' Jason asked, his eyes set on laser beam high. 'What's with all the banging? Are you all right?'

Then he saw Ashley behind the door, buckled over, alternately holding his groin and his head, groaning and convulsing.

'Jesus, Ash. Are you sick?'

'Aghhhh! Ohhhh! Aghhh!' he replied.

Jason spotted the rings on the floor and moved to pick them

up. Ashley and I found our voices at the same time.

'No! Don't touch them!'

Jason put two and two together. 'Oh, right. You goddamn idiots!'

'S... sorry ... Jace ... c ... can't ... get ... it ... out ... *ohhhhhhh* ... or ... turn it ... off.'

'What's with Ash then?'

Ashley stomped his foot on the floor and held his groin. He waved his hand showing Jason the ring. 'F... f ... fucking ... mind ... m ... mm ... meld function.' Ashley tried to pull the ring off his finger but it was stuck fast. That action, combined with all his other erratic movements, made it appear as if he was doing some sort of weird zombie dance.

Jason strode across to the bed and spun me around so my legs faced the wall. 'Jesus, I can't even have a frigging business meeting in peace.' He pulled up my T-shirt. 'Let me have a look. Turn away, Ash!'

Jason spread my legs. I felt like I was at the doctor's or about to have a Brazilian wax. He touched me gently and his hand shot back. 'Ouch! Electric shock!' He rubbed his fingers to ease the pain.

I couldn't speak, let alone put a sensible thought together. I could sense Jason's racing mind. He ran across to Ashley, seized his hand, and examined the ring, while Ashley continued to shudder and convulse. He struggled to keep Ashley's hand steady enough to examine the ring. 'Can you keep still, mate?' he said, jamming Ashley's arm under his arm pit and locking it down.

Ashley's eyes rolled back. 'E ... easier said ... t ... than ... oooh ... d ... ddd ... done ... m ... mate.'

'Here goes nothing.' Jason pressed the crystal on the ring and looked at me hopefully. I shook my head in the negative. 'Let's try this then.' He twisted the crystal, like trying to undo a screw. 'The crystal's changing colour ... to clear.' He looked at me again.

The vibrations running through me slowly petered out and I

felt a sensation of withdrawal as the device reappeared in my hand. The rings flew across the room reattaching to the device, and then the *whoosh, click* as it transformed back into a baton.

Prickly heat flowed from my ankles to my waist. My jeans were back!

Ashley's knees hit the floorboards with a *thunk* and he undertook a slow motion collapse along the floor. 'Fuck me,' he croaked.

Jason sat on the edge of the bed, took the baton, and stared at me, shaking his head.

Give me the tirade, Jason. Go on, let it rip.

'You saved us from death by orgasm. Thank you,' I muttered.

He smiled. 'I can think of worse ways to go. It's beer o'clock. I'm off to get you a nice cold glass of champagne and an icy cold beer for my mate on the floor there.'

I nodded and tried to compose a look of gratitude on my face. It wasn't easy; I was absolutely spent. I drifted off into another world, my body so relaxed it felt like rubber. Ashley groaned. He sounded liked a dying pig.

When Jason returned I was nearly asleep. 'Can you sit up?' he asked.

I stretched out an arm and a limp hand. He pulled me into a sitting position and swung my legs out over the bed. 'Nifty how it puts your clothes back on,' he said. 'Impressive. Do you want to get up or should I put you back to bed?'

I moved my mouth around trying to get speech to come. 'Up.' I feared if I didn't try and move, I would never be able to speak or move ever again.

'Up-a-daisy.' Jason pulled me to a standing position and laughed at my wobbly knees. He draped my arm around his shoulder and half carried me to the lounge room, where he plopped me on the couch, covered me with a throw rug, and put a glass of champagne in my hand.

'Thank you,' I whispered. Thank you for not giving me a hard time.

Stomping footsteps approached — Jason carried Ashley into the lounge. Ashley had his arms around Jason's neck and was kissing the top of his head. He rubbed Jason's cheek with his big paw. 'Mate. *Maaate.* You saved me ... us.'

Jason dumped him in a lounge chair near the fire. 'Cut it out. Here's a rug for you.' Jason draped it across his lap. 'You need the rug; you've still got a boner the size of China.'

Ashley peeked under the blanket. 'Really? That big? Cripes, no wonder my pants feel tight.' He undid the button and zip of his jeans, leaned back against the chair and closed his eyes.

Jason shoved a can of beer into his hand. 'This'll fix you.'

Ashley took a long slug of ale. 'I love coming home to this house.' He opened his eyes and gave me a wink. 'Oh, sweet mamma,' he said, closing his eyes again.

Footsteps echoed along the hallway and Fraser appeared.

'Here's a beer for you, mate,' Jason said.

'What's with the two grannies and their rugs by the fire?'

Jason headed back to the office. 'They've had a bit of a busy day. Come on, let's finish and then we can relax.'

A modicum of strength returned to my shaky limbs as I sat and sipped the champagne. I'd worked up a powerful appetite, so staggered into the kitchen and slapped together two ham and cheese sandwiches. I gave one to Ashley, who'd come back to life a bit too.

'Thanks. You read my mind. I'm starving.'

'Ditto,' I said, through a mouthful of sandwich. 'How good is this? Yum.'

'The best. I'll help you make a slap-up dinner tonight.'

'Sounds good.'

He rubbed the stubble on his chin. 'That device is unbefuckinglievable. I thought we were goners.'

'Indeed.'

'You tried to pull the wool over my eyes, Miss Maggie. One look at you and those knees and I knew what was going on. You couldn't resist, could you?'

I grinned. 'Curiosity killed the cat, but luckily it hasn't got me yet. I did some good stuff with the laser though.'

'You tried the *laser*?'

'It's incredible. It doesn't burn stuff; it makes things disappear. Look out the window. What's missing?'

Ashley craned his neck and looked out. 'The dead tree?'

'Yep. Gone.'

'You did that?'

'Yep. Trimmed the bloody bougainvillea too, and removed all the weeds. There's a few holes in the brick wall. I'm hoping Jason won't notice. Talking about him, he was amazingly good-natured about this, don't you think? I was expecting a tirade.'

'Yeah, I was surprised at how easy going he was.'

A bit of gloom descended on me. 'I reckon he'll blow up later.'

'Probably.'

Ashley adjusted his position in the chair. 'The vibrator thing had six rings, so seven people could participate in a shared sexual experience. God, you couldn't survive it.' He rubbed his groin and winced. 'It was so intense; more powerful than the mind meld.'

'I agree. Together we're too hot to handle.'

Ashley extended his pinkie finger and smiled. 'It's what I've always said, luv. What we've got can't be duplicated, whatever it is that we've got.'

'Beats me. I'm glad you arrived when you did, otherwise I would've been found dead and nobody would've known why.'

'Lucky you didn't disintegrate yourself. It was a pretty stupid thing to do.'

'Don't start, Jason … I mean, Ashley. But you're right, it was.'

146

'I'm right? Really?'

'Only a little bit,' I said, as I returned to the kitchen to make another sandwich.

'Yes please, luv.'

'Got it already.'

Ashley chuckled. 'I'm looking forward to the debrief tonight.'

I poured myself another glass of champagne. 'I'm not.' I returned to the lounge. How nice would it be to have a plain old, bog-standard, boring day? Would I have one, ever again?

It was just as well I couldn't perceive the answer to that question. I would've thrown in the towel, right then and there.

14 *Maggie's Playlist: Curiosity Killed the Cat — The Little River Band*

Chapter 15: Choppers & Bombs

'I know not with what weapons World War III will be fought, but World War IV will be fought with sticks and stones.' — Albert Einstein

Ashley's ring tone — *Bad to the Bone* — made me jump.

'It's Luca,' Ashley said, answering it. 'Yep, no worries, mate. I'll be right there.'

'Is he okay?'

Ashley picked up his keys. 'I think so. He's at the station. I'm going to get him on the Harley.'

'Bye,' I said, as he disappeared through the door.

The Harley's unique engine sound thundered all the way along the street. The neighbours were going to love that. Not. Two minutes later another motorbike roared down the drive. I raced over to the window and peeked out. A leather clad figure cut an impressive silhouette as he dismounted from the bike. I knew who it was before he took off his helmet because the dog sitting in the sidecar was wearing goggles. It was Schmoo. I laughed out loud and ran outside.

Schmoo sat tall and proud in his very own sidecar. And what a sidecar it was. Black and bullet shaped, it appeared antique. Silver rods ran along the length, dividing it into eight equal segments, joining at the apex. The seat was a black leather-upholstered chair with built in armrests. It was a thing of beauty.

Fox pulled off his helmet and smiled. 'Pretty good, huh?'

'My God, it's spectacular. Schmoo looks hilarious. You must've had a heap of looks along the way. I didn't know you owned a bike.' I admired the design and ran my hands over its curves. 'Gorgeous! It's a terminator bike, a cross between a motorbike and a jet engine or something. What is it?'

'It's a Ducati 2016X Diavel custom fitted with a Royal Enfield sidecar. I had a bastard of a day so decided to pull it out of storage. I haven't ridden for ages. Schmoo was so excited. He loves it.'

'I'm glad you brought it. Jason and Ashley will be beside themselves. Jason has a Kawasaki Ninja in the shed.'

'Wow. It's a powerful bike, the ol' Ninja.'

'Yep. Goes from naught to one hundred in two point seven seconds. We don't ride much these days — it's so dangerous on the roads. I miss it, but.'

Jason and Fraser wandered out the front to see what was going on. They caught sight of Schmoo in the sidecar and fell about laughing. Schmoo started to shuffle from side to side.

'Don't laugh at him; I think he's embarrassed.'

Boo came running out and stopped in her tracks when she caught sight of Schmoo. *Hubba hubba, Maggie, that's one hot dog. He looks gorgeous!*

Boo's tongue was hanging out of her mouth, and her eyes were wide and glistening.

Schmoo regained his poise and jumped out of the sidecar. He ran to Boo and they greeted with the enthusiasm of reunited lovers.

'Schmoo, come here,' Fox said. Schmoo dutifully obeyed and Fox removed the goggles.

'Wow. Great bike, man,' Fraser said.

'Fox, this is Fraser, my business partner. Fraser, this is Fox. He's a detective,' Jason said.

Fraser shook Fox's hand. 'Good to meet you. Better watch myself then.'

Jason examined Fox's bike. 'I didn't know you rode. Beautiful bike. The sidecar's incredible. My grandfather had a Royal Enfield with a sidecar.'

The rumble of a Harley reverberated along the street, and Ashley turned into the driveway. Luca had his arms wrapped around Ashley, holding on as tightly as a koala. The image was pretty much how we'd imagined it, with Luca's clerical robes flapping in the breeze.

Ashley turned off the motor, removed his helmet and kicked out the stand.

He attempted to disengage Luca's arms from around his waist. 'You can let go of me now, mate.'

Ashley assisted Luca's dismount, undid the strap on his helmet and removed it to reveal one beaming face.

Luca was beside himself. 'Oh my God, it was fantastic!'

Ashley grinned. 'Glad you enjoyed it, mate.'

I'd never seen Luca so happy. 'Ashley will take you for another ride, won't you, Ash?'

Luca clutched his robes with excitement. 'Would you?'

Ashley gave me a look. In my mind, I heard him say sarcastically, 'Thanks a lot.' 'Sure, no worries,' he said to Luca.

Luca was star struck. 'Ash is the best rider. Made me feel totally safe all the way. It was so exciting; everyone was looking at us.'

Ashley rubbed his ribs. 'You don't have to hang on so tight, Padre. I could hardly breathe.' He ambled over to Fox. 'Nice bike.'

'Thanks, mate. I'd forgotten how good it is to ride.'

'I love the sidecar,' I said. 'I've never ridden in one before.'

'I'll take you for a spin sometime, but you need protective gear. Full-face helmet, leathers, gloves, boots.'

'We have all the gear. I'll dig it out from storage. Jace, we should get our stuff out, dust off the Ninja.'

'Yeah, we should. I'm inspired.'

'Excellent,' Fraser said. 'I've been at him for ages to ride.'

'Anyone heard from Drom?' I asked.

'He texted me. He'll be here in about five minutes,' Jason said.

'Full house then,' Ashley replied. 'Better get started on dinner.'

Fraser gave me a kiss on the cheek. 'Bye, sweetheart, I'm off. Got footy practice. See ya, Jace. Bye, everyone. Nice to meet you all.'

I accompanied Fraser outside and waved him goodbye. The front gates had to be locked — I didn't want anyone stealing the bikes. Crime statistics were through the roof. The news was full of home break-ins and car jackings. It was unprecedented. People in the 'burbs were arming themselves with baseball bats and setting up vigilante patrols. In fact, sports shops had sold out of baseball bats — they were like hen's teeth. If it appeared you had something worth taking, the gangs would target you. The police seemed powerless to stop them, whilst the politicians insisted everything was fine. Yeah, right.

Returning inside, I checked out Fox's donations — a slab of beer, half a dozen bottles of champagne, plus an assortment of cheese and paté. Luca brought a bottle of Chartreuse, Dom Bénédictine, dips, olives, feta cheese and a couple of loaves of artisan bread.

Ashley said he hadn't had a roast "for decades", so he fired up the Weber and whacked in a leg of lamb. We figured it would be eight o'clock before we ate, but the head drop was going to happen prior to midnight, so the timing worked out fine.

Inside, we all kicked back around the fire. Boo and Schmoo cuddled contentedly on the rug, Schmoo with his head across Boo's back, blinking sleepily.

I was amazed. 'Check out Boo. Normally, she'd never let another dog do that.'

Schmoo's special, Maggie. He's very special.

'I think they're in love,' Jason said.

Boo gave us a look. *Could be.*

Fox massaged the back of his neck. Dark circles ran under his eyes and his face was drawn.

'Had a bad day?'

'Yep. Unbelievable. Getting nowhere fast. It's doubly hard now I know what's really going on but can't do anything about it.'

'I bet you wish you'd never come for that walk with me.'

'I'm glad I know the truth. It helps, in a way. It was doing my head in not being able to solve the cases. But now, my whole sense of reality has been turned upside down and that's proving hard to deal with. It's a nightmare.'

I looked at Luca. 'What about you? How did the meeting with the archbishop go?'

'I feel the same as Fox. I'm glad I know, but it's made life hell. I lied today. So many lies. Lying is not something I'm used to, but I know it's the only way. When the archbishop asked me if I had any idea what happened to the brothers, I wanted to say they were possessed by demonic cockroaches, hence, I had no choice but to kill them all with a crucifix and the reason there is no evidence is because they all turned into black holes and vanished.'

Fox tilted his head and sighed. 'Yeah, it's not going to fly, is it?'

The doorbell rang and Jason leapt up. He still had a gun in his pants.

'It's me,' Drom called out.

Jason opened the door, and Drom sauntered in and plonked a big hessian sack on the floor. His eyes were bright and he flashed us a big smile. 'Hi, all!'

'What's in the sack?' Ashley asked. 'More tower busters?'

Drom upended the sack onto the floor. 'I think you'll like what I have here much better. These are more traditional, heavy-duty tower busters.'

A dozen dark grey items, each with an orange stripe around the top, rolled out across the floor. They were about ten centimetres in height and reminded me of tiny Daleks from the show *Doctor Who*. However, I'd watched enough action movies to recognise hand grenades when I saw them.

Ashley sprang to his feet and picked one up. 'Bloody hell, Drom! Where on earth did you get hold of F1 fragmentation grenades? We used these in Iraq.'

'Can't say. But I thought they'd be an excellent addition to our arsenal.'

Fox buried his head in his hands and made soft groaning noises.

Ashley pointed at him and laughed silently.

'Poor Fox,' I mouthed to Ashley.

Everyone nodded, sympathising with what he must be going through.

'I'm not even going to ask. I'm *not* going to ask. Don't ask,' Fox muttered to himself.

Drom patted his shoulder. 'I wouldn't tell you anyway.' He reached into his satchel and took out a fistful of olive coloured blocks and assorted gadgets. He passed them to Ashley. 'You'll know what to do with these.'

'What are they?' Jason asked.

'C-4 plastic explosive,' Ashley said quietly.

Jason's eyes widened. 'Christ, Drom, what are you? Where'd you get this stuff from?'

'I told you, I can't tell you, so don't ask. If you don't want it, I'll take it back. I don't want you to feel uncomfortable.'

I shrugged my shoulders. 'As long as the bad guys don't get hold of it, and there's no danger of it blowing up on us, then I think we're lucky to have it.'

The feeling in my gut was strong. We were going to need every bit of it.

Ashley slapped the C-4 on the table with a thud. 'We can

lock it in the gun safe under the house.'

Jason put on a mock serious face. 'Dammit, Ashley. Be careful. You screw around with that stuff and it's gonna blow up!'

Luca moved back in his chair.

'Don't worry, Luca. Jason's similar to Ashley,' I explained. 'They're always looking for opportunities to use lines from their favourite movies. I know them all off by heart myself now.' I rolled my eyes. 'That was from *Jaws*.'

'But shouldn't you be careful with it?' Luca asked.

'Not really,' Ashley said. 'C-4 is incredibly stable. It would take a combination of a shock wave from a detonator and extreme heat to make it explode. Maggie, before I forget. I've booked you into an introduction to handguns course, next Tuesday night at the local shooters club.'

'I thought you were going to teach me.'

'I may have developed bad habits. I thought an approved course would be safer.'

'How come Jason doesn't have to do it then?'

'I asked him, and he didn't feel he needed to.'

'How come I don't get a say?'

'Don't start. I'm trying to do the right thing.'

For once I decided to button my lip, but I wasn't happy. I'm sure my face spoke a thousand words, anyway.

'Don't give me that look.'

My lip unbuttoned. 'I'm extremely sick and tired of your patronising attitude. The both of you are in cahoots, and it's not right. It stinks. Jace gets a quick rundown and he's good to go. But oh no, not Maggie, she's a girl after all, needs lots of specialised instruction. Fair dinkum, I—'

'If you don't want to go to the course, I can teach you,' Fox cut in. 'I'm police, I know everything about weapons, plus I'm a licensed instructor.'

'What about actual shooting practice?'

'I can take you to a range.'

I glared at Jason and Ashley, daring them to oppose me. 'Thanks. You know what? I'm going to take up your offer.'

'Um, yeah, why not?' Ashley mumbled. Jason shrugged his shoulders.

I knew they weren't happy. But I was. I was grateful to Fox for giving me another option. I hated being railroaded into things. You'd think they'd know by now that I was tired of being treated like a child and having decisions made for me.

'We can start now if you want?' Fox said.

'Sooner the better, I reckon. I'll start getting a few things ready for dinner and I'll be right with you.'

Ashley followed me into the kitchen. 'I know you're upset with me, about the gun training thing. I'm sorry.'

'I was looking forward to you training me, after all we'd been through and all the times we discussed this before. Plus, you *promised.*'

'Yeah, I know, but … I couldn't do it.'

'Why the hell not?'

'Because the more I thought about it, the more it worried me. What if something happened to you because of something I did, or didn't, teach you? I couldn't live with myself. I talked to Jason about it and he agreed; it would be better to get someone else, a professional, to train you. This is dangerous stuff. It's not that I don't think you're capable or that I don't want to, it's just … because I …'

Ashley's eyes glistened, and he turned away and wiped them. 'Damn hay fever.'

'What is it?'

'You know damn well what,' he said, and stomped off towards the bathroom.

Jason came into the kitchen. 'We were only concerned for your safety.'

I gave him a kiss. 'I know. But I'd just like to be asked

instead of decided for. It pisses me off. I know you had my best interests at heart.'

Jason wrapped his arms around me and kissed me back.

Ashley returned and I tried to catch his eye. He looked straight through me, before heading out to check the Weber.

'Let me talk to Ashley,' I said. 'He seems upset.' I went outside and closed the sliding door behind me. 'Ashley, I understand why you did what you did.'

He draped an arm around my shoulder and pulled me in close. The smell of roast lamb cooking in the Weber made my mouth water. We stood in silence looking out at the view. The sun broke through the clouds, and the distant horizon glowed with a soft yellow haze. New leaves on the Lilly Pilly trees sparkled like bouquets of green and bronze diamonds, and the bone white limbs of the ghost gums gleamed in the falling light.

'It's beautiful here, isn't it?' he said. I nodded.

Below us, water bubbled and gurgled in the creek Jason had designed and built. The weeping wattle I'd planted five years ago was reflected in the still water of the pond. Its leaves were the colour of weathered copper, and masses of tiny, bright blossoms covered it in a blanket of yellow.

Ashley pointed. 'Looks as though the sun has rained a million droplets of sunshine on it.'

'It's amazing how Australian natives blossom in winter,' I said.

Ashley met my eyes. 'Many things do.' He squeezed my shoulder and walked back into the kitchen.

I gazed out at the beauty of nature until the sun disappeared and the chill of twilight drove me inside.

---

15 Maggie's Playlist: Make You Feel My Love — Adele

Chapter 16: Give a Girl a Gun

'Most maidens are perfectly capable of rescuing themselves in my experience, at least the ones worth something, in any case.' — Erin Morgenstern, *The Night Circus*

Back inside, Fox had all the guns on the table ready for my instruction. He smiled and indicated the display. 'Ready when you are. Get yourself a notepad and pen.'

By the time we'd finished, I knew the difference between a revolver and a semi-automatic handgun, about ammunition, calibres, rimfire and centrefire cartridges, about double action and single action, the mechanics and parts of each gun, how to load and unload them, how to grip a gun, how to get a correct sight picture, the special way you must pull the trigger and the stance for two-handed and single-handed shooting, plus, a whole heap of safety information.

Fox taught me about gun jams and how to fix them. I learned that if you tried to keep shooting with a jammed gun, you would ruin the gun, or worse, it could explode and be more likely to take out the people *next* to you, rather than yourself. Jeepers. It was important to wash your hands after shooting because ammunition contained hazardous materials, including mercury and lead styphnate. This was all news to me.

'When we go to the shooting range you'll have to wear hearing and eye protection,' Fox said. 'As you discovered when I shot Avinash, a handgun is extremely loud and can damage your hearing.

'So that's why my ears were buzzing for hours! I thought there were hundreds of mosquitos out there.'

'Yeah, exactly. It's why you couldn't hear a thing and I had to … ah, um, keep you quiet.'

Ashley cocked his head and stared at Fox. 'Jeez, how'd you do that? It's impossible to keep her quiet. What's your secret?'

My face instantly flushed. I felt the heat rise from my neck to the top of my head. *Damn it.*

Fox kept his eyes on the gun he was cleaning. 'Simple. I covered her mouth.'

Ashley scrutinised me carefully. 'Oh, I'm sure you did, Fox.'

I turned redder still under his gaze.

'What's wrong? You've turned the colour of red silk.'

Fox shot me a look, like, what the hell's he on about?

I pulled at the neckline of my top. 'Nothing's wrong. It's hot in here. I have to turn the heater off before I die.' I scurried away to get the remote control. Damn my face. I could never lie and Ashley knew it.

I heard him say, 'Seems you had your hands full with Maggie out there.'

'Yep,' Fox grunted.

I ran to the bathroom and splashed my face with cold water. I returned to the kitchen when my face reverted to its normal colour.

Ashley grinned at me. 'Here's a drink for you. Thought it might help to cool you down.'

'Thanks.' He was baiting me again. He could be such a mongrel. He suspected something had happened and wanted to know exactly what. I wasn't going to tell him. Anyway, what happened wasn't my fault, and it was nothing anyway.

He whispered, 'What happened out there with you two? You can tell Uncle Ash.'

I glared at him. 'You're an idiot. Your imagination is out of control. Stop it.'

He mussed up my hair. 'I'm kidding around. But you can't pull the wool over my eyes, little Miss. I can read you like a book.'

'Shut up, Ashley.' I walked across to Fox.

'Ashley, do you want to show Maggie the MP5 sub gun?' Fox asked him.

'Ah … yeah … as long as you oversee what I tell her.'

Fox waved over Jason, Luca and Drom. 'Want to join us for this too?'

Ashley handled the sub gun like an old friend. 'This is a great little submachine gun. It's very easy to use; it just works. There's very little recoil, and if you use a suppressor or silencer, you don't need hearing protection. Let me show you how to fieldstrip it.'

'What's that?'

'Sorry, take it apart and put it back together again.'

Everyone sat around the kitchen table while Ashley demonstrated what to do. He placed the reassembled gun in front of me. 'Okay, you have a go.'

I took the gun and checked to see it wasn't loaded. I popped out the pin, pulled the back off, pulled out the bolt, took out the selector switch and pulled out the trigger grip. I reversed the procedure and had it all done and dusted in under a minute. I plonked the gun on the table. 'Ta-dah!'

Ashley checked my work. He put his hands on his hips and shook his head. His face crinkled into a smile. 'Jesus, you're a natural.'

I felt very happy with myself. 'I have excellent teachers. Can't wait 'til I get to push a few rounds through.'

Ashley laughed. 'She even talks like a shooter. See how the stock is collapsible? Even you should be able to shoot this one-handed … at a pinch.'

'When can we get to try these?' I asked Fox.

'I'll see if I can organise something for tomorrow night.'

'Fantastic. I'm excited.'

Jason gave me a peck on the cheek. 'It's great to see you happy. Who'd have thought it'd be about guns but.'

'What about the grenades?' Drom asked.

'You should do this training,' Fox said to Ashley.

Ashley grabbed a grenade. 'No worries.' He demonstrated how to hold it, the pin pulling technique and how to throw it from a standing, kneeling and lying position.

I picked up a block of C-4 explosive. 'What about this?'

He took it from me. 'As I said before, this stuff is incredibly stable; you can't detonate it by dropping it, putting a gunshot into it or setting it on fire. Only a combination of extreme heat and a shock wave will set it off. These blocks have a strip of adhesive on the back so you can stick it onto a vehicle or other stuff.'

He cut through the olive coloured plastic surrounding the block to reveal a whitish, putty like substance.

Jason held it to his nose. 'It smells similar to motor oil.'

'That's the C-4 explosive; it's like plasticine and can be shaped to suit whatever you need it for. You can press it into cracks and gaps in buildings or machinery. You can mould it to any shape.' Ashley pulled off a chunk and started to knead it with his fingers. He prodded, pulled and moulded it, until finally, with a big grin, he placed a model of a bunny rabbit on the tabletop.

Jason made it hop across the table. 'Very funny, Ash.'

'You explode C-4 by using one of these pencil detonators with a time delay. The explosion travels around 8000 metres per second, so there's no way you can out run it. It's not like in the movies, folks, so please make sure you're well away from the blast zone.'

'How much would one of these blocks blow up?' I asked.

'This is a standard block, a bit over half a kilo. One of these would do serious damage to a vehicle.'

'And what about these little grenades for the grenade launcher?' Luca asked.

'They're useful for smaller areas, such as shooting into a room if you want to flush out any hostiles. This little sucker will cause damage in a limited radius, about five metres. One of these shot into a room, or area, followed by fire from the sub gun will give you the best kill rate.'

Luca's mouth tightened, and he stared fixedly at the ceiling and muttered, 'Just dandy.'

I felt bad too. 'Let's pray we don't have to use this stuff. If we do, let's hope Ashley's around.'

'I think that'll do it for our lessons tonight,' Fox said. 'Don't want to give you info overload. And I agree. Let's hope we don't have to use any of it.'

'Fingers crossed,' I said, despite knowing we would use every single bit of it.

---

16 *Maggie's Playlist: A Girl is a Gun — Old Dominion*

Chapter 17: The Drop

'You're wrong. I can load a lot more than a washer and dryer.' — Unknown

We made plans for the head drop over our lamb roast dinner. It was decided Boo would go in Ashley's truck with Luca and Drom. They would park a block away, and Boo would fly in low with the head, sticking to the bushes. She'd drop it at the front door of the police station when the coast was clear.

The rest of us would follow on bikes. Jason was keen to try Ashley's Harley. Ashley was going to take the Ninja. Fox his Ducati, sans sidecar, leaving Schmoo at home to avoid attracting attention. I was going to ride with Ashley until Jason got the hang of the Harley.

My phone beeped. It was a text from the Maestro. 'Hey Jace, the Maestro said she wants to come around tonight.'

He shook his head. 'Tell her we won't be home. Ask if she can make it tomorrow night. We need to discuss what we're going to do about her first.'

By now the night was pitch black, so at 11:30 pm we set off on our mission. To minimise attracting attention with the noise of the truck and three motorbikes, we staggered our departure and met a couple of blocks away. Ashley and I were last to leave. I made sure all the security systems were in place and the front gate locked. Ashley grinned at me from inside his helmet. 'Now,

Missie, you hang onto me extra tight. I'm looking forward to having your arms wrapped around me. You look hot in those leathers.'

'You're incorrigible, Mr Beringer.'

He fired up the Ninja. 'Climb aboard, Ms. McLaine.'

I flipped my visor shut, swung my leg over and we were off with a roar. I didn't hang on to Ashley, choosing the grab bar behind me. I knew it would annoy him, but I didn't want to encourage any unnecessary body contact.

We met the others as planned, and I laughed at Jason straddling the Harley, looking like a big, tough biker. It was a twenty-minute drive to the police station rendezvous point, so we set off in convoy, truck at the front, bikes following behind.

It felt good to be back on a bike again, and the Ninja was one mean machine. I felt wild and free on a bike, despite the overabundance of safety gear. It rocked. Until you were T-boned by some lunatic driver. No. Don't think that. Enjoy the moment.

I felt safe with Ashley. He was taking it easy with me on the back, even though I knew he was dying to open her up.

We stopped at the lights before the freeway entrance. Ashley turned around and yelled, 'Hold on to me. We're going on the freeway.'

I nodded and let go of the passenger bar. The lights turned green, and the engine roared as Ashley took off at speed. I flew off the bike and found myself hovering in midair. I was suspended in space, my leather jacket pulled tight under my arms.

Why hadn't I hit the road yet? The reason soon became apparent — a big, burly thug. He'd reached across from the back of a ute in the next lane and yanked me off the bike. His arm was hooked firmly around my waist. I kicked and screamed as he dragged me onto the back of the now speeding vehicle.

My feet hit the cargo tray and I pushed backwards, sending him off balance. He let me go, flailing for a handrail. I spun around and rammed my steel capped boot between his legs. He crumpled into a heap. An acrid stink of enclosed animals hit my nostrils — a livestock truck was right beside us.

The thug started to crawl, making a move to get me. I calculated the distance of the truck, eyed off a rail on the side of it, and leapt. One hand slipped, the other managed to grab a rail.

I found myself eyeball to eyeball with a frightened sheep. I just ate one of you. I was betting my eyeballs looked wider than the sheep's as my feet struggled to find a foothold. My other hand connected with a woolly fleece and I held on tight. My legs flapped around as I tried to locate a toehold. The sound of blaring horns. Jason was on the Harley below me. His visor was up; he was screaming. 'Jump!'

Yeah, right! As if. I'd fall straight under the wheels of the truck. No way, Jose.

A pistol shot cut the air. Jason had his gun out. The ute was trying to ram him to get to me. Jason squeezed off another shot. Their windscreen shattered and the ute pulled back.

A rough Aussie voice sounded in my ear. 'Listen, darls, don't panic. Bring your right foot up twenty-four inches, and you'll find yourself a foothold.'

A sun-wizened face appeared in front of me, gouged with deep, dirt stained wrinkles. A large set of ears supported a grimy, battered leather hat. Brown eyes sat under the biggest, bushiest eyebrows I'd ever seen, and a soggy roll-your-own fag was stuck in the corner of his nicotine-stained mouth.

A hairy chest which would make a bear envious, sprouted from beneath his blue, work stained shirt and curled under his chin. It was a ghost. He floated right next to me, one grimy, weathered hand gripped a railing on the truck to stop him drifting away.

'Who are you?' I asked.

'Name's Clyde, darls, and you better move your foot before you go arse over tit.'

I followed Clyde's instructions, and sure enough, my right boot found a foothold. I jammed it in and felt blessed relief in my hands as my leg supported my weight.

'If I were you, I reckon I'd jump off at the next bend. It's comin' up. Truck has to slow there to avoid tippin' an' that. Then piss off quick down the culvert. You should be right there, darls.'

'Thanks, Clyde. How come you're still here?'

'I'm a sheep drover, darls. Like to hang around sheep, I reckon. Been doing it for a hundred and fifty years.'

'It's fine to move on, Clyde. If you want to. Go to the light. Thanks for the help.'

'Jump now, darls!'

I turned so I was facing away from the truck, arms stretched out to the sides. My triceps burned. I pulled up my knees, jammed my boots against the side of the truck and launched myself at the grassy verge.

I was channeling Drom as I tucked my head in and connected to the ground with my shoulder, rolled up and onto my feet and I was away, running towards the cyclone wire fence.

'Thanks, Clyde!' I yelled, as he vanished into the light leaving this plane behind.

I ran at full pelt — for me anyway — away from the beams of the freeway lights, heading for the cover of some bushes in front of the fence. The roar of approaching engines grew louder. The fence was bent at the top and strung with barbed wire. *Bloody great.*

I found a spot near a pole and clambered to the top. With my protective gear on, I found I could lie on the wire and get across it. I felt the barbs prick my skin, but not enough to slow me. I hung from the other side of the fence and let myself drop. My feet hit the grass with a thud, and the shock vibrated along my spine into my skull.

Headlights headed straight for the fence. Maybe it was the

guys coming to get me. I squinted through my visor, but my vision was obscured by the blinding dazzle of lights. I couldn't take the risk. I had to go. I rolled down the steep embankment and hit the concrete culvert. It knocked the wind out of me. Gasping for breath, I looked at the fence line. The headlights from a car and two motorbikes silhouetted a man climbing the fence.

I staggered to my feet and ran. I needed to hide. But where? It was one long concrete channel. What had Clyde been thinking?

My boots thudded along the culvert. I wasn't used to running. I felt my bones shake. I'd get a migraine out of this for sure.

The overpass was just ahead. I increased my speed. At the rate I could run, I figured I only had a one-minute lead. The overpass was my only chance, my only place to hide. I started to sob. The sound came from the depths of my gut. My lungs burned.

In the shadow of the overpass was an embankment of wooden sleepers. I dragged myself up them and onto an inset of pavers, which ran steeply to the underside of the bridge. Cars thundered overhead, and the smell of diesel fumes seeped into my helmet. The bridge supports had large spaces above them. I could get there, but I'd easily be seen. Along the edge of the bridge was a pipe with about an eight-inch gap above it. It ran along the side and was in the dark.

Maybe I could squeeze in there, lie on top of it. Hide in the shadows. Make like a cockroach.

Hooking my arms over the pipe, I pulled myself on top of it and pressed flat against the wall. In my poor state of fitness, it was no easy feat. My arms trembled and my body hummed with adrenaline.

God knows what else lived here. Big hairy spiders? Surely, they wouldn't survive these fumes. My lungs rattled as I tried to get air. Huge gut-wrenching sobs sought to escape me, but I couldn't expand my chest in the cramped space. I needed to be quiet.

Be quiet. Shhh, Maggie. Calm. Breathe. Dolphins. Think of dolphins.

All I could hear were my sobs and the rumble of traffic as the bridge vibrated around me.

A silhouette of a man moved below. The angle of his head indicated he was looking at the trusses under the bridge, scanning left and right. He stopped and stared directly at me. I held my breath. What for, I don't know, but I held it anyway.

He was looking at me but couldn't see me. If he had a torch, I was screwed.

Headlights illuminated the pylons of the bridge as a motorbike pulled alongside him. It definitely wasn't the guys. Where the hell were they? Surely, they'd seen what had happened.

A gruff voice with a thick accent shouted, 'She must be here. She can't have gone far.'

He sounded similar to the guy hunting Fox and me down by the river.

'Maybe she climbed back over the fence?'

'We have people on bikes out there. I go back. Get my bike. You go look. I catch up and bring torch!'

The gruffly spoken man ran back, while the motorcyclist took off along the culvert. I had two choices. Stay put and hope to hell they wouldn't find me. But if he brought a torch they would. Or run and try to get back over the fence. There was a chance they wouldn't see me. They couldn't be everywhere. Could they? I'd just lost thirty seconds thinking. I was a sitting duck. I had to go.

I squeezed out of my hidey-hole and faced the slope. Crikey, it was steep. How the hell had I got up here? Getting to the bottom was going to be way more difficult. I sat on my bum and inched forward. Instantly my feet lost their grip and I slid down the paved slope at speed.

The headlights of a motorbike approached. I figured its trajectory would coincide exactly with mine. Bingo. I hit the bottom of the culvert as it screamed to a stop in front of me. The light was blinding — I couldn't see a thing. A rabbit in the headlights.

I turned and ran, knowing I was dead already. The bike revved, took off and stopped in front of me blocking my path. The man raised his arm. He was going to shoot me! I felt my knees buckle. He lifted his visor.

'It's Ash. Get on!'

Oh, thank God.

He grabbed my arm and pulled me towards him. 'Sit at the front facing me. Now!'

Yeah, nice to see you too.

I straddled the bike facing him and he took off at speed. The engine screamed, and my helmet cracked against his. He reached into a pannier and pulled out the submachine gun with the grenade launcher attached. His face was stony as he thrust it at me. 'It's ready to fire. Use it!' he barked.

Headlights were coming up behind us. Was it a car? Bikes? I couldn't tell. What if it was Jason or Fox or Drom? I couldn't shoot.

'I can't see who it is!'

The bike screamed its guts out as Ashley put the pedal to the metal. I put my left arm around him and leant to the right trying not to block his vision. In my right hand, I held the sub gun, locked and loaded. Ashley started to weave the bike erratically. What the hell was he doing?

Pretty lights, like fireflies, swarmed around our back tyre. The ping of metal on metal. They were shooting at us!

Please, please, please, oh angel of target shooters and war heroes, help me now!

I reached around Ashley and gripped the sub gun with both hands. No single hand shooting for me. Using Ashley as a brace, I took aim and slowly squeezed the trigger.

I felt the recoil but didn't hear the pop of the grenade. Oh, my God. Maybe it was stuck in the barrel? Ashley's horror stories filled my mind. Chuck it! Get rid of it! I was about to hurl it, like I'd never hurled anything in my life, when an explosion stopped me.

Boom! The night sky lit up with a fireball as two motorbikes hit the deck and their riders rolled like tumbleweed along the culvert. One motorbike disappeared into the centre ditch, the other hit a pylon and exploded.

I'd done it!

The truck headlights were still coming. I had to use the launcher again. Ferreting around in the pannier, I pulled out another grenade. The scenery was a blur. I felt as though I were floating in space as I pushed in another round. I pulled the casing thing back to make it lock. I took aim. I pointed the gun up slightly to get a curved trajectory like Ashley had taught me. I took a breath. I held it. I braced against Ashley and pulled the trigger.

Time seemed to stop. Nothing happened. The night rushed past. And then, something did happen. The truck cab exploded. A ball of flame shot skywards.

The truck swerved drunkenly and hit the ditch. It tilted. It hovered on two wheels, tipped on its side, slammed into the concrete and then a pylon. It spun off in crazy screaming circles, heading straight for us.

'Go, Ash!' My helmet cracked into his as he accelerated. The bike responded beautifully to his touch. Just like a Ninja. Just like me.

In the distance, the truck was in flames, a glowing bonfire in the dark. Then it disappeared.

We blasted along the culvert for ages before Ashley finally

slowed. He drove along a service pathway and pulled to a stop in front of a locked gate.

I was doing a Luca, wrapped around his chest like a koala, legs and arms stuck to him like glue, the sub gun clutched tightly in my hand. He kicked out the stand, leaned back and lifted his visor. He pushed open my visor and tipped back the helmet to see my eyes. My head felt so heavy I could barely keep it upright. Ashley propped up my head with a gloved hand. 'Hey, soldier. You were awesome.' He attempted to free himself from my arms. 'You did good. Real good.'

I relaxed my legs and let them hang on each side of the bike. I was spent. Ashley climbed off and pulled bolt cutters out of the pannier. The broken chains securing the gate clinked as they hit the concrete path.

Ashley tried to prize the gun from my hand. 'You can let go now.'

I reluctantly gave it over, and he returned it to the pannier.

'Spin around, Maggie. I'm taking you home.'

I couldn't get my body to spin around. It wouldn't behave. I swung my leg over the bike and dismounted. My knees buckled, and I staggered off to one side. Ashley grasped my arm to stop me falling. He wrapped an arm around me and held me tight. Our leathers squeaked and groaned against each other.

'This is a first,' he said.

'What?'

'I'm not the reason for your weak knees.'

I felt laughter bubble in my chest.

He held me even tighter. 'I must be losing my touch.' He gripped my waist and my leather jacket groaned in response. So did I.

My knees buckled again. 'Don't worry, you've still got it, Ash.'

I could hear the smile in his voice. 'That's my girl.'

We both started as a headlight illuminated the area. A

motorbike roared along the path heading straight for us. We couldn't see who it was. Ashley pushed me behind him and pulled out a gun. The silhouette was waving. It was Fox. He slowed to a stop beside us, turned off his engine and flipped up his visor.

'You two all right?'

Ashley nodded.

'Where's Jason?' Ashley asked.

'I don't know; he's gone. I've been looking for him.'

'Jason and Fox rode into the culvert from the other end to flush out any hostiles,' Ashley said to me. 'Were there any hostiles?' he asked Fox.

'Two guys on bikes. Tried to take us out.'

'Did you get 'em?'

'Had to. No choice. How did you go?'

Ashley put his arm around me, squeezed my shoulders, and regarded me proudly. 'She took out a truck and two guys on motorbikes. Used the grenade launcher.'

'Hell,' Fox said.

A surge of fear flooded my body. 'Forget about that. Where's Jason?'

'He was right behind me. I'll go back and keep looking. I've texted the others. The drop went without a hitch. I told them to go home and we'd call if we need backup.'

Ashley zipped his jacket. 'We're coming with you. Are you right to do this, Maggie?'

I felt my strength return with the adrenaline coursing through my veins. 'Definitely, let's go!'

Please, God, don't let him be dead. What if he'd been sucked into a black hole? No. Don't think like that. Focus. We'd find him.

We travelled back into the culvert and retraced Fox's route. We rode slowly for fifteen minutes. I checked left while Ashley looked right. Nothing. There was nothing. Ashley waved to Fox and motioned with his thumb to go back. We turned around. There was no one. My heart tightened. I felt sick. Ashley gripped my knee and squeezed. He knew how I was feeling. We saw the path with the gate and veered off right, blasting back along the slope.

My heart leapt. 'Ash, there's the Harley!'

The Harley was near the gate, but I couldn't see Jason. As we approached our headlights revealed a body near the bushes. Bile rose in my mouth. I was going to vomit in my helmet. Ashley sped the short distance and slammed on the brakes. Leaving the motor running he leapt off the bike and ran to the body.

Fox and I followed closely behind. Fox pulled out his pistol. I unclipped my helmet, pulled it off and dropped it on the grass. It was Jason. He was still and deathly pale. Keep it together, Maggie. Blood trickled from his ear. His hair was matted with it, his face swollen and distorted. I felt time stop as Ashley switched into paramedic mode. He squeezed Jason's shoulder. 'Can you hear me, mate? Can you hear me?'

No response.

Ashley put his fingers on Jason's neck and then his wrist, checking for a pulse. He listened for breathing. I held mine.

'He's got a strong pulse and he's breathing.'

'Thank God,' Fox and I said simultaneously.

Fox ran to his pannier and pulled out a space blanket. He covered Jason with the shiny metallic material.

Ashley lifted Jason's eyelids and peered into his eyes. 'He's been knocked about, big time.'

My voice quivered as I fumbled with my phone. 'I'll call an ambulance. He needs to go to hospital. He could have serious head injuries. Look at him.'

We turned as Jason groaned and shuddered. I leant over his battered face and held his hand. 'Jason, can you hear me?'

His eyes opened slowly. 'I can hear you,' he croaked.

'Can you see me?'

172

He raised a blood encrusted hand and felt for my face. 'Everything … blurry.'

'I'm getting you to hospital.'

'No!' he shouted, making me jump.

He tried to sit up. 'No hospitals.'

I looked at Ashley and Fox for guidance.

'Here, mate,' Ashley said. 'Let me help you.'

'Get me up. I want to go home,' Jason croaked.

Ashley and Fox looked at me and shrugged. What to do?

'He hates hospitals,' I whispered to Fox. 'Getting him upset in this state wouldn't be good. If we get him home, Luca can check him out, or we can use a crystal.'

'We're taking you home, mate,' Ashley said.

Fox and Ashley gripped him under the arms and hoisted him to his feet.

'They jumped me,' Jason muttered. 'Four of them.'

My heart skipped a beat. 'Jesus.'

Jason patted his pockets. 'Where's my keys?'

Ashley's eyes nearly fell out of his head. 'You're friggin' kidding, Jace. You are so not riding home. You're delirious, mate. Maggie'll take the Ninja. You can sit on the back of the Harley with me.'

Fox looked at me, concerned. 'You okay to ride?'

I nodded. *Not really.*

I couldn't look at Jason. It made me too upset. There was nothing I could do. I wanted to go home. Pulling on my helmet, I clipped it tight, straddled the bike, and fired up the engine. Ashley gripped my arms. 'Are you sure you're okay to ride?'

'Yes.'

His face was solemn. He squeezed my arms for emphasis. 'Promise me you won't go fast. Promise me you'll stay near me and Fox.'

How did he know I wanted to blast off into the night and ride like a bat out of hell?

'I know you,' he said.

Jesus, he could read my mind.

'Let go. I need to ride. I need to think about something other than this.'

'Don't we all,' he said, grimly. 'Jason will be okay. You can handle this. We can handle this.'

The tedious conversation subdued my adrenaline rush, and I felt as tired as twenty women. I was in a strange state of disassociation, as if things weren't actually happening, or were happening to someone else. Not me.

'I promise I'll be safe and stay near you and Fox.'

His expression relaxed. 'Thanks, luv.'

Jason leaned heavily against Ashley's back and wrapped his arms around him. Ashley waved his arm and set off through the gate. 'Wagons Ho!'

I followed him, and Fox brought up the rear. We rode at a sedate pace, not breaking formation until we reached home and rumbled along the drive to the house. Someone had opened the gates for us, and Luca, Drom, Boo and Schmoo were waiting anxiously under the front porch light.

I pulled off my helmet. My eyes filled with tears as emotions washed over me. 'Luca! Jason's hurt. Help him, please.'

Luca rushed to Jason and helped him off the bike. Jason was disoriented and confused.

'I'll take care of him. Leave it to me,' Luca said. Ashley took Jason's other arm and helped Luca get him into the house. I felt calmer knowing Jason was in good hands.

Fox helped me off my bike while Schmoo bounded around his legs.

'Thanks,' I whispered. I could barely summon the energy to speak, and my legs wobbled as I stood. Fox held me steady.

'Sorry. Gone wobbly,' I muttered.

Fox's face split into a grin. 'You're a commando girl with wobbly legs. You've used a grenade launcher to take out a truck

174

and two bikes, plus all their occupants, all while riding on a motorbike at speed. That's an impossible feat. I should make you a member of the force. I think you're entitled to wobbly legs after that.'

My knees gave out completely and I sank slowly to the ground. 'Thanks for reminding me.'

Fox hoisted me to a standing position. 'Come on. Up!' I wobbled again, so he scooped me into his arms. 'Let's get you inside for a stiff drink. Drom, can you get the door, mate?'

Ashley came out to see Fox carrying me. 'What's happened? Is she all right?'

'Wobbly legs, is all,' Fox said. 'Probably shock.'

Ashley glared at Fox. 'Here, I'll take her.'

Fox pushed past him and carried me in through the front door. 'S'okay, I have her.'

Someone had kept the fire going, and Fox put me in the chair beside it. Staring into the flames, I felt instant relaxation. 'My favourite spot.'

'Let me get your boots off.' Fox unzipped the right one and pulled it off by the heel. 'Left.' I extended my leg.

Ashley was in the kitchen whipping up hot chocolate for everyone. He stuck his head in the lounge and gave Fox a dirty look behind his back.

'That's my job,' Ashley mouthed to me. 'Friggin' coppers.'

'Jacket?' Fox said.

I unzipped my leather jacket and he pulled it off. He grinned. 'I'll let you take your own pants off. Unless you need some help?'

Jesus. This guy had taken a leaf out of Ashley's book.

'All good. Thanks, Fox.'

Ashley strode into the lounge, pulled me out of the chair and dragged me to the bedroom. He slammed the door closed with one foot.

'What the hell are you doing?' I demanded.

'Getting you away from Fox's clutches. What's the story with him? He's coming onto you.'

'He's being caring and helpful.'

'Yeah, right. You can't see it.' Ashley rummaged through the laundry basket. 'Now, what do you want to put on? Trackie dacks?'

'I'm quite capable of dressing myself, thank you. You need to grow up. Seriously. And by the way, I don't wear *trackie dacks*.'

'I've made you hot chocolate,' he said, changing the subject. 'Take your leathers off and go back and sit in front of the fire before Fox steals your spot. By the way, I'm so proud of you, luv.'

'Thanks Ashley. Can you please check on Jason and tell me what Luca says. I can't bear to look at his poor, battered face.'

'Of course. It always looks worse than it is. He's tough. He'll bounce back.'

'I hope you're right,' I said, as he left the room.

Sure enough, when I returned to the lounge, Fox was sitting in my chair. When he saw me, he moved to sit on the floor in front of the fire. 'Just keeping it warm for you. I think I've stepped on Ashley's toes. I didn't mean to.'

'Don't worry. He thinks he owns me and he's very protective. He cares a lot.'

'I can understand why.'

Jeepers. Maybe Ashley was right. Perhaps Fox did have a thing for me.

'I care for you too, Maggie, but I don't want to cause any trouble. I think we were both revved up with testosterone and adrenaline.'

'No wonder, after tonight.'

Ashley came in and passed out mugs of hot chocolate. 'Get that into you, guys. Luca said Jason has concussion from a blow to the skull. He's going to monitor him for twenty-four hours. He thinks he'll be fine. Jason's disorientated and confused and his vision's playing up. They're standard symptoms for

176

concussion. He needs rest and quiet for a few days. If the symptoms get worse, Luca will get him to hospital ASAP. At the moment, Jason's adamant he won't go.'

'Why don't we get him to hold a crystal?' I said.

'I already tried.'

'And?'

'He wouldn't let me anywhere near him with it. He got agro, told me to piss off. Said he didn't want to waste the power.'

'He's unbelievable. So stubborn.'

Ashley clenched his jaw and drummed his fingers on the table. 'Seems to be a common trait around here.'

Boo bounded in with Schmoo hot on her tail.

The mission was a success. Not a hitch.

Fantastic, Boo. I'm sorry I haven't had a chance to talk to you.

No apology required. You've had quite a night. Ashley told me all about it.

Told you? Can he hear you?

No. I jumped on his lap while he was sitting waiting for Luca's diagnosis, and he told me all about it. He made a special point of keeping me informed. He's as proud as punch of you.

I wish he didn't have to be proud of me for blowing up people. I feel awful.

Maggie, sometimes in life we have no choice. We have to act. And you did. You did us all proud.

Boo gave me a big lick on the cheek and snuggled under my arm. Schmoo stared at me intently, waiting for an invitation.

'Come on then.' He pushed away my arm with his big head and boofed against me. 'Nothing is as comforting as sitting in front of an open fire with a dog snuggled up on each side of you,' I said to no one in particular.

'Doesn't get any better than that. Unless, you add me to the mix,' Ashley called out from the kitchen.

I looked at Fox and rolled my eyes. He smiled, and carried on staring into the fire, his hand around the back of my ankle.

Chapter 18: Jason Cops It

'Walls have ears. Doors have eyes. Trees have voices. Beasts tell lies. Beware the rain. Beware the snow. Beware the man you think you know.' — *Catherine Fisher, Songs of Sapphique*

Luca came into the lounge room and sat on the chair next to me. He patted my knee. 'You can put Jason to bed now.'

'Thanks. Don't you think we should go to the hospital? Shouldn't he get a brain scan?'

'I would prefer he did. But he's adamant. If he doesn't develop any other symptoms over the next twenty-four hours, I think he'll be fine. He needs lots of rest. He has to take it easy for the next few days.'

Jason ambled slowly into the room, holding an ice pack.

'Speak of the devil. Here's the man himself,' I said.

He held onto furniture as he traversed the room. 'Hi, all.'

'Sit here for a while. Ashley's made you hot chocolate,' I said.

Fox moved to the other side of the fire and leaned back against the couch.

Jason lowered himself gently into a chair. 'Thanks, Maggie.'

The right side of his face seemed to have copped the worst. His right eye was puffed up and had already turned various shades of purple. His nose was distorted and swollen, as was his cheek, and he had a fat top lip. Because of the swelling on one side, his face was curved, like a banana. It made me sick. Jason winced as he pressed the ice pack to his face.

Drom sat on the couch opposite and studied Jason intently. 'Can you remember what happened?'

Jason stared into the fire and seemed oblivious to the question.

'Jason?'

'Sorry, what mate?'

'Can you remember what happened? What they looked like? Where it happened?'

Jason continued to stare into the fire. 'All I remember is trying to fend off four blokes. I can't remember when or where, nothing.'

'He may never be able to recall the event,' Luca said.

'Can you remember if you injured any of them?' Drom asked.

'In the culvert. I remember I shot a guy.'

'How many shots did you fire?'

'I'm not sure.'

'Where are you going with this?' Fox asked.

Drom tapped his fingers impatiently on the armrest. 'I'm trying to understand what happened to his attackers. Did he injure or kill any of them? If so, did they disintegrate or are they still out there? Why didn't they finish him off? I don't get it and I need to get things.'

'Maybe they thought they'd killed him,' I said.

'Maybe,' Drom said. 'It appears their modus operandi is death, leave no survivors, so they must've thought they'd killed him.'

'Could it be they're getting sloppy?' Ashley said. 'Lucky for Jace, if that's the case.'

The discussion had obviously set off a chain of thoughts in Fox's brain. He rubbed his chin, something I'd noticed he always did when he was thinking hard.

Drom's foot twitched. 'Maybe your memory will come back. I hope so.' I knew the loose ends were messing with his mind.

Jason downed his hot chocolate. 'I'm going to have a shower and go to bed.' He turned and left the room abruptly.

We sat and looked at one another, our minds full of questions, but no answers. After about fifteen minutes of staring into the fire, I felt my head jerk as I nodded off. God, I was tired. I staggered to my feet. 'Think I'll turn in too. Night, all.'

I headed to the bedroom wondering if everyone felt as flat as I did.

Jason was in bed when I came in. The bedside lamp illuminated his face. He appeared marginally better now all the blood and mud had been washed off.

'How are you, Jace?'

He turned off the light and left me in darkness. 'Tired. I'm going to sleep.'

H'okay. That was that then.

I found my way to the ensuite door, hands stretched out in front like a blind woman. That simple exchange had upset me. Jason seemed so distant, so indifferent, and he hadn't said he loved me.

Luca said concussion had side effects, that Jason may behave strangely for a while. I needed to cut him some slack. It wasn't all about me. Still, it was hard having him there and not being able to talk about what I did today. It was big stuff for me. I'd killed people for heaven's sake. I felt alone without my compadre to talk to.

After showering, I returned to the bedroom, turned on the bedside light and put the dimmer on low. Jason was on his back with his eyes closed. His face was pale. I couldn't hear or see any sign of breathing.

Oh, God, he was dead.

I knelt on the bed and inched closer, staring at his face, listening, looking, for a movement, a twitch. I reached out to touch his face and, in a split second, without opening his eyes, he caught my wrist. I gasped in shock and let out a squeal.

He gripped my wrist and growled. 'Don't!'

'Don't what?'

'Touch me.'

'Sorry. I thought you were dead! How did you do that with your eyes closed?'

'Go to sleep, will you.'

My eyes filled with tears. 'Is everything all right? You're behaving strangely.'

He turned away from me. 'I need to sleep. Stop bothering me.'

'Of course. I'm sorry. I love you, Jason.'

Silence.

My bottom lip started to quiver, my foot twitched and my hand clenched into a fist. My emotions were in overload. I wanted to kiss, caress and punch him all at the same time. Every day we said I love you. We never went to sleep without saying it. *Ever.*

I couldn't make myself get into bed with him. It was as if he'd slapped me. I couldn't lay next to him feeling like I felt. It was as though we'd had a fight. As if I'd done something wrong and he was all passive aggressive. I reached out my mind to him and it hit a steel wall. That had never happened before.

I pulled on a T-shirt, grabbed a doona from the bed box, turned out the light and returned to the lounge. I could've slept on the spare bed in the office, but the fire was still going in the lounge and the couch was soft and cozy.

Boo and Schmoo were curled together on the rug in front of the fire. They were snoring, which would probably keep me awake, but better out here than in there with the Ice King.

I bundled myself in the doona and sat staring into the fire. I missed Jason so much, I ached. I wanted his arms around me, his sweet whispers in my ear, his hands on my body, his presence. His love.

I knew he was sick, but there was something else wrong. He

was lost to me. I couldn't explain it, but I could feel it. Something was broken.

I blinked back tears. I pinched my arm. Don't cry. Don't cry!

It didn't work. After everything that had happened, the wall broke and I sobbed. I howled into the doona, trying to let go of my huge, wracking sobs quietly and discreetly.

I jumped as a box of tissues appeared in front of me. It was Ashley, wearing only jocks and a T-shirt. He knelt in front of me. 'Don't blow your nose in the doona, luv. You'll have to get it dry-cleaned.'

I laughed despite myself.

He stroked my hair. 'Why are you out here?'

My chest heaved with sobs. 'He doesn't love me.'

'Why's that, sweetheart?'

I told him what happened and how I felt.

'So, you're feeling sad, lonely and abandoned?'

I sobbed some more. 'Y ... yes!'

'Things will be better in the morning. Do you want me to stay with you for a while?'

'Could you?'

'Come on, let me in under that soggy quilt of yours.'

Ashley sat on the couch and wrapped me in the doona and his arms. I knew he wouldn't go to sleep. I wasn't sure how long he held me. I remember the warmth of his body against mine, the rhythmical beat of his heart as my head lay against his chest. The fire crackled, the dogs snored, and two strong arms kept me safe and held me until sleep came.

I awoke to the smell of coffee and the sound of Boo and Schmoo barking in the garden.

Ashley came in and handed me a mug of coffee. 'You look happier.'

'I can't believe I actually slept. You're better than a sleeping pill.'

'I'll take that as a compliment.'

182

'How long did you stay with me?'

'Not long.'

'You're fibbing.'

'Could be.'

'I'd better check on Jason,' I said.

'I've checked already. He's alive and breathing.'

'How was he?'

'Pretty withdrawn. I see what you mean. He's not himself. If he doesn't improve, he should get a brain scan. I know it's hard, but try not to take it personally. I don't think it's about you.'

'Will we ever get through this?'

'Yes, luv. One way or another. Remember you're not alone. You can come to me anytime, tell me anything.'

I nodded. My eyes filled with tears again. Why was it when people were nice, it made me want to cry?

* * * * *

I had to pull myself together.

I arose and made a big bowl of Bircher-Benner muesli, the same as Mum used to make. She was into healthy eating and lived by the principals of the Swiss nutritionist, Maximilian Oskar Bircher-Benner. If we wanted to beat this thing, we had to stay healthy.

When that was done, I put on a load of washing, vacuumed the main areas, dusted, and phoned Fraser to let him know Jason had been beaten up and not to expect much from him for a few days.

I put some eggs on to boil and then cooked a big batch of homemade dog food, throwing in turkey mince, carrots, zucchini, spinach, turmeric, egg, seaweed, garlic and some left over brown rice. I made some curried egg and lettuce sandwiches using multi grain bread and soy mayo, and wrapped them tightly in cling film. Next, I made a big cheese, bacon and veggie frittata and set the table ready for breakfast.

I had an audience. Boo and Schmoo sat on the rug near the kitchen watching me cook up a storm. Their gaze was super intense, and Schmoo stacked on the pretend broken foot routine. He was master of the 'poor me, look, my leg is broken, please feed me,' act.

'You'll have to wait guys … your food is still too hot,' I said, in response to their pleading looks.

How long, Maggie?

About five minutes, Boo.

Fox came out buttoning his blue polyester shirt. Drom and Luca followed closely behind.

'Morning, guys. You've got Bircher-Benner muesli, and or, bacon, cheese and veggie frittata for breakfast. Plus, I've made some curried egg and lettuce sandwiches, if you want to take some for lunch. Do you want coffee, tea or juice? Who wants toast?' I smiled my brightest smile.

Fox seemed happier than I'd seen him for ages. 'Crikey. This is fantastic! You'll never get rid of us if you keep this up.'

'Everything's on the table. Help yourself. Who wants coffee? Hands up who wants tea?'

I was busy in the kitchen pretending to be a barista, when two arms wrapped around my waist.

'Mornin' Maggie,' my most favourite voice in the world said.

I turned around. 'Jason, you're up!' He looked forty percent better. The swelling had reduced overnight. 'You look a helluva lot better than yesterday.'

'Everything's still such a blur. Look at you. You've taken over my job.'

'Yep. Everything's under control. Have to feed the troops. Are you hungry?'

'Ravenous.'

'Sit and help yourself. I'll make you coffee. Here, can you take over this basket of toast?'

Jason smiled, took the basket, and wandered over to the kitchen table.

Oh, thank you, God. He seemed more like his old self. Fingers crossed.

'Hey, Ashley. Want some coffee?'

'Yeah great, thanks, luv. Jason seems better.'

'Yes, he's more himself.'

'See, what did I say?'

Bang! We jumped as Jason thumped his fist on the table. Cutlery and crockery rattled. Boo, who was dozing under the kitchen table, hightailed it out in fright, her paws scrabbling on the floorboards. 'Get that thing away from me! Put it away. I don't need it. I don't want it. I'm fine. Read. My. Lips.'

Drom hastily covered the crystal he had in its velvet covering. 'Sorry, I didn't mean to upset you.'

Jason took a deep breath. 'Sorry. I'm stressed. And I don't want to waste any crystal power. We need to keep it for emergencies.'

'It's fine. I understand,' Drom said.

Ashley looked at me. 'Jesus. Maybe he's got PTSD. He's erratic.'

'Post-traumatic stress disorder? You think?'

'Could be. Or the effects of concussion.'

Fox had to go and decided to leave Schmoo with us. 'I think he's in love with Boo. He seems distracted all day. I think he'd rather be here.'

'They do seem inseparable,' I agreed.

Fox mumbled something that sounded like, 'I'd rather be here too.'

'Be careful out there,' I said.

'You too. Thanks for the great breakfast. You're a legend.'

Jason came back into the kitchen and put his arms around me.

'What's happening, Jason?'

'I'm going back to bed. I don't feel in a good place at the moment.' His eyes were flat and dull. It was as if the life had been sucked out of him.

'I think that's a good idea.'

He kissed me on the forehead and headed for the bedroom. Ashley gave me a look.

'Can you come here for a minute?' Drom called to me.

I joined him at the table, and he stared at me as though he wanted to say something.

'What, Drom? Spit it out.'

'Jason's been compromised.'

'What do you mean?'

'Something's happened to him. He's being influenced by the Dark Force.'

'It's concussion. He's been beaten to a pulp.'

'No. Things don't make sense. His reaction to the crystal proves my hypothesis. He can't stand it anywhere near him. There's no way the crystal would lose significant energy to fix his injuries, and anyway, we have three crystals, so it's not an issue.'

'The thought crossed my mind when I tried to give him a crystal last night,' Ashley said. 'His reaction was weird, but I put it down to concussion and him being so anti hospital. I mean, I'd want a brain scan if I'd been beaten so badly.'

I felt a pressure in my brain. As I became aware of it, the mirror on the wall rattled, and a shadow darted in my peripheral vision. I turned to see a Tawny Frogmouth perched on the railing of the deck. It stared at me. For a moment and an eternity, I was lost in its huge, amber eyes. I pulled my gaze away from it. 'I think you're right.'

'I am?'

I rubbed my fingers through my hair trying to ease the pain in my head. 'I didn't want to admit it to myself, but I knew last night. He's not right. It's not him. What do we do?'

'You're the one they're after. They're going to use Jason to get you.'

Fear coursed through my body. 'Oh, right. Just great.'

Ashley put his arm around me. 'Move your chair closer.'

I shuffled across and leant against him.

Every day. Every friggin' single day there was something. And now Jason. 'Are you sure it's not symptoms from concussion?'

'I'm ninety-nine-point-nine percent sure,' Drom said. 'I think they're going to target you, and soon. They've had multiple opportunities to kill you, but they haven't. First they wanted the crystals, but now, in light of the kidnap attempt on the road, it appears they want you. You are the primary crystal keeper after all, but I'm still not exactly sure why they — or it — wants you.

'I've contacted someone I know who works in the field of biological detection systems. Rachael leads a team which has developed a microchip implant integrated with GPS technology. Basically, it's a more sophisticated version of the microchip they put in dogs. It's only a prototype, but she could implant you with one so that if you're taken we could track you to the source and destroy it.'

Ashley made a face. 'Sounds way too risky. Maybe they do still want to kill all of us, and maybe they still want the crystals and they'll use Jason as the delivery boy.'

'But Jason can't stand to be anywhere near the crystals,' Drom pointed out. 'The crystals destroy the Dark Force. Things have changed. They're after Maggie. I know it.'

Ashley shook his head. 'It would be a huge risk, the idea of using her as bait.'

Drom scratched his head. 'I know, but I can't come up with anything else, can you?'

'So, we let the bad guys get Maggie via Jason, track them to their HQ. And then what? Bust Maggie and Jace outta there and blow the place to smithereens? What if we can't get into the place? We don't yet have enough crystals to fully neutralise it.

We need time to find more crystals.'

'We don't have time,' Drom said. 'The tables have turned.'

I didn't much like the sound of Plan A. 'What's Plan B?'

'Tie Jason up and cover him with crystals?' Luca suggested.

Drom sounded thoughtful. 'Not such a silly idea.'

'It might kill him,' Ashley said.

'You think?' I said.

Drom shrugged his shoulders. 'Who knows? Crystals destroy the Dark Force. If Jason's infected...'

'But he's a Crystal Keeper,' I said. 'The crystals need him and have to protect him.'

'But can we be absolutely sure?' Ashley said.

I felt sick. 'So you're saying Jason's screwed?'

'I'm not saying that. I don't know.'

'Luca was roached and he beat it. He survived,' I said. 'If Jason's been roached then he could beat it too.'

Ashley looked at Luca. 'How did you overcome it? How did you de-roach yourself? I've been meaning to ask you.'

'When I was infected, I was always aware of it inside me. A couple of the other brothers were somewhat aware, the rest were completely lost to its power. I fought against it the whole time. It felt so wrong that my body and mind rejected it, similar to when a body rejects an organ transplant. If I couldn't remove it, I would've killed myself. For me, it was similar to fighting the devil. The infection was seductive and it felt good; it filled my mind with thoughts of power, domination and lust. It made me feel as though I could rule the world. It was intoxicating. But I knew it was evil.'

'Crikey,' Ashley said. 'You're one mentally strong mofo.'

Luca looked puzzled.

'It's an abbreviation of an inappropriate swear word, Luca. He meant it as a compliment. Ashley needs to clean up his language.'

'Yeah, sorry, mate. But I'm in awe of you. When I was an

addict, the high was so sublime it was like kissing God. I couldn't resist it. I couldn't tell heaven from hell. Sounds like being roached is a similar experience.'

'I think it may well be, and the more you respond, the more it gives and the more you want.'

Ashley stared at him in admiration. 'You must have an iron will.'

'It was my faith in God. And love.'

'I'm screwed,' Ashley said. 'I can do love, maybe, but God—'

Luca smiled. 'Love is God.'

'I don't want to bag you, mate, but religion is the cause of all the shit in this world and why we're going to hell in a hand basket.'

'I'm aware religion is man-made and used for power and control, but God and love are separate from religion,' Luca said. 'You can be spiritual and connected to God without religion. I think religion imposes too many mental constructs, too many filters to seeing the real truth. You're a spiritual man, Ashley.'

Ashley looked shocked and then burst out laughing. He slapped Luca on the back. 'Well, mate, I've never been called that before. Dead set, I think I'd be the most unspiritual person you'd ever come across.'

'Not true,' Luca said.

'So essentially you need super human qualities to de-roach yourself, plus have a strong connection to God,' I said.

'I'm definitely screwed,' Ashley said.

'Love is a drug. It's a chemical reaction in the brain,' Drom said. 'Being in love causes similar brain waves to a heroin high.'

Ashley shook his head and worked on deepening the two furrows between his eyebrows. 'Well, that explains a whole lot of things.'

Drom, always keen to get to the bottom of things, asked, 'Explains a whole lot of what?'

'Never you mind,' Ashley said, staring at me.

'What if we all go bush? Disappear,' I suggested. 'Lock Jason in irons and take him with us. Have a full-on focus to retrieving the crystals. According to Jason's list we could probably do it in around a week. If we split up, we could do it faster.'

'I think Jason's a GPS now,' Drom said. 'They know where he is. They know where we are. I'd stake my life on it. They'll be hot on our tail wherever we go.'

'What if we keep him drugged and unconscious?' Ashley said.

'Really, Ashley?'

'It's just a thought. We're brain storming, after all.'

'True.'

'He can't hear us can he, Drom?' I asked.

Ashley tiptoed to the bedroom. The door was closed. He opened it, peeked in, and closed the door again. He tiptoed back.

'For a big guy, you're very quiet on your feet,' Luca said.

Ashley grinned. 'Army training, mate. Jace is sleeping like a baby. There's no way he could hear us.'

'Even if we haven't fully decided on Plan A, I don't think there's any harm in me getting a chip. It's a good idea. Couldn't we all get chips?'

Drom shook his head. 'I'm lucky to be able to get my hands on one of them.'

'Let's do it then. How soon?'

'I can take you to the lab today.'

'Let's go now, before Jason suspects anything. Luca, if Jace wakes, can you tell him we've gone to the doctor with Ashley to get those combat nightmare drugs?'

'Yes. And I'll keep an eye on things.'

'Why don't we actually visit the doc and get those drugs?' Drom suggested. 'Then Luca wouldn't have to lie.'

'Yeah, yeah, Drom. Let's do it!' Ashley said. 'We'll take my truck.'

Luca looked at Drom appreciatively. 'Thank you. I've definitely lied enough already.'

190

I forgot about Luca being a priest. I forgot how easy it was to lie.

Chapter 19: Bella

We pushed back our chairs and froze as we heard a knock on the front door. Not the usual ding-dong. Just a quiet knocking.

The dogs went berserk. I looked at Ashley. These days a chill of fear always ran through me when someone was at the door.

Ashley raised his hand telling us to stay put. He pulled out his pistol, and walking to the window peeped out. 'You're not going to believe who it is.' He strode up the hall and opened the door.

'Hi, Bella, come on in.'

My stomach twisted in my gut at the name. I walked along the hallway towards her. 'Isabella. How come you're here? Why didn't you say? How's Liam? Is he here? Is everything all right?'

'Jeez, take a breath. Let her in the door,' Ashley said.

'Sorry, I'm in shock. Come in, Izzie. Do you have bags?'

'A small case outside.'

'Drom, Luca, meet Isabella, my sister. Izzie, meet Drom and Luca, very good friends of ours. We call Isabella, Izzie or Bella, as the mood takes us,' I said.

'Coffee?' Ashley asked.

'Yes, please.'

'What brings you all the way from New Zealand?' Ashley asked as he clattered around in the kitchen.

'I'm running away.'

'From what?' I asked.

'Not what, who. I'm running away from Liam.'

'What the hell happened?' I said.

Her big hazel eyes brimmed with tears. 'Nothing. That's just it. I love him, but we've turned into cell mates, not soul mates. We're best friends, but there's no intimacy anymore. No spark. I don't know what's happened to us.'

'At least you're still good mates,' Ashley said. 'That's more than some couples have.'

'I know, but it feels as if life's passing me by. Our relationship is stagnant. He doesn't see *me* anymore; he's happy in his rut. I want more. I'm dying inside.'

'Does he know you're here?' Ashley asked.

'Yes. I told him I needed to go see my little sister. I haven't seen Maggie since Dad—'

'Since Dad disappeared,' I said curtly.

Ashley knew how I felt about Bella and her lack of communication since Dad had gone missing. He said it was her way of coping, but I thought she was awful. She'd become distant towards me. It felt as if I didn't have a sister.

I felt my gut tighten with the hurt of it. 'So, you arrive when things aren't going well for you. You turn up out of the blue on our doorstep. What gives, Izzie?'

Ashley gave me a look. 'Maggie!'

'No, don't "Maggie" me. It's true. She hasn't spoken to me for months. She didn't return my calls, emails, texts, letters, so not only was I grieving for Dad, I felt I'd lost a sister too. So, what? You expect me to forget about that? Sorry, I don't know if I can.'

Bella clutched my arm. 'I'm sorry. It was how I tried to deal with Dad's disappearance. I retreated into my shell. I was depressed. I didn't communicate with anyone. But especially you. You reminded me so much of Dad. And Mum. Everything hurt too much. I know it sounds insane, but I think I went a bit mad. I couldn't speak to anyone; it wasn't only you. Please don't shut me out. You've every right to, after how I treated you, but please … don't.'

Huh. Ashley was right for once in his life. Maybe twice. Go figure. I thought Bella was stronger. She always seemed to be. My tough big sister who stood up for me and wouldn't take shit from anyone. I'd never expected she'd react that way. Now I felt bad.

Ashley gave me a smartarse look that said, 'What did I say?'

'I didn't come here because of Liam. I came here to see you. It was hard after not being in touch for so long. Please, forgive me?'

'You broke my heart; it might take me a while to … to feel I have my sister back.'

Bella's long dark hair caught the sun and shimmered with auburn highlights as she moved towards me. We hugged long and hard, and her body convulsed as she sobbed. I felt her tears run down the side of my neck and mingle with mine.

What a beautiful gift she was in a horrendous week.

Bella and I disentangled to see Ashley holding out a box of tissues. He doled out tissues to us. 'There'll be no more wiping of noses on sleeves, please.' He looked as happy as Larry. 'It's a beautiful thing, seeing you two gorgeous girls reunited. Bloody beautiful.' He turned away and hurried into the kitchen. Bella and I knew he was tearing up.

'Bless him,' she whispered.

'Wait till Jas … um, oh…' I cut myself off, suddenly remembering things were far from normal with Jason and our lives.

'Is he here?' Bella said excitedly.

'Um, yes and no.'

Ashley came out of the kitchen. 'Maggie, can I have a quick word?'

'One sec. I'll be back.' I followed Ashley to the office.

'What are we going to tell her?' he asked.

'I don't know. Talk about bad timing. She can't be here with all this crap going on. She'll be in danger. I have my sister back at the worst possible time.'

'Oh, by the way. I believe I may have been right — again?' Ashley said. 'I seem to be making a habit of it, aye, Mags?'

'I wouldn't get too carried away.'

'So, what do you want to do?'

'I'm going to tell her the truth. She can decide if she wants to stay or go. I don't want her to think I'm trying to get rid of her because of what happened between us. I missed her so much.'

Ashley held my face, his thumbs stroking my cheeks. 'If it's what you want to do then I support you. I'm happy for you that Bella is back in your life.'

I gave him a kiss on the cheek.

He moved his hand to the back of my head and, oh boy, I knew that move.

'Ashley ... no.'

He dropped his forehead gently on top of my head and sighed, before reluctantly guiding me towards the door. 'Go see Bella.'

'So, where's Jason?' Bella asked when we returned to the family room.

I pulled out a chair and sat. 'Bella. How do I put this ... um ... if I were to tell you something, something that would take your view of the world and turn it upside down and inside out and shatter your preconceptions of reality and possibly, no, probably, put your life in extreme danger, would you want me to tell you? If you choose not to know, then you can't stay here. You'd have to leave.'

Bella turned pale, highlighting the freckles sprinkled across her face. 'Jesus. What the hell is going on?'

'You need to think about the choice I've given you. This is

deadly serious.'

'You're talking in riddles. Is this a joke? Why don't you tell me what's going on and then I can decide whether to stay? I can't make a friggin' decision based on your cryptic information. And now you've got me worried.'

'It's not a good time for us at the moment.'

'You can't throw out that bombshell and expect me to walk away. You *have* to tell me what's going on. I know I wasn't here for you before, and I'm sorry, but I'm here now. Tell me. I want to know.'

'Despite the awful consequences?'

'Despite any consequences.'

'This is going to take a while. Save your questions for the end. I can't guarantee we'll be able to answer them anyway.'

It took me over an hour to bring Bella up to speed. I talked fast, and her eyes grew bigger and bigger as she listened. When I reached the part about Jason, her eyes filled with tears.

I took a sip of the now cold coffee that Ashley had made us. 'So that's about it.'

Bella sat silently and twiddled her hair around her fingers like she always did when thinking. Finally, she looked at the others around the table. 'And you can all confirm everything she said?'

They nodded.

'Jesus.'

'The detective inspector I told you about will confirm it too. And the Maestro.'

'Bloody hell. This is a joke, right? You're getting me back for all the shit I put you through.'

A loud crack made us jump. Ashley had snapped the biro he was playing with. 'It's no joke,' he said, looking at the shattered pen in his ink stained hand.

'You're fair dinkum?'

'Yes,' Luca said.

'Look, I'm really struggling to believe what you've told me.

But whatever's going on I need to be here for you and Jason.'

'You're welcome to stay here on the pull-down bed in the office. It's the only bed space left free. This is command central at the moment,' I said.

'You can have my room,' Ashley offered.

'Thanks, but the pull-down bed is fine. I could be of help, keep the house running while you do what you need to do.'

'That would be great,' I said. 'Thank you.'

'I could even help out with Jason's business. If he needs support with the office side of things until he's feeling better; you know I'm an admin whizz.'

'Are you sure, Bella? It's dangerous.'

She hugged me. 'I'm sure. Better than being in Boring Ville with Liam.'

'Trust me, you'll soon be yearning for boring and wishing you never left. Boring is beautiful.'

Bella screwed up her nose. 'I hate boring.'

'Then you'll love it here,' Ashley said.

'Ashley, Drom and I have to go out,' I said. 'Luca will be here. If Jason gets up, treat him normally. He may seem distant and odd. For God's sake, don't say anything about me getting a chip. I'm afraid at the moment you need to consider Jason as the enemy. Everyone's lives are at stake.'

* * * * *

Everything ran to schedule, for once. No hiccups. Drom accompanied me to get the chip implanted, while Ashley called on the doctor, procuring an action plan and a prescription. By the time we'd filled his prescription, it was late afternoon. Fox's bike was already parked out the front of our house when we got back.

Fox was chatting to Jason, Bella and Luca in the lounge. He smiled when he saw us. 'Hi, guys. Maggie, I'm keeping your place by the fire warm.' Boo and Schmoo were curled up next to him.

I laughed. 'You're the man. Thanks, Fox Meister. I see you've met Bella.'

'Yes, and I know how she's feeling, trying to take it all in.'

I gave Jason a kiss. 'How are you? Your face looks better.'

'Getting there slowly.' He pulled me onto his lap, wrapped his arms around me and kissed me back. 'I missed you.' He kissed me again. Hmmm. That was more like it. Maybe the old Jason was back.

'The Maestro sent me a text to say she's coming by later,' I told him.

'So, how are we going to deal with her?' Ashley asked.

'We need her to tell us the truth,' Drom said. 'We need to know who she is and where she's from. We need to know what she's doing here, what her agenda is.'

'And how do we get her to tell us all that?' Luca asked.

I had already been thinking about this. 'Pull out the baton, press the button to convert it and wait to see what she says.'

Jason looked unconvinced. 'What if she doesn't cooperate? What if she takes the baton and uses it against us? We don't know her or what she's capable of.'

'Very true,' Ashley agreed. 'When she comes in, we could pat her down for weapons, say it's for security reasons.'

Fox's face split into a grin. 'Can I do it?'

'She'd probably enjoy it. You'd have to fight Ashley for the job,' I said.

'She's all yours,' Ashley offered. 'So, we make sure we're armed but she's not. When we confront her, we have to be prepared for anything.' He looked at Bella. 'Can you use a gun?'

'I'm an ex copper, remember?'

'Yeah, but that was years ago. Want me to give you a refresher?'

'Sure, why not. Hell, I never thought I'd need a gun again. Though I sometimes wish we had them in my nursing job. We're like paramedics. We get attacked by patients all the time. One minute you're trying to save someone, and the next they or their family or friends are trying to kill you. The world has gone mad, and now at least I know why, from what you've told me.'

'Indeed, it has,' I said. 'We'll have to think of something subtler than patting her down to get her weapons off. Patting her down, as much as some of you may want to, ain't gonna fly.'

'Leave it to me,' Fox said.

'I can't wait to hear what she has to say,' I said.

'Ditto,' everyone agreed.

'I can't wait to see her,' Bella said. 'After being with Dad an' all. Hell's bells, who would've thought?'

Jason rubbed my neck. 'I've organised something special for us to do tomorrow.'

'Oh?' I said, feeling the hairs on my arms stand up.

Everyone turned to listen.

'Remember at the Hyatt, when we were going to get massages, but it never happened?' Jason smiled. 'I've booked us in tomorrow for a massage and hot rock treatment.'

'Sounds fantastic. I sure could use one. I feel as if I've been run over by a truck from all the climbing, running, shooting and fighting. I think I channeled Drom's parkour skills again last night. Did anyone see me jump off the sheep truck?'

'Yeah, we did,' Ashley said. 'You had the timing perfect. My heart was in my throat.'

'I had help with the timing.'

'Help?' Jason asked.

'The ghost of an old Aussie sheepherder called Clyde.

'You still see ghosts?' Bella asked.

'They're always floating around, but generally, they don't interact with me. I'm more aware of thought forms these days. It's what takes up a lot of my energy, blocking out people's crap.'

'She can see your fantasies,' Ashley said. 'You'd better keep check of your daydreams around here.'

Fox looked concerned. 'Can you really?'

'Don't worry. Yours are nothing out of the ordinary.'

I giggled at Fox's horrified expression. 'Just kidding. I've managed to tune you all out. My head's in pretty good shape, all things considered.'

Jason rubbed my hair and kissed my cheek. 'In very good shape indeed.'

Jeepers. Maybe we were barking up the wrong tree. Jason seemed fine. A bit quiet maybe, but pretty much his old self.

The slight shrug of Ashley's shoulders told me he was questioning our judgment too.

'I reckon its beer o'clock,' Ashley said. 'Who wants a drink?'

Everyone raised their hands.

'Beer for the blokes, champagne for the ladies?'

'Can I have champagne too?' Luca asked. 'I'm partial to it.'

'I noticed. Maggie, can you help me with the drinks?'

In the kitchen, Ashley whispered, 'Jason seems better.'

'I thought the same. Maybe Drom got it wrong.'

Ashley looked worried. 'We'll have to wait and see. I was thinking about Jason and the baton—'

'I'm way ahead of you. I have it. It's in a leg strap on my calf. As soon as Jason turned weird, I made sure I had it. I didn't want him anywhere near it if he'd been roached.'

'Good work, luv. How's the chip?'

I examined the inside of my arm. 'I can't feel a thing. You can't even tell.'

'Let's hope we won't need to use it.'

I nodded, and as I rubbed my arm, a strong intuition hit me: We wouldn't be using it. Chills ran down my spine. Why had that premonition filled me with such horror?

Ashley touched my arm. 'You've gone a whiter shade of pale.'

I took a deep breath and tried to shake the feeling. 'I'm fine.'

He searched my expression. 'You're lying. You saw

something. Tell me.'

'I didn't see anything. Simply a bad feeling. It's gone now,' I lied.

Chapter 20: The Maestro & The Truth

'What time's the Maestro coming?' Ashley asked.

'Seven-thirty. We'll all have dinner together,' Jason said. 'There'll be eight of us. Full house.'

'I make great pasta,' Luca said. 'Let me. Do you have a pasta machine?'

Jason nodded. 'I used it once to make Agnoletti. Took me six hours and a lot of VBs. We were nearly dead from starvation by the time we ate. So please. Knock yourself out.'

Drom turned up the television. 'Hey, Geraldine's head made the news.'

The banner read: Grizzly Find for Police — Severed Head Left Outside Police Station.

'They've identified it as the head of the missing park ranger,' Drom said. 'Search still on for her body.'

Fox ran a hand across his five o'clock shadow and pushed back the stray lock of hair which kept falling across his forehead. He obviously hadn't been using the lip balm I gave him. The muscles moved around his clenched jaw and his eyes were dark and troubled.

I sent out a thought form: *Turn off the television, Drom. It's freaking Fox out.*

'I think we've seen enough,' Drom said. He clicked the TV off.

I dashed to the bathroom and found another tube of lip balm for Fox. He was sitting in my spot in front of the fire.

'Am I in your seat again?'

'No, stay there.' I passed him the lip balm and smiled. 'Here. The Maestro will be arriving soon. She'll be looking for kissable lips.'

He returned my smile. 'Thanks. I left the other at work. I hope no one finds it in my desk drawer. It'll ruin my tough reputation.' He took off the cap and rubbed some on his lips.

'Nothing nicer than a man who looks after himself. Are you okay? You look stressed, Fox.'

'Yeah, the news ... it's the waste of police resources. Drives me crazy. They're looking for a body which can never be found, but I can't do a damn thing about it.' He bit his lip and rubbed the back of his neck. 'I'm split in two. I can't do my job.'

'Were you able to get the roach related cases reassigned?'

'Not yet. I can't. I'm thinking of taking leave, then someone else will have to handle them. It won't be good for my career, but I could swing sick leave. I've never taken any. If I see Doctor Howlong, I could probably get four months, easy.'

'Who's Doctor Howlong?'

He smiled. 'There are some special medicos who look after cops. They know how stressful the job is. Police tend to die young, either on the job or from stress related diseases. When we go to those doctors seeking sick leave, the doctors' standard response is, 'How Long do you need?''

'Oh, duh. Of course. Ha-ha, Doctor How Long.'

Schmoo wandered over to Fox, put his front paws on his chest and gave him a big lick on the face. Fox wiped his mouth with his sleeve. 'Yuck, Schmoo. He loves the taste of your lip balm!' He laughed, pushed Schmoo away. I noticed him wince and rub the back of his neck.

'What about I give you a shoulder massage? I'm good. I was a fully qualified masseuse.'

'Really?'

'Yep, but it was too hard, so I went on to study IT instead.'

'A neck rub would be great. My neck and shoulders feel like a rock.'

'I'll sit on the chair behind you. Sit on the floor between my legs.'

His shoulders were comparable to blocks of concrete. His musculature was incredible. It wasn't only tension; it was as if he was built out of steel. I had my work cut out for me.

'What's going on here?' Ashley said. 'Fox looks like he's in seventh heaven.'

Fox groaned as I worked on releasing the trigger points in his neck and shoulders.

'Book me in next please,' Ashley said.

'You're a lucky man, Fox,' Jason called out from the kitchen. 'I haven't had one of Maggie's massages in ages.'

'I can give you one, Jason,' Bella said. 'I give a mean massage too.'

'You're on. I'll need it after all this pasta making.'

I worked on Fox for twenty minutes until his neck and shoulders were soft. I ran my hands over his head, back and arms to finish off. 'All done.'

His eyes were closed and his face relaxed. 'Marry me,' he mumbled.

'She's already taken,' radar ears Jason shouted from the kitchen.

I hoisted Fox to a standing position. 'Lie on the couch, close your eyes and relax for a while. Don't talk. This part is important.' I put a cushion under his neck, covered him with a throw rug and tucked him in.

Jason wandered out for a look. 'Jeepers, you've received the deluxe treatment, the magic bunny rug an' all.'

Fox groaned in response. He looked blissed out.

Ashley pulled off his jumper. 'He looks pretty happy. My turn now.'

'Crikey, can I have a short break first?'

'Yes, I've brought you a fresh champagne.' He passed me a frosty glass. 'I anticipate your every need.'

'If that was the case you'd—' I was going to say, "you'd be giving *me* a massage", but thought better of it.

'I'd be what?'

Luckily, the doorbell rang and changed the subject for me.

Ashley switched to high alert. 'I'll get it.'

Fox barely blinked from the couch.

'It's the Maestro,' I said. 'I can see the limo in the driveway.'

Ashley opened the door to her familiar throaty tones. 'Hello, darling. You look gorgeous, you big hunk of a man.' Her high heels clicked across the floorboards and then she made a grand entrance into the lounge. 'Hello, lovely people.'

She wore a new cape. It was floor length purple velvet, with a large soft fur trim that enveloped the hood and flowed down both sides of the front and along the entire bottom edge. The fur was a pale golden brown, with tinges of silver. Two pleats, accentuated by three silver buttons on each side of her chest, gave the cape a beautiful fall. The only thing visible was her face, which was surrounded by the fur of the hood. She looked stunning, and resembled a Russian queen.

I glanced across at Bella who was staring open mouthed.

The Maestro smiled at her. 'You'll catch flies, my dear.'

Bella snapped her mouth shut.

The Maestro made a gentle twirl. 'My new opera cape. What do you think?'

'Gorgeous,' I said. 'What's the fur?'

'Sheared beaver.'

Drom raised his eyebrows. 'You're kidding?'

'Don't looked so shocked. The coat comes from Canada. Fur

is a sustainable, natural and renewable resource. I'll have you know, there are as many beavers now as when Europeans first arrived. The industry is strictly controlled with humane practices. I don't wear synthetics; they're made from petroleum, a non-renewable resource, which causes significant environmental problems. So, don't judge me until you know what you're talking about, sweetheart.'

'I wasn't judging you,' Drom said in his usual calm, ego free manner. 'I just didn't know they used beavers for fur.'

'Here, Maestro, let me take it for you,' I said.

She gave me a big hug. 'Maggie, my love, so good to see you again.'

I was swallowed in a cloud of soft purple velvet and fur. It felt divine, and the scent of lavender filled my nostrils.

'Sorry we couldn't make it to your concerts, Maestro. I would have loved to have gone.'

'Never mind. Another time. I know you've had a lot on your plate. Jason told me everything. You're a hero.'

I blushed. 'We're a good team.' I unfastened the Maestro's cape and helped her off with it. Unlike the other cape, this felt much lighter.

Underneath it, she was dressed in the most casual wear I'd ever seen her in. She wore skintight jeans, black over-the-knee, suede stiletto heel boots and a body hugging, dark charcoal thin knit that highlighted every sensuous curve of her body. I became aware of my own clothes — leggings, baggy jumper and thick socks covered in dog hair. Nice. Not.

Bella pulled down her top and brushed her hair with her fingers. None of the guys could drag their eyes away from the Maestro, except for Fox, who was comatose on the couch.

'What's with him?' the Maestro whispered.

'I gave him a massage and he's gone out like a light. He needed it.'

'I can hear you; I just can't move,' he mumbled from the

couch.

'Stay there, darling, don't get up,' the Maestro said.

'Wasn't going to.'

'Jason and Luca are making dinner. It's a production line in there ... homemade pasta. Drink?' I asked.

'Champagne, of course, darling.'

'I'll get it for you,' Ashley said.

'And this gorgeous creature must be Bella,' the Maestro said, walking over and extending a hand. The Maestro eyed her up and down as she pulled Bella to her feet. 'Maggie's sister. How lovely you are.' She drew Bella in for a big Maestro hug. Bella's face disappeared into the Maestro's generous cleavage. When she was released from the hug, Bella's face was flushed.

The Maestro's hugs would do that to you.

I grinned at Bella as she pulled at her top to let in some cool air.

Fox heaved himself to a sitting position, his eyes still closed. He rolled his neck from side to side. 'Maggie, you saved my life. My neck and shoulders feel so loose and relaxed.' He opened his eyes. 'I've never had a massage before.'

'Isn't it the most divine thing ever?' the Maestro said. 'Naked is better, of course. A full body massage with coconut oil. You should give him one, Maggie. He hasn't lived, the poor darling.'

Fox raised his eyebrows and Ashley gave me a look, which the Maestro picked up.

'Maggie probably has her hands full. I'll do it for you, Fox. What about now? You've a table somewhere, haven't you, Maggie?'

'Maybe another time,' Fox said. 'If I was any more relaxed, I wouldn't be able to function.'

The Maestro eyed Fox as if she was ready to consume him. 'Yes, I understand. Another time.'

Fox tugged at the neckline of his T-shirt to let some air in, while the Maestro sauntered sexily into the kitchen to view the pasta making.

'She'll eat you alive,' Ashley whispered.

'Yeah.' Fox shook his head. 'She's one red-hot woman. Too hot for me. I'll stick with Maggie.'

'Oh, thanks. Good ole scruffy Mags.'

'No! That came out wrong. I was talking about the massage…'

'Warning, Fox. Quit while you're ahead; you'll only dig yourself into a bigger hole,' Ashley said.

'I didn't mean to say you're not hot. I meant to say—'

'Quit now,' Ashley said.

'Yeah, you're right. I'm so relaxed that I don't know what the hell I'm saying.'

I giggled. 'And anything you do or say will incriminate you. It's fine. I get the hint. I'm going to get myself a makeover.'

Ashley looked annoyed. 'You don't need a fucking makeover.'

'Language! I'm also going to start a swear jar. I'll be rich in three days, the way you swear.'

'You should've seen her at the Hyatt when we dressed for dinner. She wore a short, red silk lace dress and stockings with suspenders, and black stiletto shoes. She looked hotter than hot.'

Fox shifted into interrogation mode. 'How did you know she was wearing suspenders?'

'When Jason picked her up and spun her around. Gave me a view I'll never forget.' Ashley cracked his evil grin.

My face flushed. His description made me sound like a hooker. I glared at Ashley, ready to take him to task about objectifying me, when he said, 'Maggie's the whole package, smart, savvy and lovely.' His expression told me he knew he'd just dodged a bullet.

'Those stilettos, which I hated, might I add, actually saved my life,' I said.

'How so?' Fox asked.

I ignored him and said, 'I'm going to the bathroom.' I didn't want to be reminded of Dylan. It still freaked me out.

When I came back, Fox and Bella looked dismayed. 'You told them?'

Ashley nodded, and nothing more was said. I was glad when Jason and Luca came into the lounge and broke the tension.

'The pasta's all done. Luca was like an Italian chef in there,' Jason said.

'Have you any weapons, Maestro?' Fox asked.

'Yes, why?'

'I'm interested in what you've got.'

She flashed him a sexy smile. 'I'll bet you are, my dear. I have a little Derringer .22 pistol.' She reached into the top of her boot and pulled out a gorgeous gold, pearl handled gun awash with exquisite engravings. It resembled an artwork more than a gun. She placed it carefully on the table and watched as Fox picked it up.

'Be careful. It's loaded.'

'This thing won't do much, it only takes two bullets,' Fox said.

'It only takes one bullet to kill someone.' She pulled out another gun from the back of her other boot and placed it on the table. 'I also have this. A Smith & Wesson Bodyguard .38 revolver. Be careful, it's loaded too.'

As she reached forward, the *MAESTRO* device glinted on her wrist. It looked identical to the drawing in Dad's notebook. It was a work of art too.

'Jesus,' Ashley said. 'Be careful they don't AD on you. Especially the little Derringer.'

'What's AD?' I asked.

'Automatic discharge.'

'The Derringer's fine. It was made especially for me. I'm not silly.' She stood and began to unbutton her jeans. 'I also have a little dagger strapped to my leg, and one in a pocket at the back of my jeans.'

Fox put up his hands. 'Whoa. Keep your gear on, Maestro.'

'I think that's it, Fox. Oh, wait, there's this ring of mine.' She held her hand forward to show him a huge silver and diamond ring. She began shining it on her chest. 'This thing can pack a punch.' She frowned and pursed her luscious lips. 'I do, however, feel significantly under armed. I seem to have misplaced one of my most favourite weapons.'

The energy in the room shifted. 'What weapon would that be?' I asked. I was glad that Fox now had both of her guns in his custody. *Nice work.*

'Similar to a dagger but much more versatile.'

'Something like this?' I pulled the baton from my calf holster and held it up.

She sat bolt upright, her electric eyes fixed on it. She was a cougar, ready to leap across the room and rip it away from me. But despite this she took a deep breath and made herself relax. 'Oh, you found my baton! How wonderful. Thank you.' She stretched out her hand for it.

'This is much more than a baton, isn't it?' I pressed the top. With its customary click and whoosh, it transformed into the weapon device.

She leapt to her feet. 'Don't! It's dangerous!'

Fox pulled her back onto the couch.

'Sit,' he said, quietly but forcefully.

'You don't know what you're dealing with.'

'I do actually. It's a nifty little gadget.'

She looked shocked. 'You've used it?'

I glanced at Ashley. 'In every sense of the word.' He nodded vigorously in agreement.

I waved the baton around. 'You have some explaining to do. This is obviously not of this world.'

'*Please,* be careful.' Her hands moved unconsciously to the top of her boots and found ... nothing. Fox held up her guns, and she flashed him a dirty look. He smiled back.

'Well?' I said.

'You need to level with us,' Jason added.

'I don't need to do anything of the sort. It's mine. It's inscribed with my name. Give it back.'

'You've got two chances, Buckley's and none. Not until you come clean with us.'

Drom's deep voice butted in. 'Who are you? Where are you from, and what are you doing here?'

The Maestro leapt up off the couch.

I hit the mode function for *Ignis,* the laser setting. The crystals blinked red. She retreated and sat back down. Slumping forward, she rested her elbows on her knees and dropped her head into her hands. Her long glistening locks flowed over her feet. Her fingers worked back and forth in her hair. Boy, was she upset.

Fox moved like lightening and snatched her hand from her hair. Her silver and diamond ring pulsated with light. She tried to get at it with her free hand, but Ashley sprang forward, gripped her arm and pinned her to the couch. He seemed to be enjoying himself.

When Jason made a move to get the ring, Drom beat him to the punch. He carefully pulled it off her finger and took it outside onto the deck.

'Anymore tricks up your sleeve?' Ashley asked her. 'What were you going to do with the ring? Laser beam us to another dimension? Get up!' He pulled her over to the wall. 'Hands up against the wall, and no funny business. I'm going to check you for concealed weapons.'

He frisked her hair, along her neck, across and between her breasts and around her waist, buttocks, thighs and legs. Jason seemed transfixed watching Ashley's hands. His eyes followed every move over her body. He did seem to have a thing for her. Everyone else was looking away. Jason was shameless.

Ashley made the Maestro take off her boots. He removed the dagger from her calf holster, then he undid her jeans and pulled out the thin dagger hidden in a pocket at the back of her pants.

He held out her wrist and examined the *MAESTRO* device. 'This needs to come off too.'

'You won't get it off. It's only jewellery anyway.'

'We know it's not jewellery,' I said. 'It's a *MAESTRO* device, a Multiverse Accelerator Energising Space Time Relativity Order.'

The Maestro's eyes widened. 'Oh, I see. You've found the Prof's notebooks.'

I nodded.

'Get it off,' Ashley said.

'It won't come off. It's locked onto me.'

'Dad's notes say it can be tuned or locked onto the user, but it is removable using a code.'

'We'll get the code later. Turn around and lift your jumper,' Ashley ordered. He noticed her earrings and pulled them off.

'Ow! This is highly inappropriate.'

'Since when have you cared about inappropriate?'

She lifted up her jumper.

'Higher. Over your bra.'

The Maestro did as she was told and revealed another skimpy work-of-art brassiere. Ashley put two fingers between her cleavage and pulled out a small silver ring.

'What's this?'

The Maestro looked furious. 'Can't say. Never seen it before.'

'Yeah, right. Here, Drom. Take it and be careful, for Christ's sake. It could be a booby trap for all we know.' Ashley chuckled heartily at his own joke.

'Very funny, Ash, but you're the booby.' She rubbed herself against him. 'You know I love the simple things in life.'

Ashley took a step back from her erotic movements. 'Yeah, like what?'

'Men!' she said, smashing her knee into his crotch. A collective gasp of shock issued from the men as Ashley sank to the ground. Fox and Jason were onto the Maestro before she knew what had hit her.

Drom came over with duct tape and did the honors with her legs and arms.

'Apologies, Ashley,' she said. 'I neglected to mention the steel reinforced kneepads.'

Ashley groaned and writhed on the floor. 'Fuck you!'

'Anytime, sweetheart. That's if you're ever fully functioning again.' Her laughter tinkled out gaily across the room.

Ashley staggered upright and pushed her backwards onto the couch. She plopped down, tossed her long hair back over her shoulders and stared at us disdainfully.

'Maestro, please, we don't want to be like this. We need you to be straight with us. What's going on?' I asked.

The expression on her face was that of a trapped animal. She sat silent, brooding, and so did we.

'We still have the sodium pentothal,' Jason said.

I put on a horrified expression. 'No! We can't use it!'

Good call, Jace. I'd play along.

'We need to know the truth,' Ashley said. She's obviously not on our side or she'd tell us.'

'But she's been kind to us,' I said. 'You can't do that to her.'

Jason and I had fallen into the role of good cop, bad cop.

Jason gave me his laser beam look. 'You bet we can. People's lives are at stake.'

'I know, but we can't use that drug. It's dangerous.'

'I'm getting it.' Jason headed off downstairs.

This'd be good. I hoped she wouldn't call his bluff.

The Maestro sat, stony faced. She wasn't going to give in. We were screwed.

Jason returned two minutes later holding a syringe. It flashed in the light. My blood ran cold and my skin became clammy.

Ashley had destroyed it. Why was it here? How could it be?

The room narrowed and compressed into a tunnel. My heart thundered in my ears, breath caught in my lungs and sound became distorted. Bile rose in my throat. I felt Dylan's tongue on my face and the cold steel of his gun on my chest.

The Maestro called out from a million miles away. 'What's wrong with her? Quick, help her!'

'Jason, you're a bloody idiot,' Ashley said. I felt him take my hand, lead me into the kitchen and sit me on a chair.

'I'm dying,' I gasped.

'Take a deep breath and slowly breathe out. And another. One more. Slowly. Keep going. You'll be fine; you won't die. It's PTSD, triggered by the friggin' syringe.' He unscrewed the top of a bottle of lavender essential oil and stuck it under my nose. 'Here, smell this. Keep breathing slowly and sniff it once in a while. I'm going to make you some hot chocolate.'

Slowly the room began to expand and my breath came a little more easily.

Ashley was back in a flash with a mug of hot chocolate and a cookie. 'Remember? Like last time. You'll be fine in a minute, sweetheart.'

My heart slowed and I felt warmer.

'Stay here,' he said. 'I'm going to check on what's happening.'

I nodded and sipped my hot chocolate, inhaling its aroma. I heard the Maestro shout, 'No, wait! It'll kill me. I'll talk, but you won't be enamoured with what you're going to hear.'

Ashley came back. 'She's ready to talk. Are you up to coming back in? I've put the syringe away. It was only ant killer, but he shouldn't have done that without warning you. The Maestro thought your reaction was in response to what he was going to do to her, so it made it seem authentic.'

'Oh well, that's something. Thank you for looking out for me.' My eyes pricked with tears.

'It's my job, luv. Come on, let's go back in. Now, you know

I'm waiting for you, don't you? One day, I figure you'll get sick of Jason and his antics and come back to me.' He jiggled his eyebrows which made me smile.

I took my hot chocolate and cookie with me and sat on a chair opposite the Maestro. Boo came over and hoovered up the cookie crumbs that fell on the floor as I nibbled it. I still felt out of it.

The Maestro had a genuine look of concern on her face. 'Are you all right now?' she asked me.

'Yes, I'll be fine, thanks.'

'I love you, Maggie. I love all of you. I'm not your enemy. I'll tell you everything. Although you may think differently of me after you hear this.'

Crikey, what the hell was she going to say?

I must have looked scared because Jason came over and put his arm around me. Just like the old Jason.

Ashley rubbed his sore groin. 'So, talk.'

'You're right, I'm not from here. I'm from a planet called Sonus. It's in another universe. On Sonus, the baton isn't a weapon. Unlike yours, our bodies aren't affected by sound waves. They absorb and utilise sound energies. We use the device for healing, wellbeing and sexual gratification. Sound, particularly music, sustains us, along with the vitality generated from the release of sexual energy. Sonusians are a hedonistic, peaceful race. We have open relationships and enjoy shared sexual experiences with friends and family.

'Jesus. That explains a lot,' Ashley said. 'About you, and the device.'

'It's been extremely hard for me to function in, and integrate with, your race. Your minds are so constricted by rules and religion. You're prisoners of your mental constructs. It's stifling.'

'Sonus sounds like my type of place,' Ashley said.

'You wouldn't survive. The atmosphere is similar, but the sound and sex would kill you.'

Ashley grinned. 'Good way to go but.'

Bella hadn't said a word for ages. Her eyes were like saucers, and her face was pale. Luca seemed transfixed. Drom was typing something into his iPhone. Perhaps he was recording this.

'Please, continue,' Jason said. He still had his arm around me and gave me a gentle, reassuring squeeze. I'd finished my hot chocolate and cookie and was pretty much back to normal, thank God. Or, should I say, thank Ashley. I hoped I wouldn't experience those symptoms again any time soon, or end up with combat nightmares like Ashley.

'I'm an MTJ, a Multiverse Time Jumper. I can go anywhere, anytime. The use of *MAESTRO* devices are limited to a handful of officials from the Sonus Multiverse Protection Agency.

'My partner Christos, a leading scientist on Sonus, invented the device. Such was the power of the *MAESTRO* and the ramifications of its use, or misuse, the government of Sonus kept the existence of the device top secret.

'A highly classified organisation was established to utilise the *MAESTRO* devices for scientific research and investigation. Its mission was similar to your Star Trek television show, "to explore strange new worlds, to seek out new life and new civilisations, to boldly go where no person has gone before". I love that show,' she said, smiling. 'I've met someone similar to Spock. Anyway, Christos and I were the first MTJs. We pioneered the use and development of the initial prototype devices. We risked our lives testing the technology and explored many universes, planets and time dimensions.'

'Why did you come here?' Bella asked. 'Where's Christos?'

Everyone started, surprised to hear a sound finally come out of her mouth.

'It was a combination of accident and necessity. We were on a time travel mission, which significantly overtaxed our device's energy supply. We had to find a place where we could recharge the power cells or, be stuck where we were forever. The devices are powered by crystalline energy, the same crystals you're trying to locate to use against the Dark Force.'

'Ah,' said everyone simultaneously. I could almost hear the pennies dropping all around the room.

'Our devices are able to track the nearest available source of energy and it's how we, or rather I, ended up here.

'As we jumped to planet Earth, Christo's device ran out of power mid jump. He's trapped in limbo, a type of holding dimension. We discovered limbo dimensions by accident and programmed them into the device as a safety backup for situations such as this. My mission on Earth was to find the crystals, recharge my device, jump to Christo's limbo dimension and jump both of us back to Sonus.'

'How many crystals do you need?' Drom asked softly.

I was betting he knew the answer already.

'Eleven. Ideally fifteen.'

'How long does it take them to regenerate once you've drained them of their power?' I asked.

'One year. The process comes close to destroying them, but they do recover.'

'So, you *are* the enemy,' I said. 'You're after the same thing we are.'

The Maestro fixed her gaze on the mirror in the other room. It rattled, swung to one side and hung askew.

'What is it with the mirrors in this house?' I said, getting up and straightening it.

'Mirrors and reflective objects can be a window to the limbo dimension,' the Maestro said. 'Can I show you?'

'We'll accompany you,' Ashley said. 'No offense, but I don't trust you.'

'No offense taken.'

Drom cut the tape from her wrists and ankles, and she padded across the floor in her silk socks, flanked by Jason, Ashley and Fox. The rest of the crew followed. She still towered over me despite her lack of heels. Ashley had drawn his pistol. Bella's face was tight. She had twisted the bottom of her T-shirt into a knot around her finger.

The Maestro stretched out her wrist and showed me the device. 'See this button here?' She pointed a perfectly manicured nail at a copper coloured button. 'This is the limbo dimension control. It's multi-functional, allowing us to jump into limbo or to see into areas of limbo where jumpers are held. There's no energy left to jump, but there's enough to facilitate viewing. Some people with gifts such as yours can see into limbo using their own senses. Press the button and look into the mirror.'

Jason grabbed my arm. 'Don't do it! It's a trick.'

'It's not a trick,' the Maestro said. 'I wouldn't lie to you, honey. I swear. She needs to do this.'

I placed my finger on the button and pressed. I had expected to see Christos in the mirror. What I did see shocked me to my core.

---

[18] *Maggie's Playlist: Would I Lie To You? — Eurythmics*

Chapter 21: The Mirror

'Mirror mirror on the wall, who's the scariest creature of all? Who do you see? Who looks back? Friend, or foe, ready to attack. Are they good or are they bad? Do they make you happy or sad? Mirrors hide things from our worldview. When you look in the mirror, who's really looking back at you?' — Maggie McLaine, Journey to Hell

A face stared out of the mirror at me. Its lips moved. It mouthed the word *Maggie*. Two hands pressed against the glass.

'*Dad?*'

'It's Dad!' Bella screamed, running to the mirror. The face mouthed the word *Bella*.

'How can this be? Are you saying Dad's—' I could barely bring myself to say the word, '*alive?*'

'Yes.'

'But how?' Bella asked. She put her hands over his image in the mirror.

A surge of rage stirred inside me. 'You put him in limbo! It's been over twelve months and you didn't think to tell me?'

'I didn't put him in limbo. He put himself in. It was an accident. I had a spare *MAESTRO* device, a backup, which failed. He wanted to study it, and I thought it was dead, so I let him. Somehow, the device had a residual charge left, enough to send him to limbo when he pressed the button. He's been trapped there and I can't get him out. The two people I love most in the universes are in limbo,' the Maestro said, with tears in her eyes.

Fox snorted. 'That's absolute crap. I don't know much about

all this stuff, but I'm a bloody good detective, and I can smell crap a mile off. You're a liar. You put him in there because he knew you needed the crystals to recharge your device. He figured you were going to use Maggie to get to the crystals and then steal them for your own purposes. He knew it would be catastrophic for earth, giving the Dark Force the edge. You knew he knew so you stopped him. There was no other device, Maestro. Admit it. You put him there. It's all too damn convenient, isn't it?'

Fox was in police mode. He was good.

'Absolute rubbish. You may think you're a good detective, but you know nothing about this, or me. I love the Professor. I would never do what you just said to him.' She put her hands on her hips and stared at Fox defiantly.

'So why didn't you tell Maggie?' Bella screamed at the Maestro. She clenched her fists. 'At what point did you think it would be appropriate to let someone in the family know? We've been through hell because of you!' She pulled back and took a swing at the Maestro's face. Ashley caught her wrist before it had a chance of connecting.

'Let go!' Bella screamed. She struggled violently in his arms, but he continued to hold her tight.

'Shhh. Bella, please calm down,' he said gently. 'We'll get to the bottom of this. This isn't helping,' he said, successfully dodging a backwards kick. 'Crikey, you girls are genetically feisty. Stop it!' He tightened his grip until she stopped.

'Bella, I was waiting for the right time. It was difficult. It was only recently I discovered I could get glimpses of him through mirrors and reflective surfaces. If I'd come to Maggie before, she would have thought me mad. I had no proof. Who would have believed me? Would you?'

'So, when were you planning to tell her?' Ashley asked.

'Today.'

'Rubbish,' Fox said. 'Jason had to threaten you with truth serum before you'd say anything!'

'You caught me off guard with the baton. I knew what you'd be thinking. That you couldn't trust me, because you didn't know who or what I was. I needed time to think about what to do. I didn't want to say anything which would make things worse. Please believe me,' she said, turning towards me. 'I'm telling you the truth. I love your father. I love you. I'd never do anything to hurt you.'

'Whatever the truth is, we have ourselves a serious catch twenty-two situation,' Drom said. 'She needs the crystals to get the Prof and Christos out and to get home, and we need the crystals to defeat the Dark Force. If we have to wait for the crystals to regenerate, or travel to find more, it will give the Dark Force the edge it wants and needs. We'll never be able to defeat it if we don't strike soon.'

'How long can the Professor stay in limbo?' Luca asked.

'He can stay there forever. It's getting out that's the problem. It's only meant to be a short-term solution, maybe a month at the most. The longer they're in there, the more difficult it may be for them to survive re-entry and returning to the physical dimension. Their bodies may not be able to revert properly. We don't know,' the Maestro said, her face twisting in anguish.

Fox shook his head. 'Oh, you're good.'

Bella struggled in Ashley's arms. 'A month! It's been twelve months! If we bring him out he'll die?'

'We don't know. The longest a Sonusian has stayed in limbo was three weeks. When they came out their physical being was significantly weakened, but they regenerated quickly after multiple energetic couplings.'

'Meaning they had to have a lot of sex to feel better?' Ashley said.

'Crudely put, but yes.'

'So, Dad can stay in limbo forever and live, if you call that living, or we bring him out and he could die. Great choice.' I looked around at everyone. 'If it was one of us in there, what decision would you make?'

'I'd want to take my chances getting out,' Jason said.

'Me too,' Ashley said.

Everyone else nodded in agreement.

'How do we know she's telling the truth?' Fox asked.

'We don't,' I said.

'What do you think your dad would want?' Drom asked quietly.

'If Dad thought saving him would put the planet at risk, he'd be so pissed if we brought him out. But, for me, I want to bring him back.'

'How many crystals do you need to bring back the Prof and Christos?' Drom asked. 'Forget about going back to Sonus for a minute. Could you bring them out with less crystals?'

'I could probably do it with three, but partial charging is bad for the device; it could compromise us ever getting home.'

Drom cocked his head. 'We sacrifice our three crystals to bring them out of limbo and we're back at square one. We'll have to put all our resources into finding the other crystals and three more from new locations. If Christos and the Prof survive they can help us, along with the Maestro.

'Once we have the crystals, we can generate enough energy to defeat the Dark Force. Christos and the Maestro will have to stay on earth until the crystals regenerate. Then we can fully charge Christo's device and they can use it to get home.'

Jason looked pleased. 'Great plan. Can you work with us, Maestro?'

'Yes, I can.' She touched Dad's face in the mirror, and he mouthed, 'I love you.'

Oh, Jesus Christ, Dad, you've got it bad.

'Um, one problem,' Ashley said. 'Won't it be awkward with both the Prof and Christos here together?'

'There is no problem,' the Maestro said. 'The Prof knows about Christos and our open relationship, and Christos wouldn't care. We don't get jealous like humans do. It's not in our DNA; it's how we survive. Oh, Christos will seem a little wild when he comes out, but he'll settle once I explain how things work on this planet. He'll need to regenerate fast, so be warned and be on your guard.'

'On guard against what?' Bella asked.

'On him wanting you for energetic coupling. And the warning goes for all of you,' the Maestro said, eyeing off the men in the room.

'Holy shit,' Ashley said. 'Will he be armed?'

'He'll have his baton and other bits and pieces. But I won't let him use them. He probably won't try anyway. We prefer to make love, not war,' she said with a smile.

Bella rubbed her hands on her jeans. 'Oh my, this is going to be interesting.'

That was a worry. I didn't think anyone here had had any energetic coupling for quite some time, unless you counted mine and Ashley's recent experience with the baton.

Bella looked at me. 'We're agreed this is what we want to do?'

'I can't see any other way,' I said. 'And you'll work on this together with us, Maestro?'

'Yes, I agree. You're right. It's the only way.'

'Let's get Dad out then,' Bella said.

'There should be one condition,' Fox said. 'She should take off her MAESTRO device and leave someone else in charge of it.'

'Yes, I know you still don't trust me, Fox. I'll leave it with Maggie.'

She released the device from her wrist and looked expectantly at mine. I was uncomfortable with the idea. 'It's not going to flip me off to another dimension by accident, is it?'

'No, there's not enough power.'

'That's what you thought about the other device and look

what happened to Dad.'

'I've put a safety lock on it,' she said, fastening it to my wrist.

It looked heavy, a type of chain mail construction, but it was as light as a feather. 'Wow. I can barely feel it on my wrist. Amazing.'

'Happy now?' she asked Fox.

He nodded, but he wasn't. I could tell he still didn't trust her. Maybe his policing had made him overly suspicious.

Drom collected the crystals, unwrapped them and placed them on the table. 'How do we do this?'

'Place the device on the crystal with your palm facing upwards,' the Maestro instructed. 'We'll go one crystal at a time and check the levels after each recharge. Maybe we can get away with using less.'

I felt like I needed a stiff drink. 'How long will it take?'

'A couple of seconds.'

I put my wrist on crystal number one. 'Here goes.'

For a split second, nothing happened and then the device began to glow and the crystal blasted out a flash of blinding light. I gasped in fright as the device turned molten and glowed red hot. It appeared as if it was straight out of a smelter, but there was no heat.

'Jesus, are you okay?' Jason asked.

I nodded but felt my knees start to wobble.

The Maestro held my arm. 'Sorry, I should have told you. It looks red hot, but there's no heat. It's finished now.'

The device returned to normal, and the crystal was left dull and lifeless on the table.

'Can't we regenerate it straight away using the other two crystals?' Luca asked.

'No,' the Maestro said. 'This is an unnatural process which drains the crystal to its core and damages its internal structure. It needs to be left alone to repair itself.'

Fox gave me a worried look and I returned one. I hoped the

Maestro wasn't lying. What if the process destroyed the crystals? Then we'd be putting everyone's lives at risk.

She pointed at a small knob on the device. 'The power indicator here tells us that the charge is only at ten percent. We need to be at a minimum of twenty-five percent to get them out.'

I put my wrist on the next crystal. 'Let's go again.'

We repeated the process and soon had two dead crystals. I checked the device. 'Success! We have twenty-five percent! We don't have to drain the third crystal,' I said, excitedly.

'Hallebloodylujah,' Ashley said. Everyone burst into a round of spontaneous applause.

I took Bella's hand. 'Let's bring Dad home!' When I turned to look at the mirror I could see his face a little more clearly. 'We. Are. Getting. You. Out. Now,' I mouthed, accompanied by appropriate gestures.

Ashley passed me a piece of paper with words written on it. 'Here, try this, sweetheart.'

'Oh, duh. Thanks. But won't the writing appear backwards?'

'Yes, but he'll get it.'

I read Ashley's note: *We can get you out. The device is charged. Two choices: (1) Stay in limbo forever (2) Re-enter, 50/50 chance of death. Thumbs up for out.*

'That's not a choice,' Bella sobbed.

Drom wrapped an arm around her. 'There are always choices, but sometimes the choices suck.'

I grabbed the iPad off the kitchen table. 'I've an idea. Hold the sign to the mirror. I'll take a photo of the mirror. It will put the image the right way around. We need to make it easy for Dad. He may not be thinking clearly.'

Ashley did as he was told, and then I held the iPad image so Dad could see it. He didn't respond. His brain must have been ticking over, considering all the options.

He must've felt like a puppy in a pet shop window with all the faces staring in at him. Eventually, he smiled and mouthed,

'Whatever happens, know I love you, beyond life.' He brought his fist to the mirror and paused. The room was silent, all eyes fixed on him. His fist wavered slightly, down, up, down.

Bella was making odd squeaking noises. The anticipation was intense. 'Come *on*,' she whispered.

Dad's fist rolled over and up popped his thumb. He was laughing. The room erupted in ovation. Bella jumped up and down on the spot, the Maestro had a huge grin on her face, and Jason and Ashley pumped their fists in the air. Despite the levity, I could sense everyone's darker thoughts.

I hoped we weren't celebrating his death.

My hands trembled. If he died, I'd be the executioner.

Someone touched my shoulder. 'Would you prefer me to press the button?' the Maestro asked.

'Nuh … No. I'll do it.' Dad nodded to me in encouragement.

'Okay, let's bring him home. What do I do?'

'See this button here; it's the *Limbo* function. You press it first and then this button here relates to your father. Press and hold until he appears.'

'Are we all ready?' I asked.

Everyone nodded. Bella had turned so white she looked ghostly.

Waving at Dad, I showed him the device on my wrist and nodded my head. He nodded back.

'Here goes.' I pressed the buttons as instructed.

The MAESTRO device glowed an eerie fluorescent green and extended laser beams out into the room. An energy matrix in the shape of a body appeared within its beams. The laser lights danced and flashed from top to bottom and Dad's form slowly appeared, as if he was being printed out from a 3D printer. After a minute or so the lights stopped, and there he was, standing in our dining room. He looked exactly the same as when I'd last seen him. Oh, except for the fact he had no clothes on and his skin sparkled as though he'd been dipped in fluorescence.

'Hey, Fox, he's wearing a MAESTRO device,' Ashley said.

The Maestro flashed Fox a *"what did I say"* look.

Fox shrugged his shoulders. 'I still stand by what I said. She put him in there.'

'Don't touch him yet,' the Maestro said, holding my arm as I stepped forward. 'Wait for a minute until the fluorescence disappears.'

Dad's eyes were unfocused. He resembled a statue, standing frozen still in the lounge.

'Is he all right?' Bella asked.

'We'll have to wait and see,' the Maestro said.

'Jeez, the old Prof's pretty well hung,' Ashley commented. 'I can see what attracted you to him, Maestro.'

'*Ashley!*' Bella said, sounding shocked. She'd been carefully avoiding looking in that direction. I mean, I was too. It was our dad, after all. Seeing his bits was too much information, I reckoned.

'I won't dignify that with a response,' the Maestro sniffed. 'But he does cut a fine figure for his age, doesn't he?' She leant back on one heel and devoured him with her eyes.

Fox stared at her with contempt. 'Can we get the poor bloke a dressing gown or something?'

Jason dashed off and returned with a blanket. 'Ain't got no dressing gowns. A blankie will have to do.'

We all stood and stared at Dad, watching the fluorescence fade from his body. As soon as the last glimmer disappeared, his eyes came to life, and he took a step forward and latched onto the back of a chair.

His face broke into a huge smile when he saw Bella and me. 'I'm back,' he whispered.

Bella screamed as his body shuddered violently. His eyes rolled back in his head, and he collapsed to the floor.

---

[19] *Maggie's Playlist: Coming Home — Sheppard*

Chapter 22: Christos

'A man can sleep around, no questions asked, but if a woman makes nineteen or twenty mistakes she's a tramp.'
—Joan Rivers

The guys leapt forward and caught Dad just before his head hit the floorboards. Ashley and Fox hoisted him up under the arms, and Jason wrapped him in the blanket. They headed off along the corridor carrying his limp body.

'Quickly! Let's put him in our room,' Jason said.

'He's ice cold,' Fox said.

Luca checked vital signs while we stood around watching anxiously.

'There's a faint pulse and he's breathing.'

'Thank God,' Bella said.

I looked at the Maestro. 'What should we do with him? What's the best treatment?'

'We have a different physiology to you, of course, but I would suggest keeping him warm and giving him small amounts of clear broth and see how he responds. His body needs time to readjust. He probably feels similar to your astronauts after an extended time in space.'

'He doesn't appear to have any muscle wasting,' Luca said.

'He looks the same as when he disappeared,' Bella said, going over and stroking his hair. Dad shuddered in response.

'I wouldn't do that. Any touch will be overwhelming at this

stage. Even painful.'

Bella pulled away as though burnt. 'Oh! I'm sorry.'

'Poor Prof,' I said. 'I'm so glad you're home,' I whispered. 'I'm going to make you some chicken broth.'

I raced to the kitchen. I could scarcely believe it. Dad wasn't dead. It explained why I'd never been able to get a sense of him. He'd been stuck in limbo and I couldn't reach that space.

I hoped he'd pull through. Please angels, please help him.

He would make it; I knew he would. Jeepers, how was he going to explain his disappearance? Maybe he could say he'd been kidnapped, hit his head when escaping and now had amnesia. That could work.

Ashley joined me in the kitchen and rubbed my shoulder. 'I reckon he'll make it.'

'He will. I'll make him make it. This'll be the most potent chicken broth *ever.*'

'Maggie's magic brew never fails. You fixed me last time when I thought I was dying with the flu, remember?'

'Yeah, you made a miraculous recovery. Do you think Fox is right about the Maestro?'

'I guess we'll have to wait and see.'

'What about Jason? Do you still think he's compromised?'

'Jesus … who knows? What's your gut sense?'

'Something doesn't feel right, but he's better than he was.'

'Time will tell about that as well.' He put his arm around my shoulders and gave me a squeeze. 'Hang in there, kid. We'll get through this.'

'Time will tell on what?'

We both turned as Jason walked into the kitchen. 'You two look cosy,' he said.

'I'm providing moral support,' Ashley replied.

I focused on chopping the veggies to avoid Jason's laser beam eyes. 'Time will tell if Dad makes it,' I said.

'I think he'll be fine. Do you know how much charge is left

on the *MAESTRO* device?'

'The power light indicates fifteen percent,' I said.

Jason frowned. 'We may have to use the other crystal to get Christos out.'

'The Maestro reckoned two would do it,' Ashley said.

'I'm just saying, be prepared, we may have to. Luca is looking after the Prof. We're going to bring Christos out now. Are you ready?'

'Give me five minutes to get all this stuff in the pressure cooker. Dad needs this ASAP.'

'No worries.' Jason headed back to the bedroom.

While the pressure cooker did its thing, we gathered in the lounge room ready for stage two, Christos.

I held out my wrist. 'The device is at fifteen percent. Do we need more power?'

'We can try with that amount first. The worst that can happen is nothing.'

I held out my wrist. 'Okay, show me what to press.'

'It's the *Limbo* button first, and then hold this one to bring Christos back.'

'Stand clear,' I said, pressing the buttons.

The same eerie green light erupted from the device and sent out its laser beams into the room. This time the energy matrix was much larger; the outlined form was close to seven feet tall. It appeared Christos was built like a giant brick shithouse.

Ashley and Fox simultaneously reached for their pistols. 'Jesus!'

'Relax, boys,' the Maestro snapped. 'He's a big unit.'

'You can say that again,' Jason said as a shimmering gladiator solidified before us.

Bella jumped up and down excitedly. 'Crikey, it's Yul Brynner!'

'No, it's Jason Statham,' I said.

Luca stuck his head around the corner. 'He's the spitting

image of Cary Grant.'

The Maestro rolled her eyes. 'Christos is using his power. He'll appear differently to everyone. He's using whatever he can find in your mind that is most likely to attract you to him.'

I looked at Bella. '*Yul Brynner?*'

She blushed. 'I loved him in *The Magnificent Seven.*'

Ashley rolled his eyes. 'Oh, jeez.'

Boo's thoughts broke into my mind. *He's exactly like Schmoo!*

Jason poked me in the ribs and grinned. 'Jason Statham, eh?'

'Oh, you know, I've always admired his fighting style,' I said, sheepishly.

'Ha, this is hilarious,' Ashley said.

Bella glanced at him. 'How does he appear to you?'

'Can't say,' he said, giving me a wink.

'I've told him to stop,' the Maestro said. 'What can you see now?'

Ashley appeared worried. 'He's a dead ringer for Yul Brynner! Does that mean I have a problem?'

'He does look similar,' the Maestro said.

Bella seemed very happy with herself. 'I got it right first time!'

We gazed in awe at the warrior standing before us. His skin was as white as the Maestro's and every muscle was defined and ripped. He was completely bald, with a straight nose, well-defined mouth, strong jaw and high cheekbones. Icy blue eyes stared out from under arched brows. He radiated an aura of strength and arrogance.

'Holy Magnificent Seven,' Bella whispered.

Christos opened his mouth and the word *Chiara* roared forth. The sound reverberated around the room and knocked us off our feet. I felt incapacitated, sick and terrified. It was infrasound.

Christos leapt upon the Maestro and tore off her clothes as though they were made of tissue paper. Those leather pants didn't stand a chance, I thought, as I threw up all over the floor.

The last thing I remember before blacking out was seeing the naked forms of Christos and the Maestro thrashing on the floor. I marvelled at their bodies, writhing and entwined, muscles rippling like fluid white marble, before they vanished in a blaze of light.

* * * * *

When I came to, I was sitting in an armchair in the lounge room. I opened my eyes to see the Maestro's concerned face hovering above me.

'How are you?'

My eyesight was blurry. I rubbed my eyes as I tried to focus and look around the room. Jason, Bella, Ashley and Fox were propped in chairs and looked dazed. The Maestro stood, wrapped in blanket. Christos sat in the big wingback chair, draped in my Indian sari blanket. He sat upright and silent, staring at everyone. He appeared as an Egyptian god, checking out his minions.

Crikey, he did look similar to ole Yul. Very intimidating.

I rubbed my temples. 'I have a cracker of a headache, and I've never felt so scared in all my life. Some paracetamol would be good.'

'I have them already.' The Maestro handed me a glass of water and two tablets. 'I must apologise for Christo's shattering re-entry. It's not normally so intense, but I guess because he was in limbo for such a long time, he was desperate to recharge. He didn't realise there would be aliens present.'

Huh. It sounded odd hearing us described as aliens.

'You'll all be fine. There won't be any lasting side effects. When you're feeling better, could we borrow some clothes?'

'Yeah, sure thing. Don't know if we have anything to fit Christos though,' I said, sizing him up. He was one big unit all right.

'I've probably got something to fit him. We're not too

dissimilar,' Ashley said.

Jason snorted. 'You're a legend in your own mind.'

Ashely pushed himself out of the couch. 'I'll check the truck. Crikey, it's like I've been hit by one.' He groaned and lumbered stiffly to the front door.

Christos was still sitting there silent as a statue.

'Can Christos speak our language?' I asked. 'Can he understand us?'

'Not so well now, but it won't take long. He's still recovering from his ordeal, which is why he's so quiet. He can use the language processing function on the Maestro device. I picked up the language in a couple of days.'

'Does he need to eat something?'

'He already has, energetically speaking. It's the most important life-giving source of energy for us. But because we can't satisfy all our energy requirements through coupling on this planet, we do have to supplement our bodies with food. I quite enjoy the process of eating now.'

Ashley came back carrying an assortment of clothes. 'I have overalls, tracksuit pants, T-shirts and windcheaters. They're pretty big, so should do for an interim measure.' He placed them in front of Christos.

Christo's face flexed and his mouth moved soundlessly until a deep voice finally rumbled out the words, 'Thank. You. Ash. Ley.'

'No worries. That's one helluva deep voice you've got there, mate.'

'Thank you, Ashley,' the voice rumbled again, a little more smoothly this time.

Bella was fanning herself. I laughed. Bella got off on men with deep voices. It was one of the attributes first attracting her to Liam — even more than his looks. I guessed Bella's Yul Brynner fantasy was in full flight.

Ha! Yul Brynner. Who would've thought?

I remembered Dad and Grandpa sitting with us watching *The Magnificent Seven*. We all loved a good Western. I guess that's where her Yul passion came from.

'You right there?' I asked her.

She nodded and smiled. She knew I knew what was getting her all hot and bothered.

Christos fixed his icy, alien eyes on her. The intensity of his gaze was disturbing. 'You saw me as I am, Bella.'

She flushed bright red. 'I ... I did?'

'This never happen before,' Christos said, pinning her to her chair with his gaze.

She clutched the side of it. 'Oh ... a ... and, that's bad?'

'No. Good. Very good. Rare. True pairing.'

'What's he on about?' I asked the Maestro.

'Because of the nature of our feeding habits, generally, when we are perceived by each other, or other entities, we are perceived as a reflection of what the particular entity finds most attractive. You all experienced it when Christos reentered. This function helps to facilitate coupling all the more frequently. When someone perceives our true form, it's what you would call a perfect match, so to speak.'

I glanced across at Bella who was doing a fine job impersonating the world's largest beetroot.

'So, are we seeing your true form, Maestro?'

'Yes. I don't use chameleonic mind power here on Earth. I haven't had to.'

'I can see why,' Ashley said. 'Can't think of too many guys who would find you unattractive.'

'Why thank you,' she said, seeming flattered by the compliment. 'And females too?'

'I couldn't speak for the sheilas, but I'm guessing you'd do okay on that front too. So ... you go for girls too?' Ashley said, his face reflecting his thoughts.

'We're bisexual. We have one primary opposite pairing, and

it's whatever we need or want after that.'

'Crikey moley,' Ashley said, 'I can see why you'd find our race narrow-minded in comparison.'

She shrugged. 'It's similar to how you view the Victorian era people now.'

'What was it Christos shouted when he re-entered?' Bella asked.

'Chiara. It's my real name.'

'Chiara. That's beautiful,' I said.

Luca entered the lounge. 'Chiara. It's Italian. It means light.'

'What a beautiful coincidence,' I said.

'You know there aren't any coincidences,' Drom said.

I nodded. 'How's Dad?'

'Resting comfortably,' Luca said. 'His pulse seems stronger. His colour has improved. I'm sure he's going to make it. He needs to rest and recover at his own pace. We'll slowly introduce food.'

I breathed a sigh of relief. 'Thank heavens. My broth will be ready in about ten minutes.'

We started as Christos cleared his throat and in a beautifully timbered, deep voice boomed, 'You, Bella!' He joined his hands and made a double fist. 'You, and Christos. Soon.'

Bella nearly fell out of her chair. I could see Ashley shaking with laughter.

'Christos, listen!' the Maestro said. 'No, it can't happen. Remember what I told you? It's different here. Bella can only couple with her man, Liam.'

Bella wriggled around in her chair. It appeared she wanted to say something. With what Bella had said about her marriage, I wouldn't have been surprised if she jumped up and asked Christos to take her right then and there.

Christos stared at Bella and hung his head. He looked positively crestfallen. 'Sad. Crazy planet, Chiara.'

The Maestro stroked his bald head. 'It's just different.'

A rumbling issued from Christos's throat. He sounded similar to a lion purring. Despite his forbidding size and demeanor, he was putty in the Maestro's hands.

'Sorry, no Bella,' he said throatily.

Now it was Bella's turn to look crestfallen.

Oh dear. She had it bad. The two of them, it was going to happen. I knew it. It was only a matter of time.

Ashley came over and whispered in my ear. 'We're taking bets on Bella and Christos.'

'I know which way I'm betting,' I whispered back.

* * * * *

The evening was a huge carb fest as everyone tucked into Luca's sensational pasta. Everyone except Christos and Dad, that is. Christos had one mouthful of pasta. Dad sucked broth off bread soaked in broth. He was still too weak to sit up or talk, but at least he was taking some nourishment.

Christos appeared drawn and tired.

'Do you need to lie down?' I asked him.

'You can use my room,' Ashley offered.

He nodded.

Ashley helped Christos stand. Christos seemed unsteady on his feet. He leant on Ashley, and Ashley's knees buckled with the weight of him.

'Is he okay?' I asked the Maestro.

'I think so. He needs rest.'

Ashley showed Christos to the bedroom and then came back into the lounge. He looked worried. 'I put him on the bed and he fell asleep instantly, dead to the world. Did you want to check on him?'

'He'll be fine. I'll look in later,' the Maestro said.

'You should both stay here tonight. I don't think Christos should travel the way he is,' I said.

'Thank you. I agree. I'm sorry to put you out.'

'You can both share my room,' Ashley said. 'I'll get my swag out of the truck and sleep in the lounge.'

'We can sleep on our inflatable mattress on the floor in our room and keep an eye on the Prof,' Jason said.

I was glad for Jason's suggestion. I wanted to be near Dad. I was worried about him. I'd lost him once before and didn't want to lose him again.

'I'll do the dishes,' Bella said. 'You lot turn in. I don't have to go to work, so leave it to me. I enjoy cleaning, and it'll help me feel I'm contributing.'

As we all headed off to bed, I tallied up the day's events. They were better than yesterday's, but no less stressful. I couldn't believe I had Dad back. And my sister! And now, we had two aliens sleeping under our roof — sex obsessed ones. I crinkled my brow and tried to remember what a boring day was like.

---

[20] *Maggie's Playlist: Gladiator — Zayde Wolf*

Chapter 23: Recharging Christos

'Sex is part of nature. I go along with nature.' — *Marilyn Monroe*

Sleeping on the inflatable mattress made me feel like I was camping. Jason's breath was soft, but I couldn't hear Dad's breathing at all unless I put my ear close to his face, and I couldn't see his chest rise or fall. It freaked me out because I kept thinking he'd died. My phone timer was set so I could check on him every half hour. Luca said he was stable and I didn't need to check so often, but there was no way he was going to die on my watch.

I must've been in bed for only an hour when I was awoken by the tick, tick, tick of Boo's claws on the floorboards. I lay still until I felt the gentle tickle of her whiskers and the warmth of her breath on my face.

You awake, Maggie?

Yes, Boo.

We have a potential problem I thought I should alert you too.

What is it?

Let me show you. I've been a bit of a snoop I'm afraid. I'll replay for you.

Boo had recently discovered she had the ability to replay events she witnessed, directly into our minds. She had been so excited about her head drop off mission that when she'd told us about it, her telepathic voice had disappeared and we'd received the whole filmstrip in our heads, as if she'd been wearing a GoPro camera. Everything was at a low angle, but it was fantastic to see the world from her point of view.

Ready?

Yep.

Here it is.

Bella was standing at the kitchen sink washing the dishes. A figure entered the room and tiptoed up behind her. Christos. He wrapped his arms around her waist and she jumped.

'Hi, babe, surprise!' he said.

She swiveled around in his arms, rubber gloves dripping soapsuds.

'*Liam*! Jesus, you scared me. What are you doing here?'

'I came for you. Missed you too much. Just got off the plane and came straight here.' He held her face and kissed her passionately.

She pushed him away. 'Jesus, Liam. How'd you get in the house?'

'Jason.'

Christos put his hand around her throat and ran it upwards cradling her chin. She seemed mesmerised as he kissed her again, his hands touching her breasts. He put one hand around her buttocks and the other moved between her legs. Bella groaned, tried to grab the side of the sink, missed, and plunged her gloved hand into the basin, sending sudsy water everywhere. She reached out for support and sent a saucepan flying. Christos caught it in a flash without even looking.

Oh, good work. The pot was so heavy it would've damaged the floor.

Christos pulled down Bella's leggings and undies in one swift move and was on his knees kissing the inside of her thighs.

Um, Boo, I feel like a voyeur watching this.

Keep watching.

'Christ, Liam, not here. You're crazy.' She tried to pull up her leggings with one hand and push Christos away with the other.

Christos lifted Bella and spun her around so she was bent over the kitchen bench, naked from the waist down.

'You want me?' Christos asked.

'Liam, yes, yes, I want you,' she groaned.

'You are so beautiful,' he said, ripping off his pants.

The sound of frenzied barking filled the room. Boo flew in and latched onto Christo's leg. Growling and pulling frantically, Boo's claws scrabbled on the wooden floorboards as she tried to get traction.

Bella screamed. 'Christos! Oh, my God, you're kidding!' She pushed him away and pulled up her leggings. Bella sagged, and Christos held her, whilst simultaneously trying to shake Boo off his leg.

Huh. Bella's got the same weak knee problem as me.

I wondered what you were barking at Boo. I thought you were after possums again.

A very large possum this time.

Boo was still latched onto Christos when the Maestro rushed in. 'Oh, Bella. I'm so sorry. Are you … did he?'

'I'm fine. Boo came in and broke the spell or something.' She sounded slightly disappointed.

'I told him you're off limits and can only be with Liam. He doesn't understand yet. He obviously thought if he appeared like Liam, it would be okay. Good dog, Boo.' She rubbed Boo's ears. 'You saved the day.'

'How did Boo break the spell?'

'It was the distraction. Christos couldn't hold the illusion with Boo snapping at his leg.'

'Oh. Thanks, Boo — I think,' Bella muttered.

The Maestro raised a quizzical eyebrow.

'Christos, come back to bed,' she said. 'I'll fix you. Bella is off limits, no matter what guise you adopt. Do you understand?'

'Yes,' he said, with the saddest, hangdog expression I'd ever seen.

'Oh, stop it,' the Maestro snapped. 'Apologise to Bella.'

Christos jutted out his chin defiantly. 'But I'm not sorry. I love Bella.'

'Don't worry, Christos,' Bella said softly. 'To be honest, some part of me knew it wasn't Liam. He would never do it in the kitchen.'

Christos smiled and reached out his hand. 'I will do it anywhere. Come now, I show you.'

'Christos! Enough already,' the Maestro said. 'I'm taking you home tomorrow. In the meantime, don't go near anyone in this house. Okay?'

'Okay. But Christos not happy. Bye, Bella.'

Bella was flushed and pulled at the neckline of her top. 'Bye, Christos. Oh, my God, what a crazy world I've let myself into.'

As the Maestro led Christos away, Bella sighed heavily and bent over to stroke Boo. 'Thanks, Boo. But I kinda wish you'd minded your own business. Oh, well.'

There it is. Did I do the right thing?

Yes, you did the right thing. Who knows what could have happened if Christos had done the deed.

That's what I thought. But I felt uncomfortable with my intervention as Bella seemed unhappy about it.

It's because things aren't going well for her and Liam. She's bored out of her brain and looking for something, or someone else, so she was an easy target. You did the right thing, Boo, for sure.

I will continue to keep an eye on Christos then?

Yes, good idea, Boo. Well done.

Thanks. Night.

Night.

Crikey. Boo had lost us the bet. All for the best. I drifted off to sleep thinking everyone had better be extra vigilant about anyone coming into their beds tonight. I mean, how could I be sure it was Jason lying next to me?

He turned away from me and muttered, 'Night.'

Yup. No doubt there. Definitely Jason. Boo always got more attention than me these days. I drifted off to sleep feeling as disappointed as Bella.

Sleep was short lived. I awoke with a start to the sounds of a racket coming from the other room. I leapt out of bed. 'Oh, for Christ's sake, what now?' My heart pounded in my throat. I heard Ashley shouting and hightailed it into the lounge.

'Get the hell away from me!' he screamed.

He stood wild eyed and naked in the middle of the room, shouting at Christos, who was being dragged away by the Maestro.

Oh jeepers. I could imagine what had happened there.

'Christ, I thought it was you,' Ashley hissed, as I came into view. He rubbed his mouth with the back of his hand and bent over to pull up his jocks. 'Crikey moley, that was close.'

I grinned. 'Boo saved you?'

'It's not funny. I'm scarred for life. And yes, Boo saved me from a fate worse than death. Jesus Christ, I need a drink.' He grabbed a bottle of scotch from the coffee table and chugged back a few swigs before finishing off with a good long gargle.

I giggled.

Jason staggered into the room, wiping the sleep from his eyes. 'What's so funny? Why can't I get one good night's sleep around here?'

'Christos came onto Ashley. Boo saved him in the nick of time.'

'Fair dinkum?' Jason said. 'Who did you think it was, Ash?'

'None of your business,' he snapped. 'I thought all my dreams had come true, but it turned into my worst nightmare.' He took another swig of scotch as an involuntary shudder coursed through his body. 'Brrrrrr. Jesus. I owe you big time,

242

Boo.'

The look on Ashley's face set me off again.

Ashley looked annoyed. 'It's not funny.'

'Sorry,' I said, trying to wipe the smile off my face.

The Maestro returned without Christos. 'I'm sorry too.' She looked pale. 'He's hungry, and I'm having trouble appeasing his appetite. I'm getting drained myself. I need to eat.'

'There's heaps of leftover pasta in the fridge,' I said. 'I'll heat you a bowl.'

'Yes, carbs are good. Thanks.'

Jason grinned. 'So, what stage did you get to, Ashley?'

'Shut up. Don't remind me.'

'So, it wasn't nice?' I said, feeling weirdly hurt.

'It was bloody spectacular until Boo broke the spell,' Ashley said. 'Then I felt sick. It was as if I'd been violated. I've never felt like that before.'

Ashley looked so distraught I dashed over and held out my arms to him.

He took a step backwards. 'Is it really you?'

I pointed. 'You saw Christos leave!' Ashley hesitantly allowed me to put my arms around him.

'I don't trust my own eyes now,' he whispered into my ear. 'I'm going to kill the fucker. He's ruined something special for me.'

'I can hear you,' the Maestro said.

'Friggin' perverted radar eared alien,' he muttered.

'I can remove the memory if you want,' the Maestro offered.

'You can?'

'Yes. Quickly and painlessly.'

'Right now?'

'Yes.'

'No side effects? Just erase the memory ... of waking up to ... him?'

'Yes, the whole Christos encounter. Only that.'

'Do it. Please.'

'Maggie, I'll need the Maestro device. It has enough power to do this.'

I held out my wrist and the Maestro pressed buttons and dialed knobs.

'Are you sure this is safe?' I asked.

'Absolutely,' she said, pressing a final button.

A beam of yellow light shot out from the device and hit Ashley in the centre of his forehead. It expanded into a network of light that cradled his head. A tiny spark of red ignited and then the light disappeared.

'All done.'

'What's done?' Ashley asked.

'The incident with Christos.'

'What happened?'

'He pretended he was Liam and tried to have sex with Bella.'

'Bloody hell.'

'Yes, everyone needs to watch out whoever comes onto them is actually who they seem to be, if you know what I mean,' I said.

Ashley wriggled back into his swag. 'I don't think there's gonna be much action in that department, but thanks for the heads up.'

Christos came back into the room. 'Sorry, Ashley.'

'Don't apologise to me. It's Bella you should be saying sorry to.' He pulled the swag over his head.

'After I've eaten, I'm going to tie Christos to the bed,' the Maestro said.

Jason headed off to the workshop. 'I'll get you some cable ties.'

'Good plan. Then we'll all be able to get some sleep,' I said, going into the kitchen to heat up the Maestro's pasta.

Christos was despondent. 'I will try eat too. People not like Christos in this place.'

I took Christo's hand. 'We do like you. It's just that things are different, with regards to what you should, and shouldn't, do.'

'Big rules. I cause big troubles,' he said softly, his voice sounding similar to a low growl.

'Don't sulk. It will be all right,' the Maestro said to him. 'You need time to adjust.'

Jason returned and gave her a bunch of extra-long cables ties.

'Hopefully, we can all get some sleep now,' she said.

'Hallelujah,' Ashley muttered from underneath his swag.

---

21 *Maggie's Playlist: You Sexy Thing — Hot Chocolate*

Chapter 24: Red Flowers

'When I hear a doorbell ring, it fills my heart with fear. When I hear my name called, it's a name I hate to hear. When I get a present, or see a Catherine wheel tattoo, I wonder if my time is up. I wonder if it's you.' — Maggie McLaine, Journey to Hell

The night passed without further drama, and we all managed to get some shut-eye. We had a full house for breakfast, with everyone in good spirits.

I took Dad some broth, and he managed to sip it from a spoon, which was fantastic. He even whispered, 'good morning' and 'thank you'. Things were on the up and up.

'I've made a big bowl of Bircher muesli,' Bella called from the kitchen. 'Everyone can help themselves.'

The kitchen was chaos. Ashley cooked bacon and eggs, the Maestro made pancakes, Drom did the coffees, Luca set the table, Jason fed the dogs, Fox burnt the toast and Christos sat at the table like a king, watching everything with intense interest.

He smiled. 'I watch and learn.'

'Don't watch Fox make toast,' Ashley said.

Luca sat at the table with the newspaper, giving Christos surreptitious glances. I took my coffee and sat next to him. 'How are you?'

'I've decided to leave the church.'

'That's a huge decision. What triggered it?'

'Cary Grant.'

'Cary Grant?'

Luca stared into his lap for a while and then whispered, 'Yes, he visited me last night. I couldn't say no. It was the most beautiful thing. But now…'

Oh, Jesus. Christos had been a busy boy. What the hell had happened to the cable ties?

'Christos was out of control last night. It's not your fault. If it hadn't been for Boo, Bella and Ashley would have succumbed to his wiles as well. I don't see how anyone could resist him; he becomes your fantasies.'

'I didn't want to resist him. Of course, I knew it couldn't be Cary Grant. I knew it was Christos. He made me realise I can't keep denying who I am and how I feel. The church is making me crazy. From the minute you enter the seminary you're surrounded by men and expected to be around mainly men as you go through life under its roof. There are so many homosexual bishops and priests in the church. But then you have to deny who you are … that you're gay. You have to stay in the closet and be dishonest about who you are. Last night made me realise how lonely I am. I want an intimate, loving relationship with a man. I'm glad Christos came to me. Something which feels so wonderful can't be bad. It must be a gift from God.'

Tears streamed down his face. I gave him a hug. 'It sounds as if you've made the right decision for you.'

He wiped the tears from his face with the tissues Ashley had quietly put on the table. 'A huge burden has lifted. I think I'll go back to medicine.'

Christos spoke and we jumped at his booming voice. 'I hear what you say. Sorry, we are all about sound. Our hearing very good. I am happy you are happy. Christos happy he has done good.' He banged his fist on the table and smiled like he was ready to burst. 'See, Chiara. I did good.'

The Maestro sat on his lap. 'You did well, lover.' She caressed his bald head with her long fingers and he closed his eyes in happiness.

'Luca, you want me, anytime, I'm here 'til you find your special person.'

The Maestro nodded in agreement. 'Yes, Luca, don't be shy. You'll be doing us a favour. It'll help Christos and take the pressure off me.'

'I can't get my head around what I'm hearing,' Fox said.

'Yeah, doing mine in too,' Ashley agreed.

'And mine,' Bella added.

'Congratulations on your decision, Luca,' Drom said.

'Yes, congratulations, Luca,' everyone said. We raised our coffee cups.

He beamed from ear to ear. 'I can't thank you enough for being so supportive. I'm glad you came into the church, Maggie, despite what we had to go through. It's changed my life, the bad and the good. I couldn't have survived the experience without your kindness and support. Thank you all, and thank you, Christos,' he said, looking over at Christos shyly.

A flush of pink shone on Luca's cheeks. Christos gently moved the Maestro off his lap and strode over to him. He held Luca's face in his big hands, gazed into his eyes, and then kissed him, deeply and passionately, until the Maestro suggested he stop.

Ashley leaned back and rubbed his five o'clock shadow. 'Holy snapping aardvarks. Gotta love it. You never know what each new day brings around here.'

'Ain't that the truth,' Bella said, finally closing her gobsmacked mouth. The expression on her face triggered a serious attack of the giggles in me.

'Christ. There goes Maggie,' Ashley said. 'She's got the snorts too.'

I held my sides. 'Oh, what next. My stomach hurts.'

The kitchen rang with laughter and good cheer, so much so, we didn't hear the doorbell ring. Boo and Schmoo barked madly at the door to let us know someone was there.

Who is it Boo?

A man with flowers.

'Apparently there's a man with flowers at the door,' I said.

Jason headed out the back, saying to Ashley, "Can you get it? I have some work I need to do in the shed.'

Ashley had already checked his gun and tucked it into the back of his pants. 'Yeah, no worries.'

I was curious to see who would bring flowers, so I followed Ashley to the door. 'Maybe Liam's sent you flowers, Bella.'

'Nah, he wouldn't spend the money. And if he did, he'd get me dried ones.'

A man stood at the door holding a ginormous bunch of red roses wrapped in white silk, tied with red silk ribbons. A pull string bag of red silk was tied to the flowers.

Jesus. With all the red silk, these had to have been from Ashley. But surely, he wouldn't send flowers here.

'A delivery for Maggie McLaine,' the man said.

He seemed familiar, but I couldn't put my finger on it. Tall, black hair, wide set eyes, handsome, in a rugged kind of way. And his voice. It rang a bell somewhere in my mind.

'You're Maggie?' he asked.

'Do I know you from somewhere? You're familiar.'

'Yes, same for me too,' he said, smiling a smile which didn't translate to his eyes. 'Your flowers?' he said, holding them out.

Ashley pushed in front of me and opened the screen door. 'I'll get it, mate.' He reached out, snatched the flowers and shut and locked the door again, all in two seconds flat. 'Thanks again,' he said, closing the door.

I took the flowers. 'You were rude.'

He whipped the flowers away from me. 'Not taking any chances.'

'Oi! They're my flowers.' I lowered my voice. 'You didn't send them, did you?'

'I'm crazy, but not that crazy.' He lay them on the kitchen table and examined them. 'Can't be too careful, luv.'

He passed me the card. 'Who're they from?'

I opened it. 'It says, *You are mine. Forever.*'

Bella took the card from me and examined it. 'No name. Nothing else. Do you think it was Jason?'

'He knows I'm not keen on roses. Gerberas are good. Daffodils maybe.'

'Oh, I love roses,' Bella enthused. She buried her nose in the bouquet. 'These are magnificent, and they have a scent too! Divine.' She jiggled around in excitement. 'Open the bag!'

I picked up the bag and felt the weight. 'There are beads in it.' I carefully opened the bag and pulled out a string of black pearls. When I held them up to the light they shimmered with subtle rainbow colours.

'Oh, my God. Black pearls!' Bella said. 'They cost a fortune. Wow. Someone is seriously out to impress you.'

I felt puzzled and uncomfortable. 'But who the hell is it? I have no idea. I don't like roses and I'm not enamoured of pearls. Whoever it is doesn't know me well.'

'Can I have a look?' Bella asked. She took them from me, and although she was gentle the string broke and the pearls scattered all over the floor.

She looked horrified. 'I'm so sorry! I hardly touched them!'

The pearls rolled around my feet. 'You can have them if you want, get them restrung. They're yours.'

'Thanks!'

Drom bent over to look more closely. 'They're still rolling. It's as though they're moving under their own steam.'

The pearls rolled in circular patterns on the floor, gaining momentum, rather than slowing as they should.

'Get back!' Ashley shouted. 'I don't like it.'

Fox pulled Drom away. 'Me neither.'

Boo! Get Schmoo out of here.

Boo blasted out through the dog door followed by Schmoo, his nose up her bum.

'Jason, we need you!' I yelled.

The pearls rolled lazily in ever more intricate patterns. It was hypnotic. But something was missing. Noise. The pearls began to hover silently just above the floorboards.

'What do we do?' I asked no one in particular.

The pearls stopped. We waited in anticipation. Nothing happened.

I bent to catch one, and they sprang to life making a slow ascent. I jumped back. The iridescent black orbs floated silently upwards until they hovered in front of us at chest height.

My head buzzed with a premonition. I raced into the kitchen. 'Get ready to catch!' I opened the saucepan drawer and began hurling my heavy based, stainless steel pots in the direction of my stunned compadres. 'Take one each and use it to catch the suckers!'

No sooner were the words out of my mouth than the pearls blasted forward like bullets, and the sharp clang of metal on metal sounded around the room as everyone used their pots as shields. The pearls rattled around inside the pots before flying out again. They flew erratically, similar to angry wasps, backwards, forwards, up and down, while everyone batted them away with their pots. It was pot ping-pong and looked hilarious. I would have laughed if it weren't such a deadly game.

None of the pearls seemed interested in me, so I found the lids to the pans and passed them out. I took a pot and a lid too and managed to snare a couple of beads. They banged angrily inside the pot, and dents appeared in the stainless steel.

I was glad I hadn't purchased el cheapo pots. It paid to invest in quality. Who knew our lives would one day depend on superior saucepans.

A lone pearl headed straight for Ashley. It sprouted blades and whirled like a buzz saw. 'Ashley, watch out!'

251

He leapt to one side, but the lethal pearl adjusted course and ripped through the top of his arm. His arm pulled away from his shoulder and daylight shone through the gap. Blood began to flow and his white T-shirt changed rapidly to red.

Blood. Always, blood.

He turned white with shock. 'Jesus!' He put his pot on the table and tried to push his arm back to his shoulder. Luca held the lid of Ashley's pot on with his spare hand.

Ashley looked at me. 'I'm fucked.'

I held out my pinky finger 'No! Don't say that. *Remember!*'

Luca was trying to keep the lids tight on two pots with one arm, while ripping his T-shirt off with the other. 'Keep the pressure on your arm. Move closer to me!' Luca shoved his T-shirt against Ashley's arm and applied pressure to try and stem the blood flow.

Fox stared at the large lumps appearing on his saucepan. 'The pots aren't going to hold!' he yelled. 'They're working on the metal, trying to break through.'

'Jason! *Jason!*' I screamed.

Where the hell was he?

Christos moved closer to Ashley and sat on top of his pots. This freed Luca to keep his under control. I wasn't sure sitting on them was a good idea.

Drom tried to unlock the door to the deck and keep the lid on his saucepan at the same time. He must've caught a whole pile of the deadly things as his pot was jerking around as if possessed.

Fox moved to a slightly open window and yelled his guts out for Jason. When there was no response he looked at us in frustration. 'Where is the bastard?'

It came from nowhere and he saw it too late. A pearl bullet connected, and Fox screamed. He held up a bloodied right hand and his stricken eyes stared out at me through the gaping hole. He had no palm left. He shoved the saucepan top side down on the kitchen table.

Bella crawled under the table with her pot. She pressed an oven tray against the underside of the table, roughly where Fox's saucepan was.

Good work, Bella. They'd be chewing through the kitchen table as we spoke.

Luca saw Fox's dilemma. 'Oh, Jesus! Maestro, help Fox, get something! Apply pressure. Stop the bleeding.'

She ripped off the shirt I'd lent her. 'Maggie, where's the baton?'

'It's with Dad,' I yelled.

'Get it! It might have enough power to create a shield.'

I plonked my pot on the table. 'Look after this.' I turned and raced along the corridor. The bedroom seemed such a long way away. I ran like all get out, but I wasn't getting anywhere. Looking backwards, everyone seemed so tiny. Spatial distortion. The sun broke through the clouds and floodlit the room. The illuminated air swirled with a billion particles of dust and dog hair. Yuk. I tried not to breathe. A dead fly drifted by my face. Followed by a moth. Dust on the move. Not a good thing. Dust on the move was always bad. I turned to run and slammed straight into the arms of the delivery man. He gripped my arm and pulled me towards the front door. 'I heard the noise. Come with me. We'll get help,' he said.

Why was it so dark? Where had the sun gone?

The walls turned black. The ceilings turned black. The black flowed like treacle onto the floor. It pulsated. I felt the energy push against my body.

'Jason, *help me!*' No sound. It was sucked into the void. The walls buckled and distorted around me. 'Run, everyone *run!*' A wave of coloured shapes erupted from my mouth. Still no sound. We were all going to die.

'Come. You'll be safe with me,' the delivery man said.

'No, let go! You're in danger. You don't know what you're

dealing with,' I said, hearing my voice clearly.

He smiled soullessly. 'I do know what I'm dealing with.'

'Who the hell are you?'

'You know me. We've met before.'

I felt a rising hysteria and tried to yank my arm free. 'Let go! I've no time for stupid games. My friends are in danger, dying.'

'My name is Tapakah.'

'*Tapakah!* At the church? He was only seven, for heaven's sake.'

He smiled his dead eyed smile. 'I matured into adulthood quickly. I have come for you now.'

I pulled my arm free and ran towards the kitchen. The kitchen came towards me as I ran, but I still wasn't moving. Tapakah grabbed me from behind and held me tight. I stopped trying to run. My brain was in overload.

Think. *Think.*

Yes. The self-defense technique Fox taught me. I relaxed into a dead weight, bent my knees and dropped through his arms. I stepped to one side and jammed my elbow into his guts. He buckled. I seized his left arm, pulled it rearward, and smashed my forearm against the back of his elbow.

I didn't hear his arm crack, but I felt it. His arm was bent nicely in the wrong direction. *Take that, roach man!*

Tapakah rotated his arm and snapped his elbow back into place. 'I will kill all of your friends, right now, if you don't come with me.'

'Your arm … it's not possible,' I mumbled, feeling the strength start to leave my legs.

'My body's different. Don't resist or I will kill them all.' He gripped my arm. 'I'm running out of patience.'

I felt tightness in my body. My blood pressure rose, along with the rage and anger coursing in my veins. I screamed, 'Who the hell are you to come into my house and ruin a perfectly good day? Kill my friends? I don't think so. I'm going to tear you limb from limb, you scumbag. You don't know who you're dealing with, you slimy piece of shit!' I made the assumption he had them, and kneed him in the balls.

He lurched forward, and I jammed the heel of my hand under the base of his nose. A black shadow tentacle whipped forward out of nowhere and wrapped around my wrist. It stopped me cold. I couldn't deliver the fatal blow — driving his nasal bone into his brain.

The Dark Force creature was beside me. It had drawn itself into a human shape. Dust flowed into it, hissing and sparking. Its blackness reminded me of a glittering night sky.

Every shred of resistance and rage drained from my body with its touch. I stood and swayed like a zombie injected with a mega dose of Valium.

'It adores you, Maggie. It finds your particular kind of rage delicious. You have its dark spark lodged within you. You're unique, offering it an endless, powerful source of rage, mixed with your sensitive human emotions.'

I barely had the energy to speak. 'Who are you? Are you part of it?'

'I'm Tapakah. It's in me, but I'm not it. At present, we have a symbiotic relationship, but I have my own agenda.'

'Are you going to kill me?'

'Definitely not. I want you for something special.'

I wasn't keen on where this was heading. 'What?'

'We are going to create a master race. You and me.' He jammed his tongue down my throat and ran his hands all over my body. It was like he was checking out livestock. 'I'm keeping my end of the bargain with the Dark Force. With you out of the way, the crystals won't be found and it will be unstoppable.'

He had to be kidding. Him and me? He had Buckley's. Hell would freeze over before that happened.

The only rage I was capable of existed in those few tepid thoughts. The Dark Force had sucked me dry. I couldn't resist. I wanted to wipe my mouth. I couldn't. I wanted to vomit. I couldn't. I wanted to scream. I couldn't. I wanted to shove my thumbs into his eye sockets and push his dead eyes out of his head. I couldn't.

'Will you come with me? I will spare your friends.'

'Yes.'

He caressed my face. His hands were the texture of Japanese lacquer ware. 'You won't regret your decision.' He nodded at the Dark Force and it flowed towards the kitchen table. A shadowy tendril extended, and the black pearls flowed out through the now translucent pots and hovered in the air in front of it.

Tapakah led me towards the front door. I had no power to resist. He paused mid-stride. 'You know, I hate loose ends. I think a complete break from the past would do you good. Turn around and say goodbye to your friends.'

The Dark Force stood next to my beloved friends and family and hoovered up their fear, rage and despair. They were frozen. Compliant. Unable to resist. Just like me.

'Goodbye,' I said flatly. Tapakah gripped my arm and pulled me away. I waited for the screams as the Dark Force moved to engulf them.

The last thing I remembered before the room exploded was hearing a sound I hadn't heard in a very long time.

'Get your filthy, stinking hands off my daughter, you piece of alien scum!' It was Dad. He'd staggered out of the bedroom and with a perfect, underarm bowl, he rolled our one remaining crystal right to the feet of the Dark Force.

Dad! You beauty! I'd never shitcan his lawn bowls again.

The world disappeared in a blaze of blessed light.

---

22 *Maggie's Playlist: I've Come For Your Daughter — Paul Kelly and The Coloured Girls*

Chapter 25: Where to From Here

'And this is the judgment: the light has come into the world, and people loved the darkness rather than the light because their works were evil. For everyone who does wicked things hates the light and does not come to the light, lest his works should be exposed.' — John 3:19-20

We survived, but we're back at square one. Behind the eight ball. Not a live crystal to our name. All we have is guts, determination and, hopefully, between us, a fair bit of intelligence. And by God, we're going to need every ounce of it. The quest is just beginning.

It's not all bad, I guess. We have Dad back, and Christos. The last crystal saved our bacon. It healed Ashley and Fox's injuries.

Tapakah and the Dark Force have vanished, but I'm sure they'll be back.

As for Jason, he said he had earplugs and earmuffs on, doing metal work for Fraser. Said he didn't hear a thing. Fox secretly checked out the workshop and saw no evidence of any such work. I don't know what to think.

Anyway, I thank the good powers that be, every single day, for Dad's return. And Bella's. Bella's come back to me. I have a sister again.

We've all become wiser, stronger and braver, and our brains have expanded to accept so many mind-blowing things. Things we can't tell anyone about. No one would believe us.

I'm writing this to save my sanity. It helps a bit. Mum

couldn't save hers. I'm finding out why. My editor pigeonholed this book as fiction. Yeah, whatever. No one's going to believe it's true. But it ain't fiction to us.

There's ten of us now. All fighting this thing. I'm still worried about Jason. He's definitely NQR, but with the Prof and Christos, we could do it. Restore the light. It won't be easy, but I promise we'll try. Or die trying.

Negativity is what the Dark Force feeds on. What it loves. It's what makes it strong. Be aware. Be on your guard. It's always ready to strike.

Watch your thoughts and emotions. Don't let it possess your mind, take control of you. Try thinking of dolphins.

If you do this, you may buy us time. Our fight is beginning. The darkness grows stronger every day.

Be careful of shadows. Especially the really dark ones. The ones under cupboards and in corners.

Be aware of dust. Dust = Good. Moving Dust = High Alert. No dust = Bad.

Be aware. People might not be who you think they are. Watch out for strangers coming onto you. Christos hasn't assimilated yet, and he's enjoying being out and about.

Keep a look out for those tell-tale tattoos. If you see one, *run*.

I'm a bit concerned about mirrors too. You never know who could be watching you.

Oh, and cockroaches. Don't sleep with your mouth open. Duct tape works well for that.

We're fighting for the light. We're fighting for the planet. Wish us luck.

The Dark Force is real and it's growing and Tapakah is out there somewhere. I know it.

Watch the news for the latest Dark Force update.

We'll be back.

---

23 *Maggie's Playlist: The Hammer's Coming Down — Nickelback*

Appendix — Maggie's Playlist

1. Dancing with Demons — Palisades
2. Son of a Preacher Man — Sarah Connor
3. High on Emotion — Chris De Burgh
4. Deception — Christina Grimmie
5. Storm in My Heart — Colin Hay
6. Home — Simply Red
7. Fox — Toby Johnson
8. Don't Lose Your Head — Andy Carhart
9. Collect the Trophy — 10Ft, Ganja Plant
10. 21 Guns — Green Day
11. Baton — Junip
12. Bad Dream (Live) — The Angels
13. Maps — Maroon 5
14. Curiosity Killed the Cat — The Little River Band
15. Make You Feel My Love — Adele
16. A Girl is a Gun — Old Dominion
17. Pressure Down — John Farnham
18. Infected — Garabatto, Charlee Muse
19. Sister — The Black Keys
20. Would I Lie To You? — Eurythmics
21. Coming Home — Sheppard
22. Gladiator — Zayde Wolf
23. You Sexy Thing — Hot Chocolate
24. I've Come For Your Daughter — Paul Kelly
25. The Hammer's Coming Down — Nickelback

When I hear the doorbell
It fills my heart with fear
When I hear my name called
It's a name I hate to hear
When I open a present
Or see a catherine wheel tattoo
I wonder if my time's up
I wonder if it's you —...

Who's the scarest creature of all
Who do you see?
Who looks back?
Friend, or foe ready to attack.
Are they good or bad?
Make you happy or sad?
Mirrors hide things from our world
When you look in the mirror
Who's really looking back at you

Limbo
in out

Multiverse

xtension
ings
enabl
ws to
wel

Time
Year
Date

MAESTRO

I love you like a brother
I love you like a friend
I cherish and respect you
But there it has to end
You don't ignite my soul with passion
You're not music to my ears
You don't know how to comfort me
When my mind is full of fears
I'll never ever leave you
Or hurt you with intent
But my heart belongs to someone else
And it's only here that I can vent
My secrets and my passion
No one else can comprehend
My brain's one big receiver

Red silk ribbons cutting my skin
Red silk ribbons, love or sin?
Blood and lust I see it all.
Mirrored thoughts spread their pall
minds display their secret wares
Nothing is hidden in your glass eyes
Your minds to me are an open book
Where horror lurks in every nook
What blocks it out ???...
What stops the flow ?????
Champagne + sex
It's this I know.

The Crystal Sphere Series by Ingrid Fry
Book Three: Quest for Light
Book Four — Search for Truth

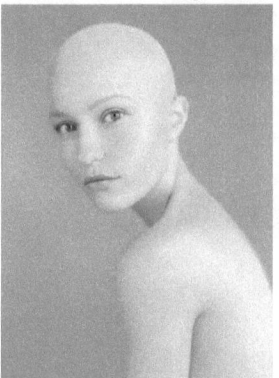

Accidental contact with a mysterious Crystal Sphere changes the nature of a group of humans and a dog, forcing them on a terrifying quest to save the world.

The frightening mission continues in book three of the Crystal Sphere series.

The pace is heart stopping as the quest takes Maggie and her Musketeers through regional Victoria, Australia. From the Mitchell River, through Bairnsdale, Lakes Entrance, Buchan and Hanging Rock, with the shocking conclusion taking place in outback Western Australia.

Can the Musketeers — a Plumber, Booze Hound, Spiritual Warrior, Catholic Priest, Nurse, Detective Inspector, two highly sexed extra-terrestrials and a Beagle-cross — save the world?

An unexpected attack makes the quest for the crystals even more urgent. The action never stops, and the sexual tension increases into the red zone.

The team have no time to take a breath, and neither will you as you join their battle in the real world and the psychic realms.

A new member joins the team and Maggie's nemesis continues to play his evil game. Aboriginal legend comes to life, and all manner of strange creatures, and nasty humans stand in their way.

Maggie faces the most terrifying challenge she has ever had to deal with. Can she withstand the relentless horror that surrounds her?
Time is running out for human kind, and it has certainly run out for Maggie.
Be prepared for the shocking outcome.

www.ingramcontent.com/pod-product-compliance
Lightning Source LLC
Chambersburg PA
CBHW050155120726
47903CB00002B/629